NEW LIFE
INC.

New Life Inc.

Copyright ©2009

Maria Rachel Hooley

Cover image courtesy of Cameron Blackwell

ISBN 978-1442180086

All rights reserved. No part of this publication may be reproduced, stored in a retrieval system, or transmitted in any form or by any means—electronic, mechanical, photocopying, recording, or otherwise—except for brief quotations in printed reviews, without the prior written permission of the copyright owner.

Acknowledgements

This book never would have existed without the support of my parents, David and Charlene Shockley, the first two people to teach me the magic of words, and the last two people I think about every night. It definitely wouldn't have taken shape without my husband, Ellis Hooley, to help me find the novel lost inside all the extra words. There would be no reason to write without my three children, Britney, Zackary, and Taylor. And writing definitely wouldn't be nearly so much fun without my writing partner, Erica Kuhn.

3

Chapter One

He'd killed the kid.

A metal trash can slamming to the ground woke Joe Ramsey from the nightmare. He'd been having that same one about Miguel dying ever since it happened two years ago. He jerked upright and looked both ways down the dark alley. A huge orange and white cat crawled inside the overturned can as it rocked slightly from side to side. The animal mewed, and the sound echoed and blossomed in the deathly midnight stillness.

Wind stirred paper and ashes from the mountains of debris around Joe, turning the slight yellow light closer to grey. Joe looked at the skeletal remains of the buildings in front of him. Uneven bricks formed half-walls. Charred metal twisted toward the sky, reaching for the moon.

"Damn dream," he muttered. His breathy words came out in a stream of gray mist before dissolving in the cold air. Joe shivered and pulled the filthy torn blanket closer to him as the December air cut through him, especially his bum knee. Christ, it hurt. He straightened his left leg out and winced as the muscles and cartilage rippled from movement, resisting as though they would break before stretching.

Three more months and the weather would be tolerable. That damn Texas wind would stop biting in March. Not that he intended to hang around the good old city of Dal-Worth until March. Joe lifted his hand and rubbed the aching muscle in his neck, instantly regretting sleeping in that half-cocked position. Just as soon as he could get a job and save enough money to slip away, he would. *You can't keep wandering like this. It's time to put down roots. It's 2175, old man*, he thought. *You're 37 and the days just keep adding up.*

And Dal-Worth, Texas, was too damn dangerous for anyone right now with the Lifers and Resisters drawing battle lines over the Lifespan Chips. From the corner of his eye, Joe took in the fragmented buildings. Just another argument between the two factions which had gone from words to works.

A small buzzing sound hovered over Joe's head. He saw a zoom scope flashing a beam in his general area. The beam came from a small, black box which functioned as a broadcaster, downloading surveillance to the Dal-Worth Federation Headquarters. *Yeah, I want to be hauled in because I'm out during lock-down. At least it would be warm.* Joe ducked under the covers, hoping he wouldn't be spotted by the Federation's patrol units. The light beam touched his blanket for a moment before leaving.

"That was close," he muttered, tired of dodging the Federation, Resisters and Lifers. Joe wiped the sleep from his eyes and shook his head. He didn't understand the controversy over the chips. True, they could increase longevity, but why was that so bad? Maybe if he ever found a job he'd get one.

A lump formed in his throat and he reached into his pants pocket. His fingers touched a cigarette lighter he hadn't used in months. The he felt a blue teddy bear. His fingers had memorized the black, button eyes and red satin ribbon tied around its neck. They caressed the soft fur and pushed the bear deeper before he pulled out his hand.

He wouldn't get that chip, even if he were a millionaire.

Joe looked down the alley at the filth and refuse piled up around him. He had made his bed deep in a corner of the pile, hidden from plain sight so both the Lifers and Resisters would leave him alone. So far, so good. Since the two factions had just torched this place last week while fighting, he figured he was safe. Besides, getting too close to most businesses wasn't a smart idea, not with the Impulse security systems everywhere. Hell, last week a drunk homeless guy had walked too close to an invisible trip-line on a jewelry store and been zapped unconscious. Joe had watched the Federation peace officers carry him away. He'd wondered how long that little sleep spell had lasted.

All of a sudden, Joe felt a gentle humming sensation in his head. He bent over and cradled it between his hands, trying to drive the feeling away. It wouldn't go. "Goddamn propagandist shit!" he seethed, knowing New Life, Incorporated was about to broadcast an advertised message directly into his thoughts. He couldn't stop or ignore it.

NEW LIFE INCORPORATED OFFERS THE CHANCE OF A LIFETIME. LIVE TO SEE ABSOLOM'S COMET IN 3050. GIVE YOURSELF AN EXTRA FIFTY YEARS. DON'T YOU DESERVE IT? FOR A MODEST FINANCIAL COMMITMENT, WE CAN GIVE YOU NEW LIFE. NEW LIFE. NEW LIFE.

As the message faded, Joe said, "Shut up," to block the traces of humming left in his mind. He lowered his hands and clenched his fists, wishing he could strangle the men responsible for mental advertisement. They still couldn't cure cancer, but they could find a way to climb inside people's heads. No laws forbade it. The Federation had ruled that mental advertisements were only thoughts projected at a certain level. These `thoughts' didn't have influential power and they couldn't change normal mental processes. They simply replaced the radio broadcasting of the 20th century.

"And what about annoying people?" Joe seethed, resting against his makeshift bed. A growling from his stomach answered him. It felt hollow, like acid had eaten through his gut. Joe reached into his pocket, searching for coins he knew he didn't have. His fingers touched the teddy bear and lighter.

I need a job, he thought, clenching his fingers into a tight ball. Unfortunately, the only job Joe Ramsey knew exceptionally well was a job he didn't want--killing people for the Federation. Even though his fingers curled into a fist, he still felt the soft bear that reminded him of the little boy who had owned it. Sweat beaded on his forehead as he remembered the medal the

Federation had given him fifteen months ago to honor his bravery.

The cold wind ripped through him, numbing Joe's hands. The throbbing in his knee worsened as though someone had punched it. If he'd had any guts, he would have left without that medal. If he'd had any strength, he would have declined that 'honor.' If he'd wanted to absolve that sin, he would have blown his brains out. An eye for an eye. Instead, he threw away his career and deserted his military retirement, leaving his medal at the bottom of Lake Erie.

His stomach rumbled louder, and Joe knew he had to eat something or he was going to be sick. With one last glance up and down the empty alleyway, Joe pulled the blanket back and stood, preparing to do something he'd never done before, scavenge food from a trash bin.

As if in reply to Joe's intentions, his stomach growled louder. Whether in protest or agreement, Joe hadn't a clue. He stood up and walked toward the dumpster, trying to ignore the cold air stirring around him. Pain sliced through his left knee, and it almost buckled. Two years and the pain wrapped its claws around him. How much longer before walking became easier?

Taking short steps, he managed to get to the silver metal wall that came to his chest. As he stuck his head over it, he smelled the mixed garbage and thought about moving from the pungent odor, but he knew better. This was the last chance cafe. No money, no meal. Unless he wanted to bum something from the Resisters' shelter a few miles away. Nobody else ran any type of good-hearted sanctuaries these days, and Joe wasn't sure he wanted to stick his face in one, had he known of any others.

He didn't deserve pity. He deserved to die.

His stomach rolled and he knew he didn't have a chance to refuse food. Even disgusting food. He had to eat. He forced himself to look inside the dumpster. All the garbage lay deep at the bottom, which meant he would have to climb inside to find anything remotely edible. After checking to make sure no one had appeared in the alley, he pulled himself over the wall and jumped into knee-high refuse.

Pain snapped through him as he landed, and when his feet slid into the garbage, the smell worsened from his body's stirring it up. The stench of some rotting animal filled Joe's lungs. *Damn,* he thought, staring at other people's trash. Living on the streets had been a nightmare when he couldn't afford to buy food. What was he becoming?

Joe bent over and dug. His numbed hands moved slowly, awkwardly. Joe couldn't feel the garbage he sifted through, and his fingers could barely pick up anything. Papers lined the surface. Joe saw advertisements from New Life Incorporated. He picked up one of the glossy sheets and saw the perfect five-star pentagram which had come to symbolize the corporation. Probably because that was the rough shape of the slight scar left on the foreheads of those who had the chip implantation installed. Free advertising.

Joe shoved aside the crinkled brochures and found a partially-burned sheet of white paper with typing on it. Curious, he brought it close to his face, trying to read the words by dim lamplight. The darkness pressed closer. Joe reached in his pocket and pulled out his lighter. Flipping it on, he held the paper up and looked at it. "dation bought out by Lifers." The first word of the sentence had been burned badly enough so that Joe couldn't make out all of the letters. He read on. "Justice can be bought for a `modest' financial commitment. Corruption can live and prosper far longer without the help of longevity chips."

Human screams broke the midnight silence. Joe ducked deeper in the trash bin as someone yelled, "Get him! Now!"

Joe's heart hammered. Had he been spotted? The small lighter flame consumed the paper. In his careless haste to hide, he had allowed the lighter and letter to get too close to each other. The flames lapped from the paper to his fingers, burning his skin. He dropped the paper and ground it deep into the trash.

Outside the container Joe heard things crashing together. "Get away from me!" a man shouted. More scuffling sounds. "I know the truth about New Life!"

"Grab hold of his arms and hold his body down," that first voice ordered. "Kneel!"

Joe listened to feet moving against the concrete. Jesus, the Lifers and Resisters were at it again. How many of each were there? He closed the lid on his lighter and shoved it deep in his pocket.

"Let me go!" the man screamed again. "Get away from me!"

A cold rock pressed down in Joe's stomach. His whole body ached from sitting still and listening too long. He forced himself to rise, carefully favoring his injured knee. He peeked over the

10

side of the refuse bin toward the scuffle.

Three men surrounded one. Two of them held the victim's arms out to the side like a crucifix. The faint moonlight played on the victim's face. Joe scrutinized it, he wanted to be sick. A damn teenager, if Joe wasn't mistaken. A kid whose voice had changed a couple of years back. Just a kid who didn't have the good sense to stay off the streets during the lock-down times. Just another damn kid caught in the middle of battle lines. Joe's fingers curled up and he felt anger work through every muscle, stiffening, tightening.

The kid's dark eyes shone in the moonlight, frightened by the flash of steel pointed at his jugular. Joe's stomach rumbled again, but not in hunger. Nausea replaced appetite as he looked at the teenager's trembling body. He swallowed the bile in his mouth and looked at the men around the kid, focusing on the one holding the knife.

About 5'10 and stocky, the guy looked old enough to be Joe's father. But his father never looked that massive and bulky as though he might have trouble fitting through a doorway. Hard, unnatural lines around his mouth, eyes and forehead defined an angry profile. In the moonlight Joe could see the star-shaped scar on his forehead where the Lifespan Chip had been implanted.

Yeah, Joe thought savagely. *This SOB is somebody I want walking around this earth another fifty years.* He looked at the kid's forehead and found another, differently blatant mark. A triangle patch fused over the skin. The badge of a Resister which blocked the chip implantation forever. The kid had made a lifetime choice, probably at the age of sixteen when getting drunk, laid or anything else which, at that moment, seemed smart and fashionably acceptable.

And the Lifers were going to kill the kid because of that badge. If they couldn't convert him, they had no use for him. Joe gritted his teeth to keep from muttering a string of obscenities. He shifted his weight and then grimaced when pain ripped through his knee.

The older guy brought the knife close to the kid's neck. "Looks like we got us a guinea pig. Maybe we should crack his skull and see what replaced his brain." He pressed the knife deeper, cutting. The kid gasped. A smile lit the old man's face. "How dare you protest the gifts of New Life!" He pulled the dagger back a bit. The youth's shoulders sagged and his head rolled forward as though he wanted to faint. "Christ," the kid whispered looking down at his pants. A growing wet spot appeared.

Joe looked back at the kid, at his tortured face. The older man moved the knife upward and flicked the point of it against the kid's left temple, drawing blood from a deep gash. He leaned close and touched the kid's face with his fingers. "Hell, maybe I should just cut that badge from your head and take it back to Caleb as a souvenir. He collects 'em, you know. Ain't like we could use you for anything else." He lifted the dagger and poised it at the top of the triangular mark.

You gonna stand and watch or fight the fight? he asked himself. His fingers slowly moved the hilt of his dagger. Three against one. Could be worse. He started over the wall and pain skewered his knee with each movement. *Then again, it could be better,* he thought. Joe Ramsey didn't care about odds. He yanked out his knife and darted behind the old man. Before the guy could react, Joe held it across the man's neck.

"I wouldn't move if I were you," Joe ordered in a softly menacing voice. "I'll cut you up so you'll need a miracle to save you, even with that chip implant." Joe saw a slight movement of hands and pressed the badge closer. "Tell them to back off and let the kid go."

Joe saw his opponent's shoulder and back muscles ball up into rigidness. "Do you know who you're fucking with?" his adversary asked in an equally quiet voice that came out between clenched teeth.

"Doesn't matter," Joe said. "This knife doesn't care who the hell you are. It'll take your head off all the same."

"It'll matter the next time we meet." The man slowly lowered the blade.

Joe pulled him back. "And what makes you think there will be a next time? What makes you think I won't kill you this time?"

"Because you're stupid enough to save a Resister. That means you won't kill me."

Joe dipped the tip of the blade into his skin and cut. "Don't be too damn sure about anything, Old Man."

Despite the cut, Joe's hostage stood perfectly still, as though he hadn't felt anything. "Ask anybody in this neighborhood about Malachette." The two men holding the youth grinned, revealing sharp, white teeth. *The pretty boys of New Life,* Joe thought disgustedly.

"And if you don't shut up, you won't be breathing long enough to worry about being a tough guy," Joe snapped at them. He looked at the youth. Red splotches covered both his cheeks, and when he saw Joe's eyes, he closed his eyes, embarrassed. In the previous second that they had stared at each other, Joe saw something that didn't resemble youth. Something broken. The kid was praying Joe would get him out of here. And Joe knew somebody else needed to be wearing the hero suit. Somebody with two good legs. Somebody who hadn't been the person Joe once was.

Joe's head hummed. Not now, he thought. Then the message came. NEW LIFE INCORPORATED OFFERS THE CHANCE OF A LIFETIME. LIVE TO SEE ABSOLOM'S COMET IN 3050. GIVE YOURSELF AN EXTRA FIFTY YEARS. DON'T YOU DESERVE IT? FOR A MODEST FINANCIAL COMMITMENT, WE CAN GIVE YOU NEW LIFE. NEW LIFE. NEW LIFE.

The guy on the right of the kid lunged. Joe started to cut Malachette's throat, but fingers grabbed his hand. A fist rammed across Joe's face, and the world turned rainbow-colored. *Jesus, I knew this wasn't a good idea.* Joe felt himself falling. He threw out his hands to soften the landing he couldn't see coming.

"Grab that kid," Malachette screamed. "He's getting away!"

Pain exploded in Joe's ribs as a foot slammed into them. "You piece of shit!" Malachette yelled. Another kick. Joe's arms moved in front of his chest and abdomen. "I had that punk. I could have taught him why being a Resister doesn't pay. Why didn't you just stay out of it?" The irrational tone quickly died and Malachette's voice softened into a normal pitch. "It doesn't matter."

Malachette bent over and grabbed a fist of Joe's hair. As his fingers knotted in it, Malachette yanked Joe's head from the ground. "You're a street rat. No home, no nothing. And you think saving a Resister is a noble deed." Venom-laced laughter filled the night.

Joe's head pounded. Pain trickled through his scalp from Malachette's death-grip in his hair. He kept blinking his eyes, trying to cleanse the blackness from them. *At least the kid got away. At least I managed to do one thing right during my miserable life.* Joe's blindness melted in time to see Malachette kick his left leg. Joe whimpered. His fingers wrapped around the damaged knee.

Malachete stopped lashing out at him, and leaned close to absorb Joe's pain. He leaned so close Joe could see the map of scars on Malachette's pitted face. Hard, angry lines made by a razor. Or a machete. A light snapped on in Joe's head. That's how he got his name.

Malachette flicked his knife at Joe's hand, leaving small, painful gouges in the flesh until Joe finally moved it. "Smart boy. At least you understand pain."

Joe lifted his leg and started to kick, but one of Malachette's thugs slammed his elbow down on Joe's groin. More pain. *What does this SOB want?*

"Do you know how much that one little Resister was worth? Ten thousand." Malachette said. "Be still and I won't hurt you. Much." Malachette's large knife poised at Joe's left knee, as though waiting for Joe to panic. The blade would sink in if he laid still. Or if he panicked. Either way Joe didn't stand a chance. He didn't see mercy as one of Malachette's qualities.

Malachette's scarred fingers flicked the blade, cutting a small hole in Joe's pants. Malachette pulled back the material and peered at Joe's knee. Then he sat back, satisfied. "Hell of a war wound, boy. Hurts, don't it?" He lifted the knife and skimmed the bruised surface, scratching the tender skin.

Pain ripped through him. Joe met Malachette's cold eyes and ignored the intense desire to look away. His fingers curled into fists. He'd rather die than talk about that war. "Fuck you."

Malachette grinned. "You ain't my type. I only like dead whores. Or soon to be dead ones."

The blade sliced in up to the hilt. Joe felt like his body had ripped in half. He screamed in a voice that he had never used before. Tears jumped into his eyes. He gripped his leg as the pain impaled him again. And again. He started to hyperventilate. *I'll never walk again.* But the frantic heart pounding against Joe's chest told him walking again wouldn't be his worst problem. Being able to breathe after Malachette finished took top priority.

Malachette bent over him and yanked Joe's hair back while laughing. "Nothing like taking something small and making it-"

The air exploded around them. Bullets rained into them.

One whizzed past Joe's ear, and all he could think was, *Here comes the war, and I might as well have a target painted upon me.*

Chapter Two

Joe covered his head as the world blurred into screams. Bullets whizzed past his body. Pain throbbed in his leg, paralyzing him. He couldn't have walked, even if he'd wanted to. *Bullets?* Joe thought. *It must be the Resisters.* They tended to pack more of the heavy stuff, since it was illegal. One of Malachette's men grunted and then toppled onto Joe, knocking the air out of him. Dead weight pinned him to the ground.

"Damn! I missed him," someone shouted. The bullets stopped snapping. Joe looked for Malachette. Gone. Joe rolled the body off his chest. He sat up and looked at the knife handle protruding from his knee. Blood quickly soaked the ripped fabric of his pants, turning the fabric black. *I wonder if the implants make you feel younger,* Joe thought, feeling painfully ancient, as he stared at the weapon and started to vomit. Five men walked toward him. *So much for hiding in the alley trash.*

From the corner of his eye, Joe sized them up. Most of them looked bigger than him, and Joe knew this wasn't a fight he could win. Not with his blade lying about fifteen feet away. He cursed the alley and his luck. He reached for the handle and started to pull it out. Any weapon would be better than none.

"I wouldn't do that if I were you."

Joe looked up and saw the youth Malachette had almost killed. "You pull it out and we might not be able to staunch the bleeding before you die." The kid walked up to him and yanked out a rag from his pants pocket. Joe forced himself to look away from the wet spot on around the crotch area of the kid's pants. Joe had misjudged him. Even if he did piss in his pants, it took balls to walk back to where someone almost slit your throat.

"The name's Henry," the kid said, looking down at Joe's leg. He knelt before Joe and began tying a rag into a tourniquet around Joe's bloody knee, avoiding the dagger as much as possible. "Not that anybody ever calls me anything but Cammo."

"I'm Joe," He grimaced as Henry yanked a knot around the wound. "Why Cammo?" he forced out between clenched teeth.

"Because most of the time he remembers how the hell to hide so that you could walk past him and never know he was there," one of the other guys said, walking toward the two. His olive clothes appeared almost brown. Short black hair ridged upward from his scalp. He wasn't particularly tall, but he strutted forward and grabbed the kid by his shoulders, yanking him up. Three other followed him.

The man quickly patted Henry down, obviously searching

for signs of injury, before stepping back, folding his arms across his chest and glaring at the kid. "What did you think you were doing back there? Did you think you could take on Malachette single-handedly? Damn it, Cammo, the next time you fuck up, I'll be digging your grave for whatever's left of your miserable body. Whatever Malachette doesn't take to Caleb."

"Take it easy," Henry said in a soothing tone. "I'm fine. He didn't hurt me. Joe stopped him."

The man stared at the wet spot on Henry's pants and then looked back at his face. "So you just peed all over yourself for the hell of it?" He shook his head. "No, I think he was probably getting ready to cut through that thick skull of yours."

The kid winced, as though the words struck him. "I'm sorry, Murray. I wanted to get him." The kid's voice softened, breaking into painful fragments. His wet, brown eyes peered at him imploringly. "I did it for you."

Murray's hands, paused in mid-air, trembled visibly. The color had left the dirty face. He lifted his right hand and raked it through short, spiky hair, before turning away from Henry and glaring at Joe. Hard, stone eyes full of rage centered on him. The triangular mark of the Resisters' branded his forehead. "I suppose I should be thankful to you for my brother's life, foolish as he is." He glanced down at Joe's wounded knee, the blood seeping through the rag. "My men and I will take you back to the Palace so we can treat your leg."

Murray strode into the darkness as two men leaned down on either side of Joe and began carrying him. *Don't do me any favors,* Joe thought.

"You're brother's got a hell of a chip on his shoulder," Joe said between clenched teeth. He looked at Henry.

Two red splotches grew on the kid's face. "Yeah, I know." He looked at Joe, his eyes wearing that same glassy expression. "He's got more than one. Malachette. Caleb Walker. New Life Incorporated. Take your pick."

Joe watched Murray walk. Even with the thick coat spoiling the clear definition of Murray's body language, Joe saw the shoulders rising upward defiantly. "Yeah, so what's the big deal? Who the hell is Caleb Walker? I mean I've heard the name twice tonight and it doesn't ring a bell."

Henry closed his eyes, as though seeing something in front of him that he didn't want. "He's the owner of New Life Incorporated. And the SOB who owns Dal-Worth and a lot more of the Federated lands than one man should."

Joe tried to ignore the pain by concentrating on the kid's words. "Yeah, so? Why does this concern your brother? I mean-"

"You stay out of it!" Murray stalked in front of him, staring with cold green eyes. Only a few inches separated their faces, but neither would move away. The gun clenched in Murray's right hand silenced Joe more than the rage, probably because he'd seen many furious men before but never that type of a gun, a Parkinson 85. Fully automatic and lethal, even to Lifers, which is what made them illegal. Ten years ago the Federation had outlawed all guns. It had been part of the peace negotiations which united the

21

three countries forming the Federation. Germany, France and the United States, all ruled by a handful of prominent men in their fifties.

Joe stared at the gun. The Parkinsons especially, because they were the only weapons which had impactifers for bullets. These not only made physical reconstruction of tissue a nightmare but also zapped the electric pulse of the chip, negating its power entirely.

So much for longevity, Joe thought, staring at the sleek silver metal weapon that all but pointed at him. "Nice gun."

Murray's mouth never twitched from the malevolent frown. Despite the lines of rage cutting into his expression, his face seemed tiny, dwarfed by the anger. His body bristled with it, like raw energy sizzling from within. What caused that much hostility in somebody? Joe wondered.

Murray took a step back. "Don't ask questions that don't concern you and we'll all be better off." His eyes strayed from Joe to Henry. "And why don't you shut your mouth. We don't know who the hell this guy is. So what if he saved your life. Piss him off and he'd probably take it quick enough." Murray glared at him one last time before walking away.

As the group walked through the sleeping town, the cold wind wrapped around Joe. And the pain filled his gut. All he wanted to do is find some place warm away from the pain. His stomach rumbled again, but this time he didn't feel hungry, just alone, surrounded by people he didn't understand.

The lightheadedness washed over him quickly,

unexpectedly. His head lurched forward, and he felt himself losing consciousness. "Joe?" Henry called. Hands touched him. "Wake up, Joe." The sounds drifted further and further away into blackness where Joe slept and dreamed.

***

"Damn it," Malachette seethed as he approached the forty-story building nestled at the center of Dal-Worth, Texas. New Life Incorporated. He looked up at the windows and found all except the one at the top dark. "Damn!" His hands balled into fists.

Two security guards glanced at Malachette and his men before nodding for him to enter. *As if I need your permission*, he thought, glaring at them. He opened the glass door and stalked inside. One closed elevator. Malachette glanced at the number above the elevator to find it was stopped on his floor.

"Caleb's going to skin us when he finds out we had the kid and lost him." One of the men behind Malachette had spoken.

"You let me handle Caleb." Gauging the panic in the faces, he knew he could still control them. That little ambush hadn't changed anything. He grinned at them, knowing his smile usually frightened people. Perhaps it was the fact that somebody with that many scars could still smile that unnerved them. "And we'll get that stupid kid. Next time he won't have a savior to free his scrawny ass."

Malachette turned and punched the button, but the door wouldn't open. Not without passing through the damn security formalities. Gritting his teeth, Malachette walked to the panel beside the elevator and pushed on it. It slid away, revealing a dark hole. Malachette leaned forward and waited for the humming. It came as a clamp latched down around his neck and held his head in place. Bright light bearing down on his forehead forced him to shut his eyes.

Seconds dragged by. *Come on and read the DNA sequence. It hasn't changed since the last time you scanned me.*

Sweat beaded upon his forehead as he thought of Caleb's impending displeasure. Not only was the fact the kid had escaped going to set him off, but finding out Murray hadn't died after all would finalize Caleb's wrath. Some days it just didn't pay to work for the man who owned New Life. He had a nasty habit of killing employees.

When the light finally went out and the elevator opened, Malachette turned to his men. "Just stay down here. I'll come back and tell you the next move." He walked to the elevator which closed in around his body. A one-man job built to keep security secure.

"What floor?" A computer-generated voice asked.

"Forty."

"How is your implant working?" the voice asked.

"Fine. Save the speech. I work here."

"As you wish."

The rest of the ride passed in silence broken only when the elevator reached the top floor. As the doors slid open, Malachette stepped off. Two guards that Malachette affectionlessly referred to as Lugnut and Spare Change patted his body down, searching for a weapon. Three knives later, they finished frisking him.

"Is everybody happy now?" Malachette asked, arching his eyebrows.

"Go on in," Spare Change said, gesturing toward the door straight ahead. "He's waiting for you. Been waiting for an hour." Calm voice. Dangerous words.

"Yeah, well," Malachette said, walking towards the door. "I got hung up."

"If you're not careful that might become a permanent state," Lugnut said, grinning. His shaved head gleamed in the bright light like a peach-colored bowling ball.

Malachette stopped before the closed door. His fingers balled into white-knuckled fists. "You think this should bother me? I've been cut like a jigsaw puzzle by bigger men than you. Cut so damn deep all I had left was breath coming in and out of my body. But it was enough. And it was more than what I left those pricks with the last time I saw them."

Malachette listened to the silence breathing behind him while he opened the door. *Everybody likes to think he's a tough guy.*

As the door swung open, Malachette stepped into a large foyer. Cream-colored carpet and dark textured walls made the room appear smaller than it was. A crystal chandelier lit the room Malachette had entered many times before. "Likes nice things, doesn't he?" Malachette muttered to himself and walked through the doorway to a much larger livingroom. More cream walls and carpet. Black leather couch and love seat.

25

Malachette sensed one of the guards following him. The sound of footfalls on the floor confirmed it. More of Caleb's standard operating procedures. Muscle boys to make him feel safe. Unfortunately it would take both Lugnut and Spare Change to equal one working brain.

Malachette kept walking. He turned his head slightly to see Lugnut following him. "Careful with your boots. Caleb might get awful damn irate if you stain his perfect carpet."

Lugnut didn't answer, Malachette noted with a smirk as he passed through the living room into Caleb's office.

"You're late."

Malachette stared at the back of Caleb Walker's leather desk chair. *Such a big seat for a scrawny, spineless man*, he thought. "Tell me something I don't already know."

"That you're fucked, my man." The chair slowly turned around until Caleb's blue eyes fixed on him. Thick blonde hair was greased back from his face. And the bluntness of his chin almost made his face rectangular. Thick bushy eyebrows drew together in the frown he wore. The narrow slants, coupled with the sneering mouth showed Caleb's obvious displeasure. "You're paid to play, but you can't deliver. I need a new errand boy, don't I? Too bad, Malachette. I thought you were a team player."

He leaned forward and began typing on the computer, ignoring Malachette. The Lifer frowned and stared at him, at the complacent way his hands tapped the keys. *I don't like this one damn bit.* He blinked, and then felt a dagger of pain rip through his head. Malachette grasped his temples and groaned. His legs

26

slipped from under him and he fell to the carpet.

"I've heard you handle pain exceptionally well, Malachette." He held a glass in his hand as he stood up and walked to the window.

"Stop it," Malachette moaned. As the pain deepened, he rolled into a fetal ball. "I'm still you're man. I got some goods. I found out something worth more than the kid."

Caleb turned to him. "No, you're empty-handed. And your brain is overloading. The chip is malfunctioning. And if you die it will look like you've simply died of natural causes." He watched Malachette writhe on the floor. The spasms of his body forced his fingernails to dig into his face. Swirling the liquid in his glass, Caleb strolled to the computer and hit one key.

Malachette groaned and his body stilled except for labored gasps. Caleb walked over to where the man lay on the carpet and kicked Malachette's shin. "Get up. Now. I'm giving you a second chance. Tell me what you know that's worth more to me than my dead wife's brother." He kicked him again and then strode back to the window.

Disoriented, Malachette sat up and took a deep breath. He stood on unsteady legs and walked toward the window to stand next to Caleb. He forced himself to bite back the nausea and grin as he looked at his boss. Blond hair. Athletic body. Damn shame no muscles would stick on that thin frame. *Yeah*, Malachette thought. *He sure was a pretty boy. But pretty boys needed other people to do the dirty work.* Five-feet, ten inches tall and a bean-pole frame that Malachette knew he could strangle the life

27

out of him with one hand. But then Malachette wouldn't get paid. And Malachette clenched his jaw and thought, *I always get paid. And then I rip his head from his body.*

The two of them stared out at Dal-Worth spread in darkness below. Some lights illuminated the darkness, but most were concentrated in the vicinity of the Palace. Two miles of rectangular brick and steel. Once it had been a prison. Now it housed everything Caleb Walker despised.

"And what is your little peace offering?" Caleb asked, turning toward him.

Malachette walked over to the bar in the corner of the room and filled a glass for himself. He looked in the mirror and his fingers dabbed at the bloodied cuts before he adjusted his rumpled clothing. "The chance to finish what you started years ago. You don't really want the kid. You want the heart of the Resisters. You want his sister. You want your wife--Murray Walker." He walked back to the window.

"Murray's alive?" His face turned red and he clenched his jaw .

"Yeah. Her brother and some other Resisters saved her apparently."

Caleb nodded and lifted his glass to a toast with Malachette. "You're right. Double or nothing, Malachette. Get Murray and you'll be a very rich man."

Malachette nodded and walked toward the door. "Oh, I'll get her all right. And I'll bring back her head for your approval." He walked back to the elevator and glared at Lugnut. "I'm still in one piece, pretty boy."

Malachette slipped through the open door and disappeared.

Caleb Walker leaned back into his leather chair and watched dawn spill slowly across the sky. Through bleary eyes, he saw the pink and sherbet clouds give way to blue. His hand still clutched his glass.

"Damn her." He knew Murray would be trouble. He just hadn't expected her to keep breathing long enough to cause problems.

Whose body had Malachette burned in that house fire? How had Murray managed to get out? And who had helped her?

By all rights she should have been dead after he and Malachette finished with her. Rope burns on her arms. Her legs. Her neck. Her back looked like a raw piece of meat.

And still she was alive.

His fingers snapped inward around the glass, breaking it into shards. Pain blossomed in his hand. As Caleb looked at his cut fingers, he laughed and tossed the fragments against a wall.

A river of blood was coming. Murray's blood.

At night he sometimes heard the screams fear had gutted from her throat, begging him to stop. Reminding him she was his wife.

Her image came to him. Naked, she knelt with her hands tied behind her back where the skin parted in gashes from his whip. Blood saturated her hands and the rope which bound them. The left side of her face beaten so that the eye swelled shut and her jaw turned black and blue. "I won't tell anyone. Please stop!"

He knelt down and touched her face. Softly. Like a husband returning from a bout of madness. "I know you won't tell anyone. I'll cut out your tongue after I kill you."

She screamed. The weak, hollow sound carried no words. Struggling, she lost her balance and fell over while trying to crawl away. Her long, black hair looked purple from the blood staining it, and the bangs matted to her face from sweat.

He watched her struggle a few feet and then turned to Malachette. "Take her to an old house. And then finish it."

The line of Malachette's lips slowly bent into a leer. Bending down, he grabbed Murray's bruised arm. She screamed. He leaned close to her face and flicked out his tongue, licking the blood on her cheek. Murray flinched and screamed louder, trying to back up. He jerked on her arm.

"Why scream, baby?" He leaned toward her ear and kissed her. "We're friends. I was your bodyguard and you trusted me."

Murray's body convulsed. "Oh, God no." She pushed at him weakly, trying to escape.

"God isn't here." He bit her lip while pulling out his dagger and moving it in front of her wide eyes. "Just the man who's going to take you apart. Inch by inch."

She started screaming again. Laughing, Malachette slammed the hilt of the blade on her head, knocking her unconscious.

Malachette let her body fall to the floor as he wiped her blood from his hands and face with his handkerchief. "What exactly did you have in mind?"

Caleb handed him the whip and shrugged. "Whatever you like best."

Blinking, Caleb banished the memory. He stood up and looked out the window at the Resisters' compound. Even then he'd known what Malachette liked best. And it had to do with a bed and a female corpse.

He walked over to the bar and grabbed a full bottle of tequila to replace the empty one on his desk. "This is your last chance, Malachette," he whispered to the empty room. "You get Murray this time and make sure she stops breathing or I'll use the implant to get rid of you."

Chapter Three

Laughter rippled in Joe's dream. Hard, angry laughter echoing loudly. Damn it was hot. That South American sun felt like it was baking him alive. Joe looked up toward the sound cutting through the air. He saw the alleyways. In front of him he sensed Miguel's tiny body. The air tasted metallic, like blood. He scanned the empty windows. Off-white curtains billowed in the hot breeze. Sweat stung his eyes. He spotted the man who was laughing at him on a balcony four stories above him.

"Good shot, senior! Do you always murder kids?" He pointed at Miguel. Sunlight glistened off his Caucasian skin and light blonde hair. The hand raised into the air sported an expensive gold watch. "Couldn't hit anything else if your sorry life depended on it, could you?"

Joe's stomach lurched as he recognized that face. Kristof Alexander, the drug lord responsible for this blood bath. He'd seen the man's book-length file.

Joe raised the gun an aimed at him. You sonofabitch.

Joe turned over, struggling to break from the dream's

undertow. *He felt the gun in his grip and his finger pressed the trigger.*

His leg exploded in pain. Joe's gun barrel dropped a few inches and discharged. The bullet splintered into the wall. More laughter. He groaned and leaned over the knee, gripping the area around the bullet hole with his free hand.

"Adios, Asshole," that voice said. Joe turned his body and saw the Spanish mercenary who had shot him. The same one he'd been chasing. Greasy black hair tumbled in the man's dark face. His smile revealed yellowed teeth with a gap between the top two teeth. Joe fired. The bullet ripped into the man's chest. Dark eyes widened. The gun dropped from his grip. His fingers twitched. His eyes closed, and he slumped to the ground.

Joe looked up at the empty window where the cream curtains billowed like ribbons. "Hablar that, you sonofabtich."

He moved his leg and bit his tongue to keep from screaming. Blood poured from his shredded knee. I may never walk again, he thought. His fingers trembled and he tried to set his hands on the ground away from the seeping blood, but it covered his skin, sticky as it started to dry in places.

Miguel.... He stared into the little boy's wide chocolate eyes. Joe's path of vision strayed the teddy lying in his slackened grip. Joe's throat constricted. "No," he whispered, shaking his head. "God, no!" What have I done?

Blackness. Joe could feel his body, the stillness of it as he lay in the residue of dreams. The pain and fear abandoned him, dissolving in the nothingness surrounding him. For once he felt warm and comfortably cocooned in the dark. So much so that he didn't want to shrug it away. He wanted to sink deeper into the midnight softness and forget his body.

Where am I? he wondered. He took a deep breath of peppermint-scented air. Fear and panic forced his eyes open. As he sat up, he came face to face with Murray's green eyes staring at him. The Resister's eyelids closed down slightly into slits and hard lines flocked around his mouth.

Is this guy just a little uptight in the ass, or what? Joe thought, momentarily taken back at the abrupt transformation in Murray's facial expression. *I open my eyes and he gets pissed.*

"Awake at last," Murray said. He pointed to a food tray sitting on the dresser beside the bed. "Hungry?"

Joe's stomach answered, rumbling loudly. "What can I say?" he muttered while looking down at it.

As Murray picked up the tray, he said, "Adjust your pillows so you can sit up, and I'll bring this over to you. After you eat we'll test that knee of yours."

Joe complied quickly. Murray set a tray full eggs, bacon and toast in his lap. Despite Joe's hunger, he first picked up the glass of water and took a long drink, draining every drop. As Joe set it back down, Murray picked it up and refilled it, watching Joe devour the food.

"How long since you've had a meal?" Murray asked, handing him the glass.

Joe finished the bit in his mouth and said, "I don't remember." Crimson flooded his cheeks. "A while, I guess." He set the glass on the tray.

"I wouldn't sleep in that alley anymore," Murray continued. He sat down and watched Joe eat. "It's a well-known target point."

"The same could be said for the whole city. Or even the rest of the Federated states, don't you think?" Joe asked. He shoved the last piece of bacon in his mouth and chewed. He noticed Murray didn't admit who started the fights or why. Or even that the Resisters were involved. Joe scarfed the rest of the food.

"Blame that on the Lifers, not me." Murray picked up the empty tray. "I'll tell Wayne you're is still breathing."

"Wayne?" Joe asked. "Who's that?"

Murray set the tray on the dresser. He folded one arm over the other. "The guy who healed you."

"Oh," Joe said, nodding. Murray quickly headed for the door. Acutely aware of the sterile walls surrounding him, Joe felt handicapped, considering the fact that he was practically naked and unarmed.

"Wait!" he called to Murray's retreating back. Joe stared at the hunched shoulders. He had remembered them as much bigger and more intimidating. "How long have I been out?"

Murray turned toward him. His eyebrows curled downward as the man thought for a moment. "About 24 hours. The first two of them were spent repairing your leg. Wayne thought you might have been playing with bombs with that much damage inside." He looked toward the blankets where Joe's knee probably was. "Were you hung up on some kind of ego trip to take on three guys

35

even though you could barely walk? Or did you just have a death wish?"

As Murray spoke, Joe moved his left leg, ignoring his words. He straightened it. A reaction to check for pain. None. "What kind of drugs you got me on? I don't feel anything." He frowned and bent his knee, knowing that would bring a sharp pain. It always did before. But this time the muscles bent easily, forgivingly, as if they had never been injured. Joe kept moving his joint, trying unsuccessfully to coax the pain from its slumber.

"You're not on drugs. There's nothing to feel anymore. Wayne took care of it." Murray watched him move his leg back and forth. "The muscles are as good as new. At least until you do something else stupid enough to hurt them." The Resister lifted his hand and rubbed at his neck, kneading the flesh in a circular pattern.

Joe stared at the hard lines etched into Murray's face. He looked a lot like Henry, except older and a lot more cynical. Black hair, the color of a midnight sky seemed to be the one feature different between the two brothers. Henry's hair was sandy instead. Joe studied Murray's frown and the stiff jaw and realized that he had finally met someone with as many dark secrets as Joe carried. "You don't like me much, do you?"

More lines deepened the frown on Murray's face. "Let's just say I don't know you well enough to like you." He headed toward the metal door. "I'll send Wayne in."

"How's the kid?" Joe asked as he pulled back the covers. "I mean, I know he wasn't hurt, but he could have been, and I think it might have scared him." Joe rubbed the callouses on his palms, pretending the question didn't have any significance.

Murray paused at the door. His gaze, once eye-level slowly lowered as he gripped the doorjamb with white fingers. Once Joe would have sworn Murray had been taller, more bulky. Without the Parkinsen he didn't seem near as dangerous. "He's fine." The gruff voice thinned to a softer one. "Thanks to you." Murray didn't wait for Joe's response, but instead slipped out the door before Joe could speak.

So that's as close to sentimental as he gets, Joe thought, looking at his knee. He touched it with inquisitive fingers, probing for lines of pain. Shadows of the war. Remembrances.

Nothing came. His fingers touched a line tracking down the middle of his knee. A scar which hadn't been there before. But it shouldn't have healed that quickly. It couldn't have. Who in the hell was this Wayne guy? And where had he gone to medical school?

Sighing, Joe moved his fingers to his face and ran them over his chin, expecting the beard he'd hated. Living on the streets didn't make shaving exactly convenient. His fingers caressed smooth skin. *One of the Resisters must have shaved me.* Joe's fingers stretched on toward his hair. It should have been long, close to his shoulders. Instead it stopped at the middle of his neck.

A flush crept into Joe's face. His back stiffened defiantly, and he gritted his teeth. Joe Ramsey had been their newest charity case. Maybe that was why Murray hadn't blown out his brains.

Or maybe it really was because of Henry?

Joe shrugged away that thought and focused on the anger. It was easier to manage. He didn't want to think about the kid. He clenched the blanket in his fingers until his knuckles turned white. *Joe Ramsey is nobody's charity case*, he thought savagely. *Least of all some damn Resister's.* Yanking the covers from around his body, Joe saw his boxers had been left on. *What a bargain,* he thought. *Next time they'll probably donate one of their damn badges.*

Joe's fingers quickly uncurled from the blanket and he tried to swallow the lump developing in his throat. *That's not funny.* He touched his forehead, searching. His fingers skimmed smooth skin. Not trusting his hands, Joe got up from the bed and hurried to the mirror hanging on the wall.

Instead of lights surrounding the silver frame, a soft white glowed from the edges of the mirror itself. He peered close to the glass and examined his reflection, looking for the triangular mark which branded all of the Resisters.

His callused fingers hadn't lied. The face staring back at him didn't have a scar. The mirror showed a thirty-seven-year-old male with ash brown hair. Grey streaks glittered throughout, especially in the sterile white light of the room.

Everything seemed sterile here.

Joe touched his face, stroking the skin of his cheeks that he hadn't felt in ages. He'd hidden under a beard. Now that someone had shaved it off, he looked younger. Alive. Painfully alive, his eyes said. He looked like the man who had become a soldier because he wanted to believe in the Federation. What he wouldn't give to be that person again. To have a chance to take back that bullet. Five seconds to remove all 'what if's' and 'too bads' from his life.

Yeah, and while you're at it, why don't you ressurect a few ashes for good measure, too.

"Moving around so soon?"

Joe whirled and came face to face with a man he assumed to be Wayne. As he looked at the canary yellow shirt with large flowers, Joe frowned. Somehow he had expected something...calmer. *You could see him coming from a mile away!* The man's shoes forced a strangled laugh from Joe. Flip flops. With socks. Joe squinted disbelievingly. "Isn't it a little cold for those?" He pointed at them.

The healer grinned at Joe and clenched a cigar between his teeth. "I've been intending to head to the coast, but you know how it is," he said, pulling the stogie from his mouth and setting it in an ashtray. "Yeah, yeah. It's winter. But I've never liked closed-in shoes. Can't feel the air or anything else with boots."

"You won't be able to feel your feet for long outside with those on."

The healer shrugged. "You'd be surprised. Besides, I don't go out much anymore, and when I do, at least I don't fall asleep. Cold feet tend to keep me alert."

Joe forced himself to stop staring at the shoes and turned his attention to Wayne's facial features. Long, silver hair splayed across the yellow knit shirt. Joe looked into his silver eyes.

39

Wayne's mouth turned into a bemused grin.

"Everyone likes the shirt." He touched one of the flowers. "I've had it for years. Hell, Murray loves it. And, uh, welcome to the Palace," the healer said, offering his hand. "I'm Wayne Williams, the manager."

"Joe Ramsey." As Joe reached out and shook Wayne's hand, the healer's grip cinched down tight. Well, hell? What had he expected? That Wayne Williams was physically weak and mentally strong? Instead of trying to answer that one, he simply echoed, "Manager? What exactly to you manage?" *A group of Resisters?*

"This place isn't just for Resisters. People who don't have a sack to sleep in come, too."

Joe's back stiffened and he stepped back. *He read my mind.*

"Yeah, I did." Wayne bobbled his head unabashedly. "Didn't find out any good stuff though, so you shouldn't be too pissed off." Wayne pushed his hair behind his shoulders. He pointed to the bed. "Would you sit so that I can have a look at your knee? I want to make sure it's healed." He picked up the stogie again, took a good draw, then set it back in the ashtray.

Joe's feet wouldn't budge. *How does....* Joe forced himself not to think.

"It's a skill, more than a gift. Someday I'll show you how it works." Wayne touched Joe's shoulder and gestured toward the bed. "I don't often use it though. Once people realize you can read their mind, they keep it clean. And what fun is that?" Amusement glittered in his eyes.

40

Joe sat down on the bed and watched Wayne kneel in front of him. Long, skinny fingers traced the seam on his knee. "I suspected the knife wound wasn't the least of your pain. I found a much older injury which had to be healed first, even before I could work with the damage done by the knife. What caused the first trauma?"

Joe's fingers clamped down on the bed and he closed his eyes. He couldn't lie about it. Wayne would know the truth, one way or another. He thought of the toy he'd carried for months and his hands felt unbearably empty without it. "An old war wound," Joe said, staring ahead. He forced himself to focus on the white walls and tried to forget the dead child.

"The knee's fine," Wayne said, withdrawing his hands. "Looks good as new." He went over to the ashtray and lifted the cigar to his mouth for one last drag before stubbing it out.

Joe nodded in agreement. "Yeah. It feels good, too. Where are my things?"

The healer pointed to a closed door. "In there." He watched Joe get off the bed and walk toward it. "Even thought your body's healed, you're welcome to stay at the Palace for a while to get on your feet."

Joe gritted his teeth and opened the door. "No thanks." He pulled on his shirt. The fabric pressed softer against his skin than it had for days, and it smelled clean, instead of sweaty. "I can't. I really appreciate what you've done for me, but I just can't."

He pulled on his pants. Wayne kept watching him from where he sat on the edge of the bed. "You still think this is about separating people into Lifers or Resisters, Joe? I didn't ask you to become an 'us' or a 'them.' I just offered you a warm place to stay until you figure out what's next."

Joe looked into those silver eyes. Wayne looked back, acknowledging him. Embarrassed, Joe turned away. He didn't want to look into anybody's eyes anymore, especially not somebody who might see the kid's body hidden there in the sharp blue of his irises. "Thanks anyway." He busied himself by putting on his boots, and quickly lacing them. "But I've got to move on."

"Suit yourself. The question is, where you moving on to?"

Joe finished tying his boots, but he felt odd, like he'd overlooked something. He'd lost something. Ice settled in his stomach when he realized his knife was missing. "Have you seen my blade?" he asked Wayne. He kept his voice casual, trying not to panic over losing the only weapon he'd had.

Wayne shook his head. "You didn't have a weapon with you when you were brought to the Palace."

"Figures," Joe mumbled. He looked up at Wayne's collar. That's as far as he could go. No faces anymore. No money, no weapon. Lady Luck had taken him to the cleaners.

Wayne got up from the bed and walked over to Joe. "I'm sorry about your blade."

Joe rolled his shoulders, trying to get rid of the tension mounting as the healer stood beside him. He felt like he couldn't breathe. He had to get out of there. He'd steal a knife if he couldn't get one any other way.

"I'm sure we've got a spare around here."

"I guess reading my mind hasn't gotten boring yet."

"Don't worry. It's not exactly exciting, either." Wayne shrugged. "It's a habit, really."

"Well, thanks. I'll take the blade. Whatever you can spare." Joe offered his hand to Wayne. "I'll never be able to repay your generosity. I mean your people could have left me there with Malachette. But they didn't...." Silver eyes rested on him. "Anyway, thanks." The last words came out fumbled together. *Doesn't matter. He can read your mind, and he knows what you meant, even if you speak like a four-year-old.*

As Joe moved toward the door, Wayne touched his shoulder. "Maybe you don't want to jump in the middle of our cause. I'm not asking you to. But someone has taken an interest in you. Someone you could help."

Joe's chest and shoulders tightened. His head lowered a couple of inches. He wanted to glare at Wayne, but couldn't, especially when Wayne said, "I'm not trying to force you into anything. I just wanted you to know there's someone here whose life you left footprints in." The healer fingers closed down gently, the motion of a friend, not a stranger.

Joe's shoulder felt like it would sink to the floor from the slight weight of Wayne's hand. *Here it comes, just like you knew it would. Nothing's ever free, is it?* "Who is it you want me to help?" Joe shrugged Wayne's hand away. "I don't recall anyone who seems helpless around here."

As Joe paced the room, Wayne stepped back and gave him

room to walk. "It's not a matter of being helpless, Joe. Helplessness is a state of mind." The healer sat down and focused on Joe's boots tapping the floor. The healer waited for each ball and toe to touch the linoleum.

"So who are we talking about?"

"Cammo."

Joe stopped walking in mid-stride. His foot stretched out and his heel touched down, but he couldn't finish the step. It would be the kid. He closed his eyes. *Another kid that I can't save. All I can do is wreck his life or get him in trouble. The only thing I know how to do is kill. Is that a gift I should pass on?*

"No," Wayne said quietly. He responded to Joe's thoughts.

Joe looked at the man, at the stillness threaded in his body. Peace. Only when the healer smiled did Joe see the crow's feet clustering around his eyes, as if time itself perched there. "What would you have me do? I have nothing to offer him." Joe touched his chest. "I'm empty."

The healer shook his head. Strands of silver hair slipped over his shoulder, glistening metallically. "Nah, Joe. Nobody's ever empty. You can teach him the art of war. That is the only way you'll ever learn peace." Wayne smiled and the skin puckered under his eyes. "Take the pain which pierces you with sharpened steel and let his youth dull it. He thinks he wants rage and revenge. Teach him to listen. Teach him to hear the same voice you now hear before it comes too late to save him." Wayne pointed to Joe's knee. "It's a simple scar. But the roots fill your body. Teach the boy to weed the garden. Teach him that they begin growing here and don't stop unless you stop them."

Joe closed his eyes and held his breath. His shoulders began to ache from keeping his body so painfully still. The image of the child came back to him. The broken body. Blood. The bear. He blinked and tried to forget the chocolate eyes which never once closed. For the first time since the war, tears pooled in Joe's eyes.

"You mean teach him not to be like me," he said softly.

Chapter Four

Joe clenched his teeth and shoved his hands into his pockets. Unable to look at Wayne's face, Joe stared at the plain silver mirror on the wall. Light seeped from around the edges of the glass. "The kid has to have somebody else. Hell, Murray's his brother. If he can't save him, what makes you think I can?"

Joe rolled his shoulders, already imagining the cold wind ripping through him as he walked away into the night. He reached for the stuffed bear, but his fingers found nothing. "Where's the rest-"

"Here," Wayne said, holding out the blue bear.

As Joe took it, he looked closely at the healer's hands. Granted, callouses collected on his palm, but the skin didn't seem weathered or old. Or even nearly as aged as the rest of Wayne Williams. Miracle hands. "Scars run deep, Joe. You, above most people, ought to know that. Murray's too blinded by anger to teach the kid anything useful. You've been where Murray is, and you've survived."

"Why don't you mind your own business, old man?" *And*

what makes you think I can? Joe thought, shoving the bear into his pocket. He walked over to the mirror and looked at the face which seemed different than his own. Clean, shaven and warm. He could stay like this. All for the price of babysitting an out-of-control kid. He raked fingers through his hair, trying to give himself something to do besides look at Wayne's patient face.

Joe waved his hand under the faucet and the water spilled out. He bent over and splashed it over his face. The cool temperature reminded him of the ice ball pitted in his stomach, growing every time he even thought about the kid.

He scrutinized his reflection again. Dark brown eyes peered back at him. Brown from all the shit he'd carried around and couldn't regurgitate. Now more baggage. *Don't get involved*, he thought. *Just walk away*.

"So that one day you'll turn around and think about him, too?" Wayne asked softly. His healer's hands folded together in front of him. "You want to change things, Joe, but you can't. Not like this. You can't save what's been left behind. Only what's in front of you. Henry."

Joe whirled away from the mirror and closed the distance between himself and the healer. "Goddamn you for reading my mind." He leaned close to Wayne until inches separated their faces. Joe's hand rested on the spot where his dagger had been, ready to yank it free if it were there.

Wayne remained still. His lips straightened into a thin, neutral line. No fear. "I don't have to read your mind. You've got enough landmarks on your body. The old wound on your leg said as much as that toy you carry with you. You want redemption, and I'm offering it-"

The door swung open and Murray walked in. His coat and hat covered his body and he said, "Damn it, Wayne. He's done it again."

Wayne shrugged and rolled his eyes. "The kid loves jokes. I told him not to do it." Wayne waved his hands in the air. "But you shouldn't have gotten so uptight the first time Henry put the snake in your bed."

"Forget the snake. He's taken off again."

Wayne's hands dropped from each other to his sides. "It's nothing new. Don't come unhinged about it. When was the last time anybody saw him?"

Joe glanced at the clock on the wall. Four a.m.

Murray pulled out his Parkinsen and checked the status of his ammo. "An hour, give or take. He's out in the middle of Lockdown with Lifers all around him. What does it take to make you panic?"

Wayne scratched his head. "A sexy blonde in my bed telling me she's a friend of my ex-wife which means she's probably well armed and I'm naked." He pulled out a cigar and lighter from his pocket. "Calm down, Murray. We'll find him. We always do."

Murray gritted his teeth. "God, I had those things," he said pointing to the cigar. "And that shirt."

Wayne rolled his eyes. "Bitch a little more, why don't you? You sound like a woman." He reluctantly stowed the cigar back into his pocket.

The kid slipped out during lock down again, Joe thought. Every muscle in his back ached from stress. "Is he alone?"

Murray's response came out as a cold, mirthless laugh which didn't fill his eyes. "Yeah, he left alone. But he probably didn't stay that way, not considering the fact that he's a `Resister.' in a world full of Lifers." The angry smile vanished quickly. "He'll be lucky not to be killed." His voice thinned. Murray shook his head and looked at the ground. "Maybe that's what he wants. I don't know." Murray quickly looked at Joe with those cold, green eyes. "So are you gonna make yourself useful and help look or get more beauty sleep?" He holstered the gun and headed out the door.

Wayne's silver eyes met Joe's dark ones. "It's not easy growing up in this world of hate and rage, Joe. Especially when hardly anybody teaches anything different. So are you in?" Wayne followed Murray.

Joe looked at Wayne's thongs, and shook his head. *Christ, what a thing to wear in a world like this. His feet are gonna be freezing.*

Joe hung his head and closed his eyes, cursing the image which came to mind. The boy he'd killed. Except this time he saw Henry's eyes. His hands trembled visibly. Muttering a string of obscenities, Joe picked up his worn-out coat and headed after them to find the kid. First he had to find another blade.

***

The night cut through Joe's worn-out coat. He'd been

scouring the streets and alleyways for an hour. In the inky blackness all of them had begun to look the same. He half-expected pain to splinter his knee like always. Instead, he felt it creeping in his fingers and toes, keeping his whole body chilled. He'd wandered through enough alleys to last a lifetime. The one he'd been walking was dark, but Joe could see bodies lying on the ground.

Glancing at one face, he noticed the pentagram on the forehead of a man. A Lifer. His hands stretched over his body, as though reaching for something above. His glassy-eyed stared peered back at Joe as he patted the corpse down, ignoring the dried blood staining the ground and everything else. The faces looked ashen in the moonlight like waxen figures, not bodies. Welcome to hell. A place where alleys suffice as graveyards.

Joe bent over and started to go through their pockets when a voice said, "Don't bother. I already took what they had. Not that much was left."

Joe yanked out the borrowed sword and whirled around. Henry stood, holding Joe's weapon, offering it to him. "I saved this for you. I thought you might want it." The kid proffered it more firmly, looking at the ground, instead of Joe.

Dumbfounded, Joe sheathed his new blade and accepted his old one. "Don't tell me that's why you skipped out of the Palace during lock down, kid. To find my sword."

Henry flushed and looked up at the sky. He walked over to an old mattress lying on the ground and sat down. "Nope. I grabbed it right after Malachette left."

"Oh, thanks." Joe followed the path of Henry's gaze toward a horizon of blue and pink. "Tell me why you're here then."

Henry pointed at the sky. "To watch that."

Joe shook his head and gritted his teeth. *Oh great. A romantic.* "Jesus, kid. That's what windows are for." Joe rubbed the bridge of his nose.

Henry glared at Joe. "No, they're for hiding behind. The sunrise doesn't look the same behind a pane of glass." Henry stared at the sky without blinking for a long time. His hands hung limply at his side and his breathing dwindle to a small, regular rhythm as though he were sleeping.

Joe held his sword and watched the sunrise with the kid. From the corner of his eye, Joe saw the thin body which still didn't look like a man, and Joe knew the healer had been right. Whatever Henry had learned, it hadn't been how to protect himself. Or why. And Joe's throat tightened and he wished to hell nobody had to ever teach him. Especially not Joe.

Once the sunrise had transformed the sky into its normal blueness, Joe touched Henry's shoulder. The kid blinked, as though coming out of a trance and his breathing sped up. "You've got to quit sneaking away like this. Murray's probably going to have your ass for this stunt." *And mine, too, for not dragging you back sooner.* "The world's a lot safer behind the Palace's walls." Joe started walking and motioned for the kid to follow him.

"Yeah, so you've said," Henry replied glumly. "Maybe you think everything looks the same behind a pane of glass, Joe. But I can't smell the morning air like that."

At least you won't get killed that way, Joe thought. But he didn't say it as they walked together. People began to walk the streets. As Joe scanned the faces, they blurred together. The women looked like men and the men looked like women. Baggy clothes, mostly in blacks and greys brushed past him. Lots of short, spikey hair and bald heads. And lots of pentagrams on foreheads.

Joe looked at the daggers and knives sheathed at most of the citizens' waists. Another Federation law. Being armed required only that the blade be kept at the waist in visible sight.

Dal-Worth, Texas had enough blades to rebuild the fallen Statue of Liberty in silver, Joe thought. A woman shoved between Joe and Henry. She stood out because of her tight, black dress and stiletto heels which nobody wore anymore except prostitutes.

Two men rushed past Joe and the kid, jarring them both to the side into other people. Joe mumbled an apology to the woman he'd bumped into and then glared ahead. The dark olive clothing and drawn guns the two wore immediately alerted Joe they were Federation peace officers, chasing a suspect.

One of them sprinted through the crowds and caught her. The peace officer tackled her and bore down on her back with his weight. Joe stopped walking and watched the two of them fall together. The woman's body hit the cement first, breaking the impact for him. She groaned as her head slammed to the ground.

A crowd gathered and thickened as people watched one of the Feds pull her to her feet and the other run a small silver box up one arm and down the other. She screamed and tried to move her arms, but couldn't. The box had paralyzed them.

A bruise started to flower on one of her temples, just a few inches away from the pentagram scar. Her hair fell into her heavily-made up face and she screamed, "I wasn't out during the lock-down! Leave me alone."

One of the Feds grabbed her arms and hauled her off, while the other followed behind, watching her walk. He looked at the crowds and said, "Clear out everybody. You all know what happens if you're out during lock-down." He smirked at Joe, as if to say, "And don't let me catch you next."

Joe looked away and tapped the kid's arm. "Let's get back to the Palace."

Henry rolled his eyes as though bored with the Feds' arrest. Joe sighed and tried not to think about how difficult it was going to be to make a lasting impression on this kid.

The thick, wire gates of the Palace swung open as Joe approached, weeding through the crowd of protesters already gathered.

"Is that kid your son?" a woman asked, shoving a "Lock Up the Resisters" sign in Joe's face. "Did you make him get that badge?" She stepped in front of him.

Joe moved around her. "I didn't make anybody do anything." Joe and the kid entered and waited just inside until the gates closed. No Lifers followed them.

He stared at the huge grey, brick building looming in front of them. Two thick steel gates swung open, waiting for them to

53

step inside. Joe touched the kid's back and propelled him in front. "Let's go, Henry. I think your brother's probably ready to explode."

Murray and Wayne met them at the door. Although Murray had been pacing away from the entrance of the Palace when Joe and the kid had walked in, the minute Murray heard the door slam, he turned and stared at the kid first. Then Joe.

Murray stalked toward Henry. His green eyes narrowed to ugly slants. He circled around Henry silently. The kid's Adam's apple moved as he swallowed nervously. Henry refused to look at the ground. He stared ahead at Murray, waiting for his brother's reprimand. Silence filled the room. He shifted his weight from one foot to the other. Joe, too, felt his nerves unraveling. He straightened his left knee. An old mannerism built on alleviating the pain of a shattered knee. Sometimes Joe's body didn't remember he'd been healed.

Murray finally stopped striding when he reached Henry's back. He leaned close to the kid. So close that Henry's hair moved every time Murray inhaled and exhaled. So close that Henry's back grew rigid like a piece of wood. So close that Joe was afraid he'd knock the kid into tomorrow.

"So you aren't dead," Murray said in a quiet voice. "You just walked into the night again and forgot that Malachette almost killed you."

Murray began sauntering again. This time he stopped in front of the kid. "God, there are times I want to kill you myself." He gritted his teeth.

54

"I'm sorry," Henry whispered. His shoulders rolled forward and he looked like a sapling bent permanently by the wind.

"Sorry," Murray repeated. He kept his fists at his hips and shook his head. "You think that makes me forget the nightmares I wake from about you? I see your death in ways you can't imagine, and you tell me you're sorry." Murray reached up and grabbed Henry by the shoulders. "You aren't going on any runs with me." Murray turned and moved toward the window, giving Joe a clear look at the kid's dropped jaw and wide eyes. "In fact," the older brother said, "You're not going anywhere for a while."

"You've got to be kidding," Henry sputtered. His shoulders straightened rigidly. He jerked off his coat and glared at Murray. "Damn it! You're not my keeper. I'm almost a man."

Murray whirled about and stalked toward his younger brother. As he came close to Henry, he thrust out his hand and savagely jabbed a finger into Henry's chest. "Are you?"

"Ye-"

"Then why don't you act like it? Why don't you know the difference between being brave and being stupid? Wayne taught you to heal. I taught you to fight." Murray withdrew his hand and stepped back. The angry red splotches on his cheeks shrank until the color disappeared and left his face pale. He touched his brother's shoulder. "But I guess neither of us can teach you to think, Cammo. You want revenge so badly. And so do I. But not if it means you might get killed in the process."

Henry jerked away from Murray's hand. His jaw clenched defiantly. "I'm not gonna die."

55

Murray rolled his eyes and folded his arms over his chest. "I know you're not. Because you're gonna be sitting on your butt for a while." He walked toward the window and stared out again.

"Murray-" Henry protested. His brother didn't let him finish.

"The discussion's over Cammo." He kept staring out the window as he spoke. His back stiffened into an impenetrable wall. He leaned against the window sill, both hands pressed to its metal surface. Sunlight trickled though his spiky hair, giving each ridge a blue-black shine. "You're late for Group One."

Henry closed his eyes and shook his head in disbelief before stalking through the doorway, deeper into the Palace walls.

"He's a good kid," Joe finally managed. Wayne caught his eye, smiling as he left behind Henry.

Murray shifted his weight from one leg to another. "Yeah. But he's still just a kid."

"Give him a break, Murray," Wayne said. He popped a piece of gum in his mouth and began chewing abnoxiously. "He's a teenager. He's hormonally challenged. He's forgotten how to think."

Murray glared at the healer. "You always take his side."

"That's because it pisses you off." He stuck out his tongue and blew a huge bubble. Once it popped and he'd cleaned his cheeks up, he shrugged and said, "In the absence of women and beer, I become impossible. Come on, Mur, take me to a strip bar and I'll be a good boy."

Murray rolled her eyes. "No, you'd become hormonally challenged." He pointed to the door. "Go impale somebody with something so you can heal them. Better yet, take a cold shower."

"I'm going. I'm going," Wayne muttered, heading out the door.

Joe looked out the window at the crowds forming. At least a hundred people stood outside the entrance to the Palace. Most carried signs with variations on the same theme: "Help Resisters to an early death." or "Get rid of the Resisters." Scanning the crowds, Joe spotted several peace officers standing in the background. Most of them smiled openly and approvingly at the protesting crowds.

Joe walked up next to Murray and asked, "Friends of yours?" in a sarcastic tone.

Murray rolled his eyes and replied, "Maybe we should have checked for brain damage, considering that last wisecrack." The lines around his mouth seemed softer, leaving an impression of concern instead of anger at Joe. "They don't even know what they're protesting. It's amazing how much stupidity breathes in this world."

A short, portly man stepped from the crowd outside and carried a large doll forward. The doll was dressed in black, and long silver hair flashed in the sunlight. Holding the toy in one hand, the man wrapped a string of firecrackers around it and lit one before throwing it to the ground and backing away.

As the firecrackers started popping, the doll arched in the air convulsively. Up and down. Up and down. The hair caught on fire and burned. Then the body. The whole time the small fire consumed it, the man looked into Joe and Murray's eyes. He

57

smiled coldly at them and pointed to the doll, saying, "You're next. You're next."

Murray closed his eyes and turned away from the window. "Maybe I should have let Cammo stay to see that." He turned toward Joe. The normally wrathful green eyes had dulled with fatigue. "Where did you find him?"

Joe kept watching as the protesters stomp on the doll until the fire died. In his mind, he saw Henry lying there as one foot after another beat the life out of him before he forced himself to look away. "In an alley." He closed his eyes and remembered Henry's face as sunrise washed over the sky. The kid's words came back quickly, unexpectedly. "Maybe you think everything looks the same behind a pane of glass, but I don't. I can't smell the morning air like that." He forced himself to exhale the air burning his lungs.

"Are you listening, Joe?" Murray's voice demanded loudly.

He opened his eyes and saw the man staring insistently at him, tapping his foot as he waited for Joe to reply to an unheard question. Murray frowned impatiently. Joe rubbed the bridge of his nose and said, "I'm sorry. I didn't catch that. What were you saying?"

Murray muttered an obscenity and sauntered over to the bar and pulled out a bottle. Grabbing a glass, he filled it with amber liquid and looked at Joe. "You want some?"

Even staring at the liquor made his stomach queasy. He raised his hand and declined his offer. "Too early."

Murray put the bottle down and drank the liquid in one

58

gulping swallow before refilling. As he lifted it to his mouth, Murray caught Joe shaking his head. "What's that about?" He lowered the glass and set it on the counter.

"In the last hours you've shattered every myth I ever heard about Resisters. Starting with the religious part and ending with the cloistered thou-shalt-not image."

"Good." Murray smiled at him, toying with the glass. "It's nice to know some people can be educated." He glanced out the window toward the protesting crowd. "Why don't you go spread the word to those good-hearted folks?" The smile died as he lifted the glass and emptied it again.

"We both know they won't listen. They don't want to hear it."

Murray put the bottle away. "Yeah," Murray grunted. "Tell me something I don't know. Tell me what my brother was doing when you found him." His voice sounded sharp, like brittle leaves breaking.

Joe sat down in a chair facing away from the mob outside. "He was watching a sunrise. He had my knife. Said he picked it up for me." Joe pulled out the sword Murray had loaned him and set it on the table. "Thanks for letting me borrow it."

"Keep it." Murray paced around the room, muttering something Joe couldn't hear. He rubbed his temples, as though trying to ward off an approaching headache. "Seems like you've made quite a friend, Joe. How long are you planning to stay with us?" Murray's green eyes stared right through him as though turning to icy waves which would dissolve everything except the

59

truth.

He opened his mouth, but quickly bit off the first answer. It would have been, "I'm not staying." But, as Joe shifted his sitting position, he knew he would. If only to keep Henry from becoming that doll. Whatever it took--for however long it took--he'd be there. He reached into his pocket and touched the bear again. The softness of the fur made Joe retract his fingers quickly from his pocket. "For quite a while Murray." *At least until the kid learns whatever I need to show him.*

The man's head snapped up and he looked at Joe. His eyebrows raised in amazement, and his lips parted slightly. Finally, Murray nodded and said, "Then I'd better show you around. It's not often we get stragglers."

"Stragglers?" Joe echoed, rising from the couch.

Murray nodded and pointed to Joe's unblemished forehead. "Yeah, the people who haven't decided which side of this war they're on."

Joe snorted despite Murray's glare. "This isn't a war. It doesn't have to be."

Murray pointed out the window at the screaming mob. The peace officers simply watched the people walking around the doorway to the Palace. "Tell them that. Tell them that New Life Incorporated has been lying to them and butchering them like cows being prepared for a slaughter." Sweat beaded on the triangular mark on Murray's forehead. He lifted his hand and brushed it away, leaving a glistening trail upon his skin where the seam of flesh ridged noticeably.

"Why do you despise New Life so much?" Joe asked, walking toward Murray. "I mean it's just a choice.

Murray walked away from him. "Yeah, you would believe that. Just like everybody else who has been brainwashed by New Life Incorporated. You'd believe it because you don't know the truth about the implants, the truth they aren't telling in their mental advertisements."

Joe caught his arm. "So tell me about it. What do you know about New Life that I don't? What makes you think you need to fight the whole world to stop them? What makes you think New Life is slaughtering people?"

Murray laughed loudly. "Don't you get it? It's all in the implants, Joe." Murray said, glaring at him. He raked his fingers through his hair. "They aren't adding years to people's lives. They are simply serving New Life Incorporated's purposes."

"What purposes?" He released Murray's arm.

"I don't know. But it's sure as hell not what New Life is telling everybody."

Chapter Five

"You can't-"

A rock smashing through the window of the Palace interrupted Joe. It hurled past them and thudded against a wall. For a second, Murray just stared at the gray stone. A piece of twine tied a white note to it. Then he closed his mouth and rage supplanted the surprise, twisting his lips into a snarl. "Damn stupid sheep. New Life leads them around by their foreheads."

Standing by the window, Joe watched the peace officers dispersing the crowd. The cops looked from the mob to the inside of the Palace, waiting for hell to break loose.

Murray picked up the rock and unwound the string. Once he pulled the paper loose, he unfolded it and read the note. Joe watched the lines in Murray's forehead deepen as he read. Once the Resister finished, he snorted softly and muttered, "They can't even come up with an original threat." He shoved the paper into Joe's open palm and walked through the doorway, saying, "I'll show you the Palace. And then we'll talk about New Life, Incorporated."

Joe followed Murray's impatient steps while reading the note. "Your time is at hand." Joe crumpled it into a ball and waited to find a trash container. "Nice hate mail."

Murray stopped walking in a hallway. "You're a real comedian, Joe." He pointed at a long corridor of doors. "Those are all sleeping quarters for the people who live here. You know, the ones you call Resisters. You never thought you'd have such strange bedfellows, did you?"

Murray didn't wait for a response. Instead he started walking in the opposite direction of where he'd just pointed. The hallway opened up and divided three separate ways. As Murray took the first turn to the right, Joe followed. "Why haven't I gotten any mental advertisements from New Life since I've been here?"

"Because we've blocked them." Murray stepped toward a room. When their feet first crossed the threshold of the room, lights flooded the area. Although rather large, the silver walls enclosing the area seemed to shrink the size. Two gurneys in the center also broke up the spaciousness. A cabinet on the east wall held numerous small vials and medical equipment, such as syringes and bandages. More silver equipment lined the walls.

Joe's left hand touched his thigh as he remembered the absent pain of his knee. "Let me guess. This is The Doctor Zone." He touched one of the gurneys.

"Actually, we call it the RCU. The Recalibration Unit."

"The doctor zone," he confirmed. Joe walked around the room, taking deep breaths. He expected the damn antiseptic scent which he remembered from the clinic where his leg had first been treated. Instead he smelled lemons.

Murray raised his hand to his chin and rubbed it while grinning sheepishly. "Just because it's a medical room doesn't mean it has to smell like one." He walked over to the wall and raised a seemingly invisible panel. "If you don't like lemon, try the scent of a rainstorm." Murray pushed a button.

The citrus smell evaporated and the air thickened like a storm approaching. Joe could smell the raindrops which never came. The air was weighted with it.

"Nice, huh," Murray asked.

Joe opened his eyes and nodded. He looked down at the torn place in his pants where Malachette had wounded his left knee. As if to test it, he shifted all of his weight to it. "How did Wayne do it?" he asked, forcing himself not to see the dried blood around the rip and instead glancing around the room. He shifted his weight back to his right leg and tapped his left foot, seeking the pain. It didn't come. "I've seen doctors, specialists, quacks and more doctors. Nobody could do a damn thing about the pain in my knee. They said it was all in my head."

Murray slid the wall panel back into place. "We both know it wasn't just in your head. Wayne said places in the scar tissue were infected. Unfortunately, it looked good on the outside and they didn't want to have to open it up without a good reason."

"So how'd he cure it? I mean I don't even feel any pain. That doesn't seem possible." Joe crossed his arms over his chest.

"It's not a miracle. And even if it were, I don't think you'd believe it." Murray walked to the medicine cabinet and opened one of the glass doors. He leaned forward and scanned the jar labels. Once he found the one he sought, he picked it up and held it out to Joe. "Here's what he used."

Joe reached out and took it, turning the vial as he brought it toward him so he could read the label. "Trianna Solution." As Joe moved the vial around, the clear gel inside remained stuck in the same spot. "It looks like petroleum jelly."

"Well, it's not. Not by a long shot." Murray tapped his foot against the silver floor. "Once you were brought in here, Wayne used a laser to open the wound. He cleaned it and then applied that ointment to it. He seamed the incision with the laser, sealing the wound."

Joe unscrewed the lid and pulled it off the vial. Bringing it up to his nose, he took a deep breath and gagged. He quickly screwed the lid back into place. "Whew. What does this stuff do, besides smell like piss?" He held up the vial and scrutinized the thick mass clinging to the same spot inside the glass walls, even when Joe tilted the vial from one side to the other. Bored with the lack of motion, Joe handed it back to Murray.

"It has a biogenetic re-growth accelerator in it which attaches to the damaged tissue and reconstructs the weak areas. The gel stimulates tissue regeneration at a high speed." Murray took the vial, set it back into the cabinet and closed the door.

"How effective is it?" Through the closed glass door, Joe kept staring at the vial he'd just held.

Murray headed toward the door. "It depends. Sometimes it

doesn't work at all. Some tissue won't respond to it. Some people, like you, heal completely, leaving the faintest scars. That's the trouble with this 'miracle.' We never know when it will work. We don't know how to improve it. We don't know what triggers the tissue's response. But we're working on it." Murray walked out the door. "Come on. I'll show you the rest of the Palace."

As Joe followed Murray, the lights flickered and then shut off. Farther down the hallway, the two of them stopped in front of a huge Plexiglas window. Inside, several people in white lab coats worked in various stations of a brightly lit room.

All the wiring, metal casings and monitors made the room look like an electronics warehouse. At least until Joe saw an unconscious woman lying on the gurney in the midst of the computers. Wires were attached all over her scantily-clad body. Following the wires from her body to the computer monitors, Joe noticed that each of the five screens flashed a different image. Three of the screens displayed different angles of a human skull. The other two showed random numbers flashing in sporadic patterns. Looking past the monitors and at least fifteen men, Joe also spotted monitors which displayed the woman's slow, regular heartbeat patterns.

"What is this?" Joe asked, pointing to the woman.

"Our research team." Murray leaned close to the glass and watched the screens with slightly squinted eyes.

"What are they researching?"

Murray backed up from the glass and reached deep into his

pants pocket. When he pulled his hand out, he opened his palm, fiddled with a small silver box and pulled out a small disc, a frisbee sized for a doll. "This. It's the answer to everyone's prayers--the way to live on borrowed time. Take it. Have a good look at the lie."

Frowning, Joe reached out and plucked the disc from Murray's hand. As he looked down, he noticed Murray's shirt sleeves had pulled upward sharply. Thin horizontal scars tracked up the inside of his forearms. Wayne's words came back to him. "Murray's too blinded by anger to teach the kid anything useful. You've been where Murray is at, and you've survived."

Murray pulled down one sleeve and then the other, as though he had read Joe's mind. "Take a look at that," Murray said in a gruff voice. "It's everybody's miracle."

Swallowing a lump in his throat, Joe forced himself to look away from the faint pink scars, but his thoughts remained there. His fingers clutched the object tighter and tighter until he could feel every muscle in that part of his hand and wrist working, reminding him he hadn't tried that solution, even though the thought had crossed his mind.

Joe opened his fingers and looked at it. "The Longevity chip?"

Murray nodded and looked back at the lab boys. "Supposed to be. But it's not a chip at all. It's a disc. It doesn't monitor the body's rhythms the way it's supposed to so that it can even out the stress patterns." He looked back at the disc. "It's not even made for that."

Joe flipped the disc over, took a good look and then gave it back to Murray. "How can you be so sure this is an implant? Where'd you get it?"

Murray accepted it and pointed to the woman. "People like her. She's a `Resister' as far as her heart is concerned Joe. But she volunteered to get the implant, just like the person this one came from."

Joe watched Murray shove the implant deep into his pockets with a trembling hand. "So what happened to that other volunteer?"

The color drained from Murray's face and he focused on the men inside the lab, refusing to meet Joe's eyes. "She died. When the guys tried something new with the implant, it killed her."

Ice slid down Joe's spine, and he braced his shoulders more stiffly, trying to ignore the tension threading there. Murray's pale, shell-shocked face didn't help a damn bit, either. "I thought the Federation regulated this kind of stuff."

Murray snorted and crossed his arms over his chest. "Aren't you listening? That depends on who owns the Federation, doesn't it?"

Joe lifted his hand and massaged his left temple where a slight pain was beginning to bloom into a bigger one. He closed his eyes and remembered the leering smiles of the peace officers watching the protesters outside the Palace. "New Life has taken control of the Federation?"

Murray clenched his jaw and watched the lab boys moving around the computers and the woman. "Yeah, we think so. Isn't that what everyone wants? Except the Resisters. And who cares about them? They are mentally unbalanced." He looked back at Joe with eyes colored like spring leaves with ice frozen over them. "Isn't that what you thought? What you expected? Sorry, but we haven't lost our minds, just the way to get rid of the implants."

Joe felt his cheeks redden and he had to look at the floor. He had thought those things once. Now he didn't know what to think. "So what is the implant made for? And what is New Life gaining by installing it into everyone?" Joe looked at the computer screen and watched the image of the skull change slightly. Arrows pointed to different sections of the forehead.

Murray's eyebrows raised questioningly. "You're one of the few stragglers I know who hasn't accused me of blasphemy. Nobody wants to hear the truth. It's funny how people will believe anything which is packaged attractively enough."

Murray lifted his hand to his short, spiky hair and tugged through it. Even after his fingers moved on, the strands lifted back into the spiked ridges as they had stood before. "We don't know what the implants are doing. All we know is that they are recording some kind of data onto these discs. We've been trying to find a sort of play-back mode for the data, but haven't been successful."

"What about that one?" Joe asked, pointing to Murray's pocket. "I mean you've got a prime example of one right there."

Murray nodded in agreement. "Yeah, but the disc only seems active while in the host body. We've been able to do certain things while the person with the implant was alive, but nothing very conclusive. We've stumbled onto accessible spots in the software, but when the data starts coming, all we find are numbers and we don't understand the code behind them. Then the program simply shuts off and we've learned absolutely nothing...."

Joe noticed Murray's voice dying away, but he was too busy staring at the woman waking up on the table to respond.

She tried to turn her head, but the three-pronged device holding it still, wouldn't let her move. She blinked repeatedly.

"Damn!" Murray swore. He took two rapid steps toward the door and tried to yank it open. The knob wouldn't turn to let him in.

"What is it?" Joe asked, watching Murray slam his fist on the glass. "What's wrong?"

None of the men in the lab looked at them. "Jesus! Sedate her! She shouldn't be awake for this!" He kept slamming his hand against the window, even though none of them heard him. His face flushed as he watched the woman struggling against the leather straps holding her to the gurney.

"Damn it, sedate her. Christ, she shouldn't feel trapped like a damn lab rat. Why don't you just get away from her and let her breathe!" His voice dropped to a growl and his whole body looked taut like a drawn bow. Finally, he stopped pounding the glass. Instead, he leaned his head toward it and tapped his forehead against it and stayed there. His whole body trembled and the fingers splayed against the glass withdrew into fists.

The woman's eyes fluttered shut. Stillness. Joe's heart sped up, and he looked at the monitors to confirm she was still alive. The monitor displayed a constant wave pattern. Seeing this, Joe felt his chest burning from the air he'd been holding. He exhaled and looked at Murray. The Resister's head still touched the glass, and his eyes were closed.

"It didn't seem to hurt her to be awake," Joe said softly, staring in wide-eyed amazement at Murray's emotional state. Glancing at Joe, Murray's eyes looked disoriented. Sweat beaded upon his forehead and dripped down his temples, giving his cheeks a tear-stained look. His mouth parted into a disbelieving oval.

Murray pulled his arms away from the window and took an uneven step toward Joe. Reflexes made Joe lift his hand to offer support, but Murray caught himself before he lost his balance completely.

Murray looked at the floor. "It's not about the pain. It's about the nightmares she'll wake from if she survives this hell. You don't get it, do you? You've never had a dream you couldn't wake from, have you? You wouldn't know fear if it came knocking at your door." His voice sounded small and breakable as though he had been locked away in a box and couldn't escape. The words thinned and trickled around Joe's ears like invisible wind chimes, tapping against each other, but unable to resonate because the breeze blew too softly.

You're wrong about that, you SOB. I have just as many bad dreams as she'll ever have. Probably more. As Joe felt the tension threaded through his body, his headache worsened. And yet, what bothered him more was watching this man so fueled by anger reduced to pain from a source Joe still hadn't found. Had he loved that woman?

Joe wanted to reach out to Murray, to say he understood the rhythm of pain and that it sometimes slept. Even if it stirred now, it would sleep again. He stood beside Murray. Simply touching his shoulder might say something Joe couldn't. But Murray's rigid back told Joe pity would be unacceptable.

Instead, Joe pointed to the unconscious woman. "She's back out. No harm done. She won't remember that brief span of waking."

"No harm done?" Murray turned toward him slowly. He shook his head. Crimson splashed his cheeks. "The only reason you think no harm was done is because it wasn't you strapped to that gurney. It isn't your brain that's going to overload because someone is toying with the implant you volunteered to get to find out what New Life is doing."

"I didn't mean-"

"I know what you meant," Murray snapped, stepping backward. His boots tapped loudly against the floor. His hand rested on his belt, close to the Parkinsen. Fingers fidgeted against the black grip. "But until you're fucking tied up and someone else is holding that pretty weapon of yours threatening to cut your balls off, don't tell me no harm's been done." He turned and headed down the hall. "Tour's over, Joe. Have a nice day." His seething tone made the words difficult to understand, but Joe caught them anyway. And the glaring go-to-hell look that came with them.

Murray's slow steps mounted in speed. Before he reached the end of the hall, Murray had broken into a run that slowed only long enough to allow him to turn through the doorway and disappear from sight. For a few seconds, Joe heard Murray's boots clattering on the linoleum. Then silence.

What in the hell did I say? Joe wondered, staring at the empty hallway in front of him. He leaned against the cold rock wall. His head wanted to explode from the pain and all he could think was, What the hell happened to him? Murray had to be the strangest person God had ever made. And it had nothing to do with the fact Murray chose to be a Resister, either. Joe just wanted to understand what made him such a damn live wire, ready to rage or suffer but unable to simply exist.

Chapter Six

Joe lifted his hand and massaged his temple, trying to ease the pain rapidly turning into a migraine. Closing his eyes, he saw lines cutting through the blackness. *Damn! A migraine for sure.* Someone touched his shoulder, and Joe instinctively reached for his blade. He opened his eyes and held the weapon ready.

"You keep waving that thing and you're liable to hurt someone. There's really no need for it here."

Joe looked at Wayne's blank face and quickly replaced his knife. "Says you," he muttered, trying to clear his distorted vision. "I keep saying the wrong things to Murray and I'm liable to get a knife rammed into my back." *And I don't even know what I said or did that actually pissed him off this time.*

"Nah, Mur is just barking as usual. You'll understand everything soon enough." Wayne pointed to Joe's head. "Nasty headache you got there. Want something for the pain?"

"Does the word privacy mean anything to you? Like staying out of my thoughts?" Joe asked savagely.

Wayne scrunched his nose and shrugged. "No, not really.

Let's get back to the RCU so we can get some meds."

Joe grimaced as the throbbing increased. "Yeah, you've probably got some wonder drug here, right?"

"Just aspirin, Joe. It still works."

As they began walking to the RCU, Joe tried not to stare at the red shirt with large blue tropical flowers all over it because it made his head worse. "Don't you have any...normal shirts?"

Wayne pulled out a cigar and stopped to light it. "Do I look like a normal person?"

"No, just an eyesore."

Wayne inhaled, savoring the taste. Smiling, he started walking. "I'm a healer. I fix people. Most of the time, I use medicine. Sometimes, things like ridiculous shirts work. Especially with someone like you or Murray." He raised his eyebrows knowingly. "Think about it."

As they started walking again, Joe took one last look at the lab. Five minutes ago everyone had been seated at their different stations, watching the computer monitors. Now they all converged around the gurney.

"What's going on?" Joe asked, stopping.

Wayne looked in, closed his eyes and sighed. "Another failed attempt."

Joe looked at the EKG monitor. A thin straight line of light. Cardiac arrest. He looked back at the gurney toward the blond woman's face. Her eyes remained open, looking toward the ceiling.

At once Joe had to close his eyes, too. "Can't they do

anything?"

Wayne grabbed his arm, pulling him further down the hallway. "There's nothing they can do for her. At least her suffering is over."

Joe stopped walking. With every breath he felt like his chest would simply cave in from the way the air hurt to breath. He balled his fingers into fists and glared at Wayne. "So that's it? Her life is over and you don't give a shit?"

"Yes, frankly, I do give a shit." Wayne tilted his head forward, and the long silver hair spilled over his shoulders. He stared at the ground. "I'm a healer, Joe. I heal whatever I can. I take away pain when I can. But sometimes there's not a damn thing I can do."

Wayne lifted his arms and gestured to the walls. "I own this place. I run it because I keep thinking we're going to be able to destroy New Life Incorporated and its lies. But first we have to find out what kind of lies they are telling." Wayne looked inside the lab where the technicians covered the woman's body with a sheet. "And to do that sometimes people die. Even if I don't want them to."

He started walking again. His shoulders and back straightened into a rigid line. "Come on, Joe. Let's go find something for your headache."

Joe stared at the men shutting down the computers, turning off lights and thought of Murray's words. "The only reason you think no harm was done is because it wasn't you strapped to that gurney. It isn't your brain that's going to overload because someone is toying with the implant you volunteered to get just to find out what New Life is doing."

Forcing himself to look away, Joe walked with an impatient step, as though trying to out-maneuver the devil. Joe Ramsey now understood the harm. The next step he wanted to discover was how to stop it for good.

Wayne walked ahead of him into the RCU and strode over the cabinet. He yanked open the door and pillaged through the various bottles, finally picking up a small one. With a deft twist, he pulled off the top and then poured two tablets into his hand. Turning half-way around, he offered them to Joe. "This ought to do it."

"Thanks." Joe accepted the tablets Wayne dumped into his hand. He tipped his head back and swallowed the dry tablets, ignoring the way they stuck to his throat on the way down.

"You're welcome." Wayne put the bottle up and closed the cabinet. His fingers stayed on the steel handle as Wayne stared vacantly at the floor.

"Wayne?" Joe prompted, waving hands in front of Joe's path of vision, trying to flag his attention. "Hello?"

Wayne blinked and slowly raised his head. Taking a deep breath, he lifted his fingers to his eyes and rubbed the inner corners of them. "Yeah, what?"

"What were you thinking about just then?"

Wayne released the cabinet with his other hand and turned toward Joe. As Wayne stared at him, his jaw clenched and the vein in his temple stood out, as though his body were straining.

"Aeriadnie...the woman who just died. I was thinking of her." Wayne started to walk out of the room and Joe followed close behind.

Joe stared at Wayne, at his tense shoulders and the way his chest barely expanded each time he inhaled. "How long was she here?" he asked, trying to break the strained silence.

"Since we opened the doors eight years ago. She was a ten-year-old runaway then with nobody to care for her." Wayne stopped walking and rolled his shoulders, trying to get rid of the invisible weight pressing down on him. He looked at the ceiling. He exhaled softly and the air came out a trembling gasp. "Eight years is a long time to love somebody only to be reminded that person is on loan."

Wayne shoved his hands into his pockets and started walking again. Joe followed, and, as they passed the lab, Joe peered in. It had shrunk in darkness. The only thing reflecting the hall light was the silver around the edge of the gurney. The computer screens sat in charcoal blankness.

Aeriadnie must have been close to Murray, Joe thought, remembering the raw pain on Murray's face as he tried to yank open the door.

"Like the sister Murray never had," Wayne said, touching the glass. His fingers splayed apart on it, as though reaching for something on the other side. They trembled and lifted as Wayne backed away from the glass and started walking deeper into the compound where Joe hadn't been before. "Come on. The others will be waiting for us."

Silence wrapped around them as they continued down the corridor until it ended in a T. Wayne turned left and stopped in front of a closed steel door. Lifting his hand to a numeric keypad beside the door, he punched a sequence of buttons. "Aeriadnie was the sister we all never had. Murray didn't want her to get the implant. He knew what the odds were of her surviving. Murray wanted to get it himself."

"Why didn't he?" Joe asked, watching Wayne open the door.

"Because Murray would have been dead the minute he walked into New Life Incorporated's front door. Caleb Walker would have slit his throat without batting an eye." The healer gestured for Joe to go in front of him.

Joe cocked his head to the side and looked curiously at Wayne. "The infamous Caleb Walker again. Why do I keep hearing his name?"

"That's Murray's story, Joe. Not mine."

Joe took about five steps before coming to another closed door with a numeric keypad. Murray walked around him and punched more buttons. He reached down and opened the door for Joe.

Walking into the room, Joe noticed a large group of men sitting around a table, covered with paperwork. Maps and photos covered the walls. One of them glared at him. He looked up to meet the gaze and realized he had come face to face with Murray.

"What in the hell are you thinking, Wayne? He's a drifter, a straggler. Probably a player to the highest bidder." Murray pointed at Joe. "He shouldn't be here."

Joe rolled his eyes and put his hands on his hips. "I didn't take bids for finding Henry, even though I'm certain Malachette would have paid me. It wasn't about money then and it isn't about money now."

Murray put down the sheets of blue prints he'd been holding. "We healed your leg for saving my brother, Joe. That debt's been paid in full."

Joe pulled up an empty chair and sat down. "Yeah, well, there's another score I have to settle. Malachette doesn't seem to have any manners, and someone needs to teach him. He's connected with New Life, which means I want in."

Joe scanned the room. Everyone else was looking at Murray or Wayne, waiting for one of them to speak. "Whatever you're trying to accomplish against New Life, it seems to me you need all the helpful bodies you can get."

Murray slammed her fist down on the table. "You don't have a clue-"

"What he's dealing with?" Wayne interrupted, his silver eyes staring intently at Murray's frown. He sat in a chair beside Joe. His long hair fell in front of his shoulders, covering the large flowers. "He just took a knife in his knee for the hell of it? Malachette won't forget Joe, which means he's one of us anyway, and Malachette will have to be dealt with. We do need all the people we can get. Especially for this," he said, pointing to the blue prints which had curled back into a roll.

"For what?" Joe scanned the room more closely, noticing all the pictures on the walls were of the New Life Incorporated building, taking both during the day and at night. The maps looked to be layouts of the interior.

"Breaking into New Life Joe," Murray said, spreading the blueprints across the table.

Joe looked at Murray's hands lying on the blue-printed basement section. He thought about the Federation and Murray's comment about New Life owning it. "Count me in."

Again the other men looked to Murray and Wayne, waiting for one of them to speak. Wayne offered his hand and Joe took it. "Thanks, Joe. Want one of my shirts?"

"So what's the plan?" Joe asked, ignoring the healer's last comment as he scanned the blueprints. "What exactly are we looking for and how are we going to get in?"

"First we start a little distraction just far enough away from the building to lure the guards." He pointed to a section approximately 100 feet from the building. Murray pointed to the blueprint. His finger touched the basement. "Then we get in here, after dodging the first perimeter alarm."

"Which is?" Joe placed both elbows on the table and cradled his chin between his hands.

"A heat sensor." Murray's green eyes flashed at him in impatience and annoyance. He looked back at the blueprint. "The alarm system is located in the basement of the building." He skimmed his finger across the east wall. "Probably in here. It's the only wall attached to the interior of the building. Once the location of the alarm is discovered and it is neutralized, then we can get our team inside where will go to the fourth floor."

Joe watched Murray's finger rise up match the location he'd just spoken. "Why the fourth floor?"

"That's where the research and development section of New Life is located." Murray pulled out the disc he had shown Joe earlier and set it down the table. "We're going to hack into the computers and figure out what this data is and what New Life is doing with it." Murray turned toward the skinny man sitting to her right. "Explain what happens next, Larry."

Larry pushed his glasses higher on his nose and said, "After we get inside the system, we're going change all of Caleb's codes to deny access to him. Then we will install a link between his system and ours. That way we can transfer the data from here."

"A back door." Joe leaned back in his chair and crossed his arms over his chest. "So when is this going down?"

Murray leveled his cold eyes at Joe. He took a deep breath and exhaled, never once looking away from Joe as though he expected Joe's eyes to reveal some sense of treason. When it didn't come, Murray finally said, "In two days."

No, I don't think you'll ever be completely ready to take on something like New Life Incorporated, he thought.

Wayne touched Joe's shoulders. "Yes, we'll be ready in two days. Now that you've joined us. Until then, Murray can take you on a run with him. Give the two of you a chance to work through your attitudes."

Murray's shoulders tensed. His eyes narrowed to slants. "You're not my father, old man."

Wayne nodded, and as he bobbed his head, the light flashed

on his silver hair. "Yeah, I know. But sometimes you forget that not everything revolves around you. Joe didn't come to piss you off. Granted, he's got a knack for it. But this is about New Life, Mur."

"What's a run?" Joe asked.

Murray rolled up the blueprints and stood up. "It's a moonlit stroll, Joe." He picked up the folders and stacked them neatly. "We often go out during the Lock-down times, looking for the Lifers strike groups. It's usually a pack of six or eight bullies, trying to force people to get the implants, even though they can't afford them. Sometimes it becomes more about authority than anything else."

Joe shifted uncomfortably in his chair. "Why doesn't somebody stand up to them?" he asked.

Murray's harsh laughter drew everyone's attention. "Because the people being threatened are the ones who don't count. They don't have enough money to eat, let alone get the implant."

Joe drummed his fingers against the table. "So it sounds like they're barking up the wrong tree. I mean if they can't get the money, the Lifers are wasting their time with threats."

Murray nodded. "Which is why the strike groups are so dangerous. They often leave bodies behind, Joe." His eyes narrowed to slits. "And the Lifers get away with it because nobody can prove anything. The people they kill don't have family. Nobody's going to file a missing person's report after a few days. They just die."

Joe's fingers abruptly stopped tapping on the table. They cinched down on the edge as he thought of Malachette's scarred face leering at him while thrusting that blade into his knee. At first Joe couldn't place the gleam lighting Malachette's eyes. He'd seen it all right, but on other men's faces--the men who were honored for their parts in the war. They had been decorated with metals because they'd killed the enemy. Never mind the fact that sometimes the enemy happened to be two years old and didn't know how to use a weapon. Never mind that sometimes the murder was necessary to win. Never mind that men like Malachette loved inflicting pain.

The Federation had trained them and New Life had turned them loose in the country. Joe tried to ignore the hollowness in his stomach. "Why would pushing everyone to get the implant be so important to New Life anyway?"

Wayne shrugged. "We don't know yet. It has something to do with the data stored on the discs. The same data we can't read. Until we can transfer the information to a readable format, we won't know much. That's why we're breaking into the New Life Building."

"So when are we going on the run?" Joe stood up and stretched his legs, even though every muscle in his body felt stretched to the max and it had nothing to do with exercise.

"Tonight at midnight," Murray answered him.

"Where's Henry?" he asked softly, touching his head, searching for traces of the pain.

"In Group Two probably," Murray replied. "We'll probably

have to lock him up to keep him inside the compound. I certainly don't see him staying of his own free will."

Joe groaned inwardly as he realized Henry's future frustrations with walls. Correction, Joe thought. A new headache has just taken the old one's place. "You can't lock him up."

"Yes, actually I can," Murray said, glaring at him.

"We're not running a zoo here," Wayne argued, standing next to Joe. "You can't just keep him locked up like an animal. Let Joe talk to him."

Murray rose up quickly from his chair. "If it'll keep him alive, I don't care what species he turns into." His voice rose to a shout.

"You can't shield him," Joe said, tapping his hand on the table. "He's not a kid anymore."

Murray clenched his hands into fists. "What do you know about kids? Hell, what do you know about anything? This isn't your brother. So stay out of it."

"Maybe I am a stranger, but I won't stay out of it." Joe shook his head. "One way or another he'll go, even if he has to sneak out. At least like this I can keep my eyes on him." Joe rolled his head, trying to unwind his shoulder muscles.

"Joe's right. And I'm with him." Wayne pulled a cigar out of his pocket and slid it between his teeth. Clicking on his lighter, he lifted it to the end of the cigar until it burned. He leaned against the chair and thrust his hands behind his head.

"Thanks, Wayne," Murray seethed, glaring at the healer before turning on him. He snorted softly and scooted his chair.

"You're both so damn generous with other people's lives." He headed toward the door. "I'll go tell Cammo the great news."

Chapter Seven

"What have we got here?" Caleb Walker asked, leaning back into his black leather desk chair. He watched the monitor mounted on the wall, instead of Gabe Renault's face, even though Gabe stood in front of his desk, holding a thick binder and a handful of computer discs. Caleb was too busy staring at the screen and watching a New Life Incorporated doctor install one of the Longevity Chips into a patient. "I asked a question, Gabriel. What have you brought me?"

Gabe's shoulders stiffened from the harsh tone. In another life he might have told Caleb that Gabe wasn't short for Gabriel. In another life, it might have mattered. In another life the world might not have revolved around Caleb Walker and New Life Incorporated. But in this one it did, and Gabe didn't have the guts to ram his fist across his boss' face, even if he wanted to. "It's the data from last month's installations."

Caleb pointed out a corner of the desk to set the discs and binder. "Have all the other facilities sent the data, as well?" Caleb asked, watching the laser cut through the skin of a male patient.

87

His fingers drummed on the desk. "I hate tardiness. You know that." He picked up a remote control from his desk and switched to a different channel. Another doctor, another laser, another patient. Fifty channels full of the same thing. Putting his hands behind his back and smiling, Caleb reflected on how perfect everything was. Except for Murray.

The smile vanished as he glared at Gabe. Sweat beaded on Gabe's forehead. He lifted his hand and wiped it away, then brushed his hands on his slacks. "Twenty-three of the twenty-five facilities you own have forwarded the data, as you instructed."

Caleb's path of vision alternated between Gabe and the monitor. "And the other two?" He spoke in a calm, thin voice that felt like ice drifting down Gabe's spine. It was always that tone which ordered murders. Gabe tried to swallow the lump wedged in his throat. Everything was business to Caleb. Even death.

"The other two should arrive within the week," Gabe finally said, taking a step back, trying to put some space between the two of them. He reached up and adjusted his shirt collar, annoyed by the choking sensation.

Caleb leaned forward and reached for the disks. As his hand skimmed across the desk, his fingers touched the ancient dagger inside a glass orb. It was often used cut open things.

Gabe held his breath, waiting. The fingers moved on to the discs and binder. "See that mistake isn't repeated in the future. It could prove to be quite painful if it does."

88

Gabe slowly exhaled. His heart rammed against his chest painfully. "Yes, sir. I'll do that."

Without bothering to look at Gabe's face, Caleb picked up the disc and inserted it into his computer. "You're excused, Gabriel. Shut the door on your way out."

"Thank you." Gabe forced himself to walk slowly, half expecting to feel that letter opener rip into his back. Even when he reached the door, he didn't feel safe. But who did when they were in the room with Caleb Walker?

From the corner of his eye, Caleb watched Gabe's shoulders sag forward as though relieved. He kept watching as the Vice-President of New Life Incorporated opened his door and hastily exited. Caleb smiled. *It's difficult to be an executive lab rat here at New Life, isn't it, Gabriel? We both know that the Vice President title is empty. It's just words to make the company look safe to corporate America.*

People weren't afraid of New Life as long as they thought it was a majority thing. He'd made the advertising look safe. Each facility had separate `visible' owners. But Caleb was the common denominator. He was the invisible owner, the money man. And he would soon be the key behind the Federation, even if nobody outside the company knew it. Seven of the ten council members already had implants. Just three more and he would command the world. And then all the miserable Resisters would die.

Caleb smiled and flipped the channel to see Gabriel riding in the elevator. Sweat trickled down the VP's temples and Gabe yanked out a white handkerchief to blot away the perspiration.

"You're a nervous wreck," Caleb muttered, tapping his fingers on his desk. "Which means one of two things. You'd like to leave New Life, which I can't allow. Or you're afraid even your best efforts to please me will fail, which you can't allow."

Caleb turned to the computer screen and scanned the icons. He lifted his hand and touched the phone image in the left-hand corner.

"Whom do you wish to call?" a computerized female voice asked. The screen shifted to blackness with white, blinking lines at the bottom, waiting for his vocal instructions.

"Malachette."

"One moment, please." Silence. Numbers filled the blanks, dialing.

On the third ring Malachette answered and his face appeared on the screen. "Yeah?" He brushed through his rumpled hair and glared at the screen through bleary, red eyes. "What is it, Mr. Walker?"

"You look like hell," Caleb snapped, leaning closer to the computer screen. "Any news on Murray yet?"

Malachette rubbed the bridge of his nose. "Not yet. Soon."

Caleb laughed raucously. "You know I'm not a man of patience, Malachette." He glanced at the binder. "Since you haven't got any news, then you can give me one of your men for a job. Someone who is adept at tailing."

Malachette pulled out a cigarette from his pack and lit it. "Yeah. And who's he gonna be tailing?"

"Gabriel Renault."

Malachette took a drag and exhaled a thick plume of smoke which obscured his image in the computer monitor. "You want me to tail the VP of New Life?"

"No," Caleb said, his tone tightening with irritation. "I want you to get me Murray's head. Preferably away from her body. Leave Renault to one of your men."

Malachette tapped his fingers on his arm, over the tatoo of a rose with a serpent wound about it. "Whatever you say, Mr. Walker. I'll get the ball rolling."

"That's what I like to hear," Caleb muttered and disconnected the call. The screen went dark and then the icons flashed back onto the screen. This time Caleb reached for the New Life Incorporated pentagram.

The screen shifted to a white background decorated with grey pentagrams. The words "Enter Password" appeared on the center of the screen.

Caleb smiled and pushed a few keys. The New Life Insignia flashed on screen, along with a scroll-down menu with five options: patient records, DNA sequencing, projected DNA combinations, compliance ratio, and patient labeling.

He touched the first option and smiled. "Time to get to know my patients. And weed them out."

***

For the second time that day, Joe found himself in parts of the Palace he hadn't been before. He sighed and kept walking, giving himself the tour Murray had reneged on. From time to time he still expected pain when he extended his left knee, especially

91

walking on the concrete floors. None came.

He passed through the small quarters while searching for Henry. Although the bars had been taken out, along with some walls, and the place had been painted and redecorated, Joe still recognized the roughened starkness of prison rooms.

He smiled at the irony of using a prison to headquarter the Resisters. They were the people fighting to understand what the Federation, now owned by New Life, planned to do to 'its citizens.'

He glanced at the rooms in passing. Each one had at least one computer, a bed and a desk. Sleeping quarters, he presumed. As Joe passed the Resisters, he got used to seeing the badges. He even preferred them because now he could at least understand that choice. Over the last few days he had come to understand a lot of things.

The hallway ended in a large cafeteria which Joe ambled through. "Just past the cafeteria you'll see the way to the yard," Wayne had said while pointing him in this direction. "Henry'll be in the yard working on his swordsmanship."

Confident he was headed in the right direction, Joe made his way through the cafeteria to the door on the other side. As he stepped through it, he found himself outside in a huge, grassy area. Looking up, he saw a huge, clear dome which had once separated the prisoners from freedom. Now it protected the Resisters from the Lifers.

Joe scanned the yard, searching through all the people in white uniforms practicing fencing skills with one another.

Sunlight filtered through the dome, sparkling off the daggers and swords. Thrust, parry, block. Joe watched the movements, recognizing them as maneuvers he had learned long ago. He frowned at the ancient rituals of hate. His hand slipped downward, touching his scabbard. *Damn reflexes*, he thought, lifting his hand and resettling it at his hip. The Federation had taught him well and it would take a lifetime to undo the lessons.

Despite the large area, the air smelled of sweat and grease. Through the swords arching through the air, Joe finally spied Henry. The youth was paired off with a much bigger man. Joe focused on the dance of the two weapons. Henry's offensive strokes were constantly blocked by a trained arm, much stronger and more patient. The kid's mouth deepened into a frown with each deflected stroke. He thrust and met blade. Henry slashed and met steel. He lifted his sword and felt his opponent knock his legs from under him with a single kick.

"Damn!" Henry said as he landed. His blade slipped from his fingers and slid away. His sparring partner held the sword tip to Henry's throat, keeping him from moving.

"You weren't focusing, Cammo. Anybody else would cut your throat right now." The teacher lowered his blade and offered a hand, which Henry grudgingly accepted.

"I was, too." The kid bent over and picked up his sword.

"You focused on your rage, not your energy, and the only thing anger does is puts you in the ground." The man looked at Henry, trying to force the kid to look at him. "Did you hear me?"

Henry glared at him. "Yeah. I heard every word." As he

walked back to his instructor, Henry saw Joe. A flush crept across his face. But Joe didn't look at the kid's face. He looked at the soft, untrained body standing next to that seasoned warrior who taught him. In that split second Joe wished he could take back his idea about taking Henry on the run. His fingers clenched into fists and he thrust them deep into his pocket to hide the useless frustration as he walked up to the two of them.

The teacher met Joe's stare with cool eyes before glancing at Henry. "We'll finish practice later, Cammo. Maybe then you'll remember how to concentrate."

Henry rolled his eyes and looked at Joe like he'd heard the same speech a million times before. The kid waited until his teacher walked off before pulling out a cloth and wiping his blade. "I hear there's a run tonight," Henry said, glaring at Joe.

Joe frowned, watching the kid clean the blade repeatedly, polishing the steel. The repetitive motion was careful, practiced. Too damn practiced. "Yeah, there's a run tonight."

Henry lifted his sword and watched sunlight skim across the blade, double-checking his polishing to make sure it was clean before putting it inside the sheath and laying it on the ground in front of him. Although he had released the sword from his grip, his fingers didn't stray far from the hilt. "I'm going on this one. I don't give a damn what Murray says."

Joe stared at the kid's stubborn chin and straight back. Granted his chip wasn't as large as Murray's, but that didn't rule out the genetic factor. And given time, it was sure to grow. "You ought to." Joe sighed and walked over to an empty section of the yard where he sat down and toyed with a blade of grass while watching the others spar.

Henry scowled and followed him. He stopped in front of Joe and leaned on his sword. "Why should I care about what Murray thinks? Because he's older? Because he knows how to fight better than me? Because he's my brother?" Henry stood upright, his fingers clenched around the sword hilt. "I'm not a kid. I won't be treated like one." He sat down next to Joe. "Those damn Lifers are gonna pay. I'll have Caleb Walker's blood on my hands. If it's the last thing I do, I'll have it. Promise."

Didn't anybody ever teach you not to make promises you can't keep? Joe thought. "Sit down," he said quietly. "Please."

Henry's nostril's flared, but he looked away from Joe's gaze and sat down next to him. "Oh great. Now you want to lecture me, too. I thought you were different."

Joe watched the kid's shoulders rise tensely. Henry's eyes narrowed slightly, distorting his face to a less-than-kind expression. Where did all this anger come from? Joe thought back to the previous night when Henry had stolen away to watch a sunrise, and then looked at the person in front of him. The two extremes didn't seem to go together. He sighed again and popped his knuckles just to keep his hands busy. "Sounds like you've been taking lessons from Murray-"

"Shut up!" Crimson flooded Henry's cheeks. His fingers curled around the hilt like he wanted to draw the weapon. "I was so wrong about you. I thought you understood about me, but you don't. You don't have a clue about me. Or Murray. So why don't you get out of our lives."

Nice going, Joe. Pissing him off is really going to be helpful. Joe looked up at the sky and remembered why he'd never wanted to be a parent. Making mistakes was difficult enough. Watching someone slam into the same wall felt impossible. "I'm sorry. You're right. I'm an outsider looking in." He reached up and touched Henry's shoulder. "I'm not a Resister, and I'm damn sure not a Lifer. So what does that make me?" He kept his hand in place, despite Henry's muscles stiffening. "So why should you trust me, right?" He lowered his hand and reached into his pants pocket, pulling out the bear.

"I'll tell you why you can trust me, Henry. This." He held out the bear to the kid. "Take it." Henry exhaled loudly and stared off into the distance with disinterest plastered on his face. "I said take it!" Joe barked.

Henry jumped . A few of the Resisters sparring nearby stopped moving and stared at them. Joe met their gazes with disdain, as though saying, "This is none of your concern." He raised his hand higher toward the kid. "Just take it."

Henry slowly reached forward. His fingers encircled the bear, picking it up. At first he looked at it curiously, but his expression quickly changed back to boredom. "It just a toy."

Joe nodded and looked down at the blue bear. Most people would have looked at the face to see the cute features, but Joe focused on the ear. The blood-stained ear. "Yeah, it's a toy. Pretty stupid for a thirty-seven-year-old to carry it around, right?"

Henry looked from the bear to Joe and nodded. "So why do

you keep it?"

"To remind me." Joe's voice dwindled to a whisper. "It belonged to a Spanish boy. Probably one of the few things he ever owned." *Breathe, Joe. Just keep breathing.* It was probably a good thing he was already sitting, because healed knee or not, he just knew it would give out under the weight of those god-awful memories.

"How old was he?" Henry's voice had calmed and softened.

The image of the child came to mind. Soft, dark curls around a chubby baby face. Flushed cheeks from the unforgiving sun. "Wrestle with me!" he chirped, holding out his arms. "Tickle me!" He lifted his hands high into the air, daring Joe.

"How old was he?" Henry asked again, louder, as though Joe hadn't heard him.

Joe swallowed the saliva pooling in his mouth. "Maybe four. At most. I had been assigned to defend the Federation's embassy in Spain." Joe spoke in a mechanical tone. He kept telling himself it was just a bunch of words. No meaning.

The image in Joe's mind changed from the toddler standing in front of him to a red ball the size of a cantaloupe bouncing toward him, just like that first time. In reflex Joe bent over and picked it up. The boy came running up to him, holding out his hands for it.

"That's my ball."

Joe looked up at the kid, holding out his hands. He grinned. "What do you say, kid?"

"Pleeease." The boy stared at the ball with worried eyes.

"Why are you speaking English?" Joe stared at him, at his definitely Spanish features.

"'Cause you don't know no Spanish." The boy put his hands on his hips. "My mommy told me about you gringos."

Smart kid. "Yeah. Well, what's the Spanish word for please?"

The kid grunted in protest. "I know it."

"Then tell me."

"Por favor."

Joe threw the ball back to him. The kid grabbed it and took a mock bow. "Gracias."

Joe grinned. "De nada."

Joe closed his eyes, blanketing the image with blackness, trying desperately to forget. It was the eyes which wouldn't disappear. Ever. Chocolate brown.

"So what happened?" Henry asked.

Joe took a deep, sharp breath. It filled his lungs and left an ache flowering in his chest. He didn't want to talk about this. Didn't want to have to say it. But he had to make Henry understand how familiar rage was to him. And how useless. It would consume the kid if he didn't let it go.

Joe cleared his throat before speaking. "I had been chasing a rebel through the alley after he had opened fire on the embassy. As I stopped and looked down one side, I heard a sound from behind me. It sounded like the safety switch on a gun." Joe took another deep breath. More saliva pooled in his mouth. He swallowed, but gagged as bile sat in the back of his throat, waiting. Sweat. He started to breathe faster, but it wasn't enough. He couldn't get enough air.

"What happened?" Henry touched his shoulder, just like Joe had done to the boy earlier. The hard lines of anger had melted from his face, leaving a softer embarrassed frown. And in that moment Joe saw the kid who liked stars.

And remembered the one he'd killed. "I turned and fired. Point blank." Joe cradled his head in his hands, his fingers rubbing his scalp to break the stillness clawing at him. "I didn't know it was the kid. He had been playing with a toy gun. Bullets ripped through his body." He kept his eyes open, trying not to see the kid or the teddy bear lying in his hand with the small card attached. The kid had written "For Joe" in an uneven childish scrawl.

"It wasn't your fault."

Joe lifted his head and wiped away a thick sheen of sweat on his forehead. "I killed him, Henry. I didn't know it was him or that he had followed me from the embassy." His voice thickened. He looked at Henry's ashen face.

"What about the rebel?"

"I leaned over the kid, trying to stop the bleeding, even thought I knew it was too late." Joe's fingers moved to his healed knee. "That SOB plugged a shot in my leg before I killed him. Months later I got a stupid medal for it, for killing that guy." Joe remembered the gun discharging, remembered the body falling, remembered the damn ceremony. But those didn't matter. It was the kid's body and the grave that made him want to vomit. And he thought about the way he'd picked up the bear, pulling its ear from the pool of blood. He closed his eyes. "That scum I shot was higher on the food chain than I could have dreamed."

Henry sat up straighter. "You're a hero!" he gushed.

"I'm no damned hero!" Joe snapped. "So wipe that smirk off your face."

Henry squirmed uncomfortably. "But the medal?"

Joe leaned over and gripped the kid's shoulders, barely restraining the urge to throttle him. "I killed a kid, Henry. Someone who trusted me. And I carried his ghost with me. Still do." He reached down from Henry's hand and picked up the bear. "I carry this with me to remind me about choices. Yeah, I did my job, but look at the cost. Would I do it again? I don't think so."

He looked at Henry. The kid's face looked so damn innocent and frustrated. "Everything is about choice, Henry, and which ones I make. What I can live with. What I can't. I don't know about your demons. Or Murray's, either. But rage won't erase them. Blood won't absolve them. You have a past, and maybe it hurts like hell. But don't let it become your future."

Joe's shoulders sagged forward and fatigue came on him quickly. He closed his eyes and rubbed his temples as he stood up. "I've said enough. Maybe too much. You're right. You are going on the run. But go because you believe in what you're doing. Not because you want to spill somebody's blood."

Henry's face had turned white. He'd released his sword completely. "So why are you coming? You aren't a part of either group."

"Because of this." Joe gripped the bear and shoved it into his pants pocket. "Because I think the Federation is doing something wrong. I don't know what it is."

Henry started to smile, convinced that he had turned Joe into a Resister. "So you want-"

"No," Joe interrupted. "I'm not ready to be a Resister. I'm ready to be me. I don't always agree with the way you people do things either. But at least I understand what you're doing. Not joining either group doesn't mean I don't believe, Henry. It just means I haven't figured out what I should believe yet."

He started to walk away but then stopped and turned back. "One last thing. Whatever you do, don't look into a dead man's eyes. They will stay with you." He thought of the small brown eyes. "And they'll change you. They'll make you hard when you want to be soft and soft when you would cut off your hand to be hard." He took a few more steps.

"Joe?"

"Yeah?"

"What was his name?" Henry had stood. His fingers clutched the sword, almost like he wasn't sure he should be holding it anymore. He leaned forward, as though he wanted to go to Joe, but something stopped him. His eyes looked glazed, as though he wanted to cry, but had taught himself not to.

"Miguel." Brown eyes. As Joe walked away, he started limping. It was a subconscious movement, not based on pain. He tried to stop it, but his body refused, as though it hadn't given up the child ghost either.

Chapter Eight

As Joe left the yard, he still battled the urge to side with Murray and lock the kid up. "I need some air," he muttered, heading toward the entrance of the Palace.

Stepping out into bright sunlight hurt Joe's eyes. He blinked repeatedly to adjust. As usual, a crowd had gathered at the gate. Joe eyed the protest signs and as the people noticed him, the protest screams grew louder. The angry voices jumbled together, mixing words to form noise.

Joe stopped walking and watched the mob for a moment. *Jesus, the only thing worse than getting into the Palace is getting out.*

Without realizing it, Joe's hand crept to his knife, checking. As he started through the gate, he noticed someone else exiting in front of him--Murray. He started to call out, but then realized he couldn't speak loud enough to be heard over the mob. He quickened his steps, trying to reach Murray.

Most of the people moved aside, even if they were cursing Joe and Murray, but a particularly burly fellow stepped right in

Murray's path. Murray's shoulders snapped upward and his back straightened like a wall. "Excuse me," he said, trying to sidestep the Lifer.

The Lifer matched Murray's direction and stepped closer. "There ain't no excuse for you. You're trash." He leaned over and spat on Murray's shoes.

Murray looked down at the drops of saliva, and then back at where they had come from. "Is that supposed to intimidate me ?"

The Lifer pulled out a knife and held it in his beefy hand so that sunlight gleamed off the steel. "What does it take? A hole in your throat?"

Joe slipped through the gate and walked up beside Murray. "That's enough."

The Lifer looked up instantly. Although he'd gritted his teeth as if he wanted to chew on Joe, when he saw Joe's unscarred forehead, his expression changed abruptly. The burly man eyed Joe but stepped back.

"What the hell you doing with this scum?" he asked Joe. The blade wavered, but he didn't put it away. "You ain't no Resister. You don't belong with him." His eyes seethed angrily at Murray while he spoke.

"It doesn't matter." Joe's voice came out calm amid the angry lynching comments from the mob around them. Murray brushed past the Lifer, continuing unscathed through the crowd. "I have the right to choose, the same right you have." He walked after Murray and even when the left the crowd behind, he had to double his speed to catch Murray.

103

"Where are we going?" Joe fell in pace beside Murray.

He stopped walking and glared at Joe while pointing at the Palace. "We're not going anywhere. You're going back to the Palace. Or somewhere else." He started walking again. "Anywhere else besides with me. You pick."

Undaunted, Joe followed and grabbed Murray's arm. "What are you hidding Murray? Why are you alone? We were damn lucky that bozo back there didn't pick a fight, considering how badly outnumbered we were."

Murray stepped away from Joe. "I didn't ask you to come with me, did I?" Silence. Murray looked at the crowd, able to see the guy who had almost cut him. The Resister's jaw was so damn tense, it must have hurt to grit his teeth.

The silence grew, leaving Joe's question unanswered, annoying him. He tapped his foot waiting, but not for long as Murray took a few more steps to a locked hover jet. Murray pressed his hand over a place in the driver's door and the metal rose upward slightly, shaping around Murray's hand. A quiet chime sounded. Murray removed his hand and the door slid open.

As Murray climbed inside, Joe raced to the other door and opened it. "I'm coming with you." He sat down and slammed the door behind him.

"Suit yourself. Just don't say I didn't warn you."

As Murray guided the craft into the air and took off, Joe held onto his seat. "I've been warned lots of times for lots of reasons. What makes this one so special, Murray?"

Murray pulled to the side and looked at him. The frothy

green eyes scrutinized his face, searching. His breath went in and out in shallow gasps, as though he was furious.

Joe knew the game. He didn't look away. He met Murray's rage head on and didn't back down. "I used to be really good at covert operations. Still am. So you can't hide a damn thing."

Murray looked out the windshield and floored it. "Why should I trust you?"

"Why shouldn't you? I'm not a Lifer." Joe pointed at his forehead. "Or didn't you notice?"

"You're not a Resister either."

Joe nodded. "Yeah. And I still don't know why I should be. I don't know what New Life is doing, but you do. Somehow. You can trust me now. Or later. But you damn sure can't get rid of me. So you might as well talk."

Murray stared at the slower traffic ahead and adjusted his speed. "I'm going to meet my contact from New Life." His fingers tapped on the steering wheel in short quick spurts.

"Your contact?" Joe leaned forward.

Traffic picked up speed. "Yeah. Who do you think's been leaking to us about New Life? Where do you think we get the info from?" Murray shot him a cold glance.

Those eyes are cold enough to freeze the sun. He shrugged off Murray's sarcastic tone. "It makes sense." He turned away from the driver, toward the buildings and watched them blur together during the flight. "Where are we meeting him?"

"On the east side of Dal-Worth at Saints And Sinners." Murray turned left at Rockwell Boulevard. The rest of the flight passed in silence. Although Joe stared out the front windshield, he also watched Murray with his peripheral vision.

Murray's straight back leaned away from the seat. His fingers kept tapping nervously. They didn't stop moving until the jet pulled up across from what had to have been the seediest joint in Dal-Worth. Saints And Sinners. The words flashed in a blood-red neon haze. Well, only half the letters flashed. The light bulbs in the other half had burned out. White lights outlined the figure of a naked woman next to the name of the bar. Inside her face, blue lights flickered on and off to simulate blinking. And red lights formed her lips in two different expressions. During one flash, her full mouth was closed. The next showed it open.

Joe looked away from the harsh neon glare. The brown brick building had seen better days. On the east side black soot covered the top of the wall as though a fire had started there and charred that section. In other areas, some of the bricks had fallen away, scarring the wall's surface. While there were some windows, many had been broken and boarded over with plywood. The ones still intact had turned a smoky black color.

Saints? Right. At least we won't have to worry about Lifers here, Joe thought. *Nobody in this rat trap could afford the implant, even if they wanted it.* Joe felt his head start to buzz as New Life's mental advertising formed.

WE NOW OFFER A MORE AFFORDABLE PACKAGE FOR THOSE WHO CANNOT AFFORD THE FIFTY-YEAR IMPLANT. GET AN IMPLANT FOR FIVE YEARS. AS YOUR BUDGET ALLOWS, YOU CAN EXPAND YOUR

LONGEVITY IN FIVE-YEAR INCREMENTS. IT'S EASY. AND CHEAP. CALL NEW LIFE TODAY. WE MAKE LIVING LONGER OUR BUSINESS.

"Yeah, right," Murray muttered, shaking her head. "That's one good thing about the Palace. They can't broadcast their messages inside. We've managed to stop it." He reached into the console compartment between seats and pulled out a small, less visible version of the Parkisen, which he shoved into his shoulder-holster.

"Expecting company?" Joe asked, touching the hilt of his sword to make sure it was in place.

"Always." Murray reached into the console and pulled out a second gun. "Here." He offered the weapon to Joe.

A ball of ice weighted Joe's stomach down as he stared at the black plastic, remembering the last time he'd used a gun. Miguel. Joe shook his head. "No. I'd rather stick with a blade." He cinched his fingers into fists.

Murray laughed hollowly. "Then you might as well tell me where you wanted to be buried. You won't get a chance to use it before they blow you away."

Joe stared at his stone face and forced himself to uncurl his fingers and accept the Parkinsen.

"Smart move." Murray pulled out an extra clip and handed it to him. "You might need this."

Joe loaded the clip and shoved the gun into his pocket. The pocket opposite from the one holding the bear. "You ready?"

"Yeah."

As they walked into Saints And Sinners. Joe took mental notes about the clientele coming and going. Despite the cold, most of the women weren't wearing much. Leather straps covering the bare essentials. Leather, leather, and more leather. Joe looked up at the neon letters forming the word Saint and shook his head, thinking, It must all be in the interpretation. Which made him really nervous about the word Sinner.

Murray walked through the door, not bothering to wait for Joe. He didn't even look back to see if Joe was there, instead stalking to the front counter and setting down enough credits to cover them. Joe followed, bustling through the thick crowds. Heavy strains of synthesized music pulsed in the air. Red and blue lights flashed sporadically, illuminating a stage full of female strippers gyrating with the rhythm.

"I hate this crap," he muttered, keeping Murray in his sight as he made his way through moving bodies. Once Murray broke through the crowds, he stopped in front of a section of tables and scanned the people through the smoke-filled air. He looked at the strippers and frowned.

Joe peered toward the stage and grinned. His fingers drummed the table he leaned against as he admired the women dancing. "At least the scenery is good."

Murray snorted disgustedly and yanked some credits out of his pocket. Frowning, he handed them to Joe. "Make yourself at home. Why don't you get a drink and cool off?" He turned away from Joe and started scanning the room again. As Murray spotted his contact, he walked over to the table. Joe hung back, waiting and watching as Murray sat next to a suit and tie. Correction, Joe thought, staring at his sweaty face, A very nervous suit and tie.

The man blotted his face with a handkerchief, but in the glare of colored lights, more perspiration gleamed. A bar girl came over to their table and the suit lifted his glass, asking for a refill. She nodded, took his glass and headed back to the bar.

Joe followed her to the bar. Leaning toward the skinny, balding bartender, he said, "I want a shot of whiskey."

"Show me the credits first."

Joe set them on the bar and waited for his drink. Nodding, the bartender took three of the five credits and fixed the shot. As the small glass was set before him, Joe smiled and picked it up. He downed it and savored the taste spilling down his throat. *It's been too long.* Setting the glass back on the bar, he turned back to check on Murray.

The Resister was talking, and, judging from the frown on his face, the conversation was far from pleasant. They spoke for a moment longer before Murray stood and headed toward Joe. Murray didn't stop walking or talk to Joe. As he passed, Joe said, "That was short."

Murray didn't answer as he began squeezing through the crowds again. Joe followed. He kept sight of Murray's back until a bottle whizzed past Joe's head, crashing into the guy standing next to him. Beer and blood splashed Joe.

Fists and knives tangled in the air as a bar-room brawl erupted. A knife came down toward Joe. Stepping aside, Joe grabbed the wrist of his assailant and snapped it before yanking the guy to the floor and moving on, dodging elbows and blades.

Couldn't they have waited five minutes to start a fight? Joe thought, twisting his body to fit around people. After clearing the crowd, he looked for Murray in the ocean of faces. Joe couldn't have found Murray if Joe's life depended it, which it very well might considering Murray had the keys to the Jet.

Maybe he went outside, back to it. Joe turned and walked outside. The cold air stung his eyes. He slid his hands into his pockets, not only to keep warm, but also to grab the gun. He started back to the Jet, but paused at an alley when he heard voices. He stopped, leaned against the wall and listened.

"How long did you think your new identity would cover your ass?"

A dull thud echoed in the air, sounding like a hand slapping flesh. But that wasn't what chilled Joe. Instead, he focused on the easily-recognizable pitch and accent of the voice. Malachette. Joe groaned and laid his head against the wall none too softly. *Who was he terrorizing this time and why?*

Joe held his breath and slowly peeked around the wall. But what he saw forced the air from his lungs in a surprised gasp. It wasn't possible. With one arm Malachette held Murray, pressing Murray's back into Malachette's chest. With his free hand, Malachettte held a dagger tip pointed at Murray's throat. Blood trickled from a small wound.

"You didn't answer me, whore. How long did you think it would take for me to find you?"

Joe's fingers gripped the rough brick wall and ducked back

behind it. He shook his head. What the hell was going on? Whore? Confused, he peered from around the corner again. Malachette smiled at his victim and ran his tongue across Murray's face. "You were good last time."

Joe ducked back and leaned against the wall. That was what had bothered him all along. He was a she, and he'd suspected it. She'd acted the part of a man, but deep down he'd recognized signs about her gender. He'd always known, even if he didn't consciously realize it.

"Shall we pick up where we left off last time?" Malachette asked coldly.

He leaned out and peered at them again. Her eyes were closed and she seemed unbelievably still, as if the simple act of breathing would break her body. The stance validated what Malachette's words implied. She'd been here before, and had disguised herself as a man hoping that she wouldn't ever return. *She'd rather die first.* Joe's stomach rolled as he imaged what had happened. No wonder nobody ever revealed her secret to him. No wonder she hated the world.

No wonder she didn't trust him.

"No answer, huh? Turning mute on me? I can think of other uses for you tongue." Malachette pricked the dagger deeper into her skin. Murray's eyes opened. Her lips rounded into an excruciating oval as if silently screaming.

He frowned, disappointed by her self-control. He wanted her to scream. At least once. He pushed the dagger into her skin a little more, giving her an added incentive. "Yeah. Let's get back to where we were. Caleb only wants your head. That leaves the rest for me." He grabbed the collar of her shirt and ripped it.

She cringed and tried to fight his hands. Her fingers clutched like a woman, as though her body finally remembered she was a female. Joe gritted his teeth as he saw all the hope go out of her. She was giving in because she thought she'd be better off dead. To her anything would be better than this.

Joe stared at her face. All the features had lost the hard lines or rage and determination. They had softened into shadows of fear. She tried to pull away, but Malachette gripped her body harder, twisting her against him. She screamed. He snapped his hand over her face, cutting the sound off to a gurgle. Joe swallowed hard

"Hey, Malachette!" he called. "She's not alone. She's got enough guys out here to finish you off and serve you for desert."

" I didn't see her little artillery when she went inside. And they didn't help her when I grabbed her." He laughed raucously. "I don't think she's got backup. If you're it, you're late."

"You're a dead man."

"You think that'll get her loose. It doesn't matter. She'll be dead in a moment. Then you'll die with her."

Joe forced himself to laugh loudly. "Yeah, that's what you said about me the last time. Except you didn't kill the kid and you didn't finish me then, either."

"My mistake. It won't happen again."

Joe peeked around the corner to find the blade deeper in Murray's neck. "Damn it!" he muttered, yanking the Parkinson out. One of two things would happen when he used it. Malachette would finish impaling her throat or he would fumble. Fifty-fifty odds were all he had, and he knew if he didn't shoot, he would be taking Murray back to the Palace in pieces.

He pointed the gun at the wall close to the two of them and fired. As Malachettte jerked away from the blast, his dagger slipped away from Murray's throat, and his grip around her body slackened. Murray yanked free and turned to kick him in the groin. Then she took off, running the opposite direction as Joe.

"Murray!" Joe called. "Wait." He watched her disappear around a corner and he shook his head.

Malachette, still clutching his balls, rose to his knees. "I'll get that bitch."

"I wouldn't count on it." He lifted the gun to aim it at Malachette. "You won't be getting anybody anymore."

"Who's gonna protect her after you kill me and get sent to prison for using that gun. Hell, you'll die for murder because you used that gun on me in front of so many witnesses." He pulled his hands away from his groin and slid his knees under his body so he could sit upright. When he looked up at Joe, he grinned, just like when he had stabbed Joe's wounded leg. "I'll get Murray. And then I'll get you."

Joe's body screamed with tension. His shoulders ached from not beating the shit of out him. "You won't be around, old man." He applied pressure to the trigger. *Shoot him, Joe. Just pull the trigger and blot his sorry ass out forever.*

"We'll see. Won't we." Malachette leered at him. "I had her

before. I'll have her again. I cut you before, and I'll cut you again. People like me don't die Joe. We just get better."

Joe could hear shoes hitting the pavement as people came running. He kept his finger on the trigger, knowing it would only take one good shot to put this scum out of his misery. But Malachette had pointed out he didn't have that shot. Not without witnesses. Fifteen people were running toward him. They weren't close enough to see the gun yet so he put it up.

Chapter Nine

"She's running like the devil's chasing her," Malachette leered. His laughter echoed in the alley.

"Shut up."

"Sometimes you just can't catch people. They fall too far over edges, if you know what I mean. And then they might as well have died. It would've been better for them if they had," Malachette continued as Joe walked past him.

"I said shut up."

"I don't care. Enjoy what's left of your life because I'll be breathing over your shoulder."

From the corner of his eye, Joe saw Malachette rise and slip into the crowd gathering outside the alley. Joe turned and looked down the alley both ways, searching for Murray. In the distance he saw her. Chills swept down Joe's spine as he realized she was running from past demons. He had to catch her before she met up with a few present day ones, like more of Malachette's men.

"Murray!" he shouted. "Wait."

His voice made her run faster. With a grunt, Joe sprinted

after her, thanking his lucky stars Wayne had healed his knee so completely. With each step, he gained on her. He was within an arm's reach when she turned left, and cast a panicked glance at him. Her eyes had widened. Tears. *God, what in the hell had been done to her?*

Joe ran faster. A burning sensation stabbed his chest. He turned left, darting inside a doorway. Something slammed into his head, darkening his vision.

"What the hell are you following me for?" Murray screamed. She tried to punch him again, but Joe caught her wrist

"Stop it, Murray." He cinched his fingers on her wrist, trying keep hold of her, but she yanked free and swung again.

"Get away from me! Now!" Her body exploded with rage. Joe deflected most of the blows. One got through and slammed into his eye.

"Murray, stop it!" he yelled, grabbing her hands.

She fought like a hellcat, taking Joe off balance and throwing him to the floor. *Jesus, somebody taught her to fight. Malachette must have taken her off guard.* Joe jumped to his feet.

"I hate to do this," he muttered. Murray slammed her fist across his jaw before he struck the back of her head. As she lost consciousness and slid to the floor, Joe caught her and swung her body over his left shoulder before putting the gun back into his pocket.

He carried her back to the Jet, pushed his hand against the body to unlock it and then laid her in the passenger seat. As he started the Jet, he looked at her and rubbed his jaw. "Hell of a punch, Murray."

As he flew back to the Palace, he snooped around the console and spotted a screen with the triangular mark of the Resisters centered on it. Curious, Joe pressed it.

Wayne's face appeared on screen. He frowned. "What are you doing in Murray's Jet? Where is he?"

"You mean she, don't you?" Joe replied accusingly. "Why didn't you think to mention this little bit of information earlier?"

Wayne shrugged. "Because asking her out on a date would gotten your balls cut off." He tapped his cigar against an ashtray. "Now you know. Tell me what happened."

"She just got done tangling with Malachette right after we met her contact from New Life." He glanced at Murray. "Right now she's a bit out of things, and I'm gonna need some help getting back inside the Palace with all those damn Lifers standing outside the gate." He could just see trying to carry her in with a bunch of them picking fights.

Wayne nodded. "How quick will you be here?"

"In five minutes."

"We'll be watching for you."

The screen lapsed back to blackness before the triangle reappeared. Joe leaned against the seat and tried to ignore his aching muscles. When he thought of Malachette's leer, he forgot the minor aches of his body and remembered the cold eyes.

He looked back at Murray. Her head rested against the window and wisps of black hair rose against the fogged glass. Her lips parted slightly. He stared at the bruise flowering on her temple and cringed. What in the hell had they done to her? And how exactly did Caleb Walker fit into her life?

***

Leaning against the medicine cabinet, Joe watched Murray sleep in the Recalibration Unit. He remembered the first time he had seen her and the intimidation he'd felt then because of her weapon. Now he didn't feel intimidated at all, and she'd probably hate that. Obviously she'd felt secure in her disguise.

Until Malachette had taken it away.

"What happened? How did Malachette get her?" Wayne asked, cleansing the wound in her neck.

"I don't know. A fight erupted in the bar. She got outside before I did. He must have caught her off-guard." Joe stared at her face, at the way sleep smoothed away the emotion, leaving only peace. Long, dark eyelashes contrasted against her skin. Without all the added bulk of coats, she looked smaller.

Wayne went to the cabinet and grabbed a vial of the Trianna solution. He put some on a piece of gauze and wiped it on her neck. "Yeah. Somebody surprised her. Otherwise she would have blown him away and asked questions later."

"Yeah." Joe watched Wayne cover the wound with a bandage. "Why is someone trying to kill her?"

Wayne's hand stopped moving. He looked up abruptly. "For two reasons. First, Murray knows way too much about New Life that she shouldn't. She just needs the proof to go public and ruin the Longevity Implant." He finished putting the bandage on and replaced the medicine in the cabinet.

"What's the second reason?"

Wayne's shoulders stiffened. He looked down at Murray and touched the bruise on her forehead. "Because she's Caleb's wife. She's his property, and if she won't come back alive, he wants her dead."

Joe's throat constricted. "I see. Malachette tried to kill her before, didn't he?"

Wayne's fingers moved to stroke her short hair softly. "You ask a lot of questions, Joe."

Joe paced around the room. "So. Tell me about it."

The healer touched the bandage on her throat. "She likes her privacy."

Joe stopped walking and glared at the healer. "Tell me."

Raising an eyebrow, Wayne shrugged. "Yeah, Caleb was there to help. She was raped, beaten so severely she couldn't move and then left in a burning building to die."

Murray stirred slightly and Wayne moved his hand. At the absence of his touch she drifted back to sleep. "So how did she survive?"

Wayne looked at him. "Cammo and I were friends. He came and got me and some others who distrusted New Life. We barely managed to get her out of there." He folded his hands together as though they needed something to hold onto. He looked at the cabinet where he'd put up the Trianna solution. "If I hadn't discovered the secret of that healing gel, she wouldn't have made it. Her body was so broken in so many places if the skin hadn't been holding it together, she would have fallen apart."

He took a deep breath and swallowed hard. Joe watched his Adam's apple move. "Sometimes I just wonder if she'd been better off dead. Maybe if I'd had something like the Trianna for her spirit, she would've been okay. But you can't break down that much of the body without breaking the spirit, too."

He adjusted the blanket around her body. "Let's get out of here and let her get some rest. She'll need it before the run."

Joe glared at him. "She can't go on the run."

Wayne walked out of the room and Joe followed, watching the lights automatically flip off. "It's her choice, Joe. The run might be the only thing that keeps her from going over the edge after this." He took a cigar and lighter out of his pocket. "Besides, it'll help her get back into her disguise."

"What good is it? Malachette knows she's alive. So does Caleb." His voice rose slightly.

Wayne lifted a finger to his mouth and gestured for Joe to be quiet. After slipping the cigar in his mouth and lighting it, he took a puff and said, "It matters Joe. It makes her feel safe. As safe as somebody can feel who's been raped and beaten." He began walking and gestured for Joe to follow along. "When Murray wakes, you can't treat her differently."

"But she knows I've found out her secret." He rubbed his jaw where she had left proof.

"Consider yourself lucky that was the only thing she hit." Wayne shrugged. "She was out of things, Joe. You said so yourself. Maybe she does. Maybe she doesn't. But if you act like you always have, it might salvage her pride. She doesn't need your pity."

Joe snorted. "Well she damn sure needs something. Malachette and Caleb aren't going to let go on like nothing's happened." He shoved his hands into his pockets. He found the bear and the gun.

"That's why we're going to find out what New Life is up to when we break in." Wayne touched his shoulder. "Be patient, Joe. We'll get those bastards."

Joe pulled away from Wayne. "What then? So Murray's got revenge. What's going to keep her from going over the edge then?"

Wayne threw up his hands. "Your good looks." As Joe rolled his eyes at the healer, Wayne shrugged and said, "I don't know. I'm taking this one crisis at a time."

***

Malachette stood in front of Caleb's desk. Behind him, two of his men held Gabe Renault in place. "Here's the leak, Mr. Walker. This guy's been a little friendly with the wrong people."

Caleb stood in front of his window, watching the sun set over the Palace, bathing the world in an orange-sherbet glow. "Which people?"

"Murray."

Caleb moved his glass around in a circular pattern and watched the amber liquor rotate like a whirlpool. "Is that true, Gabriel? Have you been associating with my beloved wife. The same wife who was supposed to have died in a tragic fire a little while back?"

121

"I-I just talked to her, Mr. Walker." He pulled out a handkerchief and blotted his forehead. "I didn't tell her anything."

"Nor did you tell me she was still breathing." Caleb raised his hand to smooth his blond hair. As he moved his hand, sunlight glittered off his gold watch.

Gabe yanked free of the two goons holding him. "She's afraid of you. Afraid of New Life."

Caleb slowly turned and smiled. Gabriel stared at his perfect white teeth and shuddered. "I just didn't want to get her into trouble."

"Perfectly understandable," Caleb said. He smelled the liquor and then took a small sip. "You saved her from trouble and bought it for yourself." He looked at Malachette. "Kill him."

Gabe's face turned white. He staggered forward. "But I'm your VP, Mr. Walker. Haven't I done my job well for New Life?"

Caleb took another drink and nodded. "Why of course, Gabriel. Just think of this as a wonderful, paid vacation. After all, I am paying Malachette to dispose of your miserable body."

"No, Mr. Walker. Please." Gabe fell to his knees. "I didn't give her anything. I swear."

Caleb nodded to Lugnut, who unrolled a long piece of clear plastic and covered the floor with it. Caleb opened his desk drawer and pulled out a cloth and some gloves. As he pulled on the gloves, the plastic rubbed against itself noisily. Caleb picked up the Parkinsen lying in his desk. "Nice gun, Murray. Too bad you won't be needing it anymore."

He snapped the clip into place and looked down at Gabe,

still flinching from the sound of the gun being loaded. "Now, Gabriel. One last chance. What did you give my sweet wife? What did you tell her?"

Sweat drenched the front of Gabe's white, button-down shirt. "I didn't give her nothing. I promise. Please don't do this, Mr. Walker. I'll make things up to you." Sweat beaded above his lips.

Caleb lowered the gun and aimed. "Oh, you're about to. This is my wife's gun. Her fingerprints are all over it. And the slugs from it are going to be found in your body. So you see even if I can't kill her, I can put her in prison and then kill her. Thanks so much for...dying."

Caleb smiled at Gabe. The brilliant sunset outside his window made his teeth look yellow. His blue eyes shone in excitement.

"Mr. Walker, NO!"

Caleb pulled the trigger.

***

"Let's get back to where we were," Malachette seethed in Murray's ear. His hot breath smelled like his mouth was rotting away. One of his hands cinched down around her waist, holding her still. But the knife at her throat enforced it.

Oh, God. Not again! I'll die first.

Murray fought hard and fast, thrashing her arms and legs furiously. She felt the agonizing slow dance of the blade impaling her throat. And then blackness.

"Mur?" Wayne's voice broke the webbing of dreams. She opened her eyes to the stale, fluorescent lights of the RCI and

Wayne leaning over her. She looked down at her hands clenching the blanket. She kept replaying the image of the knife at her throat and her left hand reached up and touched a thick fabric.

What had happened? Her mind felt numb as though a fog had washed over it. And her head throbbed in back. What had stopped Malachette? "My throat?"

"Does it hurt?" Wayne asked softly. He leaned over her and touched her hand.

Murray flinched and moved away. "No. It's fine." She took a deep, shuddering breath and tried to focus, replaying her last waking minutes. She'd been in the alley with Malachette. She closed her eyes and remembered. The knife at her throat. Bullets someone had fired.

Joe. He knew. He'd been there. Murray's chest stiffened until she could barely breathe. He knew. Heat filled her cheeks. She couldn't face him. "Where is he?"

"Malachette is gone," Wayne said, pulling off her bandage. His fingers touched her skin.

"I don't give a rat's ass about Malachette. Where's Joe?"

Wayne traced the thin scar where the wound had been a couple of hours ago. "He's checking out your underwear and bras to see if you have anything he might fit," Wayne said, rolling his eyes. "He's with Cammo, sparring in the yard." Wayne tossed the gauze into the trash. "Looks like the Trianna did it's job."

"I want him out of the Palace. Now." Her hands clenched the blanket again, drawing it tightly to her body.

"Why can't you be like every other female I've met and get

married to a man before you want to throw him out?" He went over to an ashtray and picked up his cigar. "I mean no judge is going to give you one cent of his money like this."

Murray gritted her teeth and glared at him. Her fingers ran through her hair. "I'm serious, Wayne."

Wayne's silver eyes stared at her in open disbelief. "We can't just throw him out, Mur. He's done nothing wrong. Besides, he wants to help us fight New Life. And we need his help. Cammo-"

Murray sat up sharply, despite the pain clawing the back of her head. "Damn. What the hell did he hit me with?" She winced as dizziness and nausea rolled over her in waves.

"His hand. He didn't see any other way to subdue you."

She flinched at his verb choice. Her stomach felt lined in acid. "I want him to go. Now!" she demanded loudly.

"No, Murray. He did you a favor. He got you away from Malachette. He could have cut loose then and left you to him, but he didn't. What does that say about him?"

Murray waved her hand in front of her face. "God, I hate your cigars. Can't you turn on the sensory switch?"

Wayne smiled and took a bow. "Well, for you, I guess I could. What's your pleasure?" He walked over to the panel and reached for the knob.

"I don't care."

"That's not an option."

"Lemons!" she seethed, gingerly caressing her head, searching for knots where Joe had hit her. She clenched her jaw and brushed through her short hair. "I don't care if he did do me a favor."

Wayne put the cigar in his ashtray before he walked over to her and touched her hand. When she tried to pull away, he held on tighter. "Yes, you do. You care because you know he's different from Caleb, and that frightens you. It took you months to believe in me while you healed. You built up so many walls. But I cared for you. I healed you." Wayne smiled at her. "And I'd kill anybody to keep you safe. You're the daughter I didn't have. Would I have let Joe stay so long inside the Palace if I didn't believe he would be on our side?"

Murray didn't answer. Staring off in the distance, she suddenly looked surprised and she frantically patted her stomach, relieved when she realized all of her clothes were still on. "The disc. Where's the disc?"

"What disc?"

She reached into her panties, searching. When she touched a square plastic box, she closed her eyes and muttered in relief. She pulled it out and opened the lid, checking to make sure Renault hadn't lied. That the disc really was in there. Then she handed it to Wayne with trembling fingers.

Wayne took it. "Yeah. Just what I've always wanted. A little black box."

"I got this from Gabe. He said it had important data."

Wayne took it and looked at the disc. "Did he say what kind of information? Or how we could use it?"

Murray shook her head. "No. He said we'd know what it

was when we saw it."

Wayne shut the case. "Are you sure it's there? I mean what if your contact is lying?"

Murray thought about Renault, about how he'd practically begged her to get him out of New Life. Said Caleb was watching him. He was one of the few men she'd liked at New Life, even when she'd been with Caleb. Maybe because he needed to get out of there. But nobody ever left New Life. At least not while they were breathing. The only reason she had made it out was because Caleb thought she was dead.

"So maybe this is our Godsend. Maybe this will tell us what New Life is doing with the implants."

Murray nodded. "Yeah, but we've got a different problem. New Life just dropped the price of the implants."

Wayne arched his eyebrows. "They're making them affordable. For some reason they think everyone should have them?" He rubbed his chin. " I guess this isn't about money anymore?"

"It never was. Caleb Walker has enough money to buy the whole world. He wanted something else. Something twisted." She shuddered and took a deep breath, trying to regain her composure.

"Yeah, well, he's not going to get it. We're going to get to the truth and expose Caleb for the scum that he is."

Murray looked at the floor. She pulled away from Wayne's hand and yanked the covers from around her. "What time is it?"

"Eight."

"I'm going to get ready." She put her feet on the floor.

"You don't have to go tonight. Not after dealing with Malachette." Wayne touched her shoulder.

Murray moved his hand. "Yes, I have to do this for me."

"He's going with us, Murray." The weight of Wayne's silver-eyed stare rested heavily on her.

Joe knows, she thought. She rubbed her shoulders, suddenly feeling exposed. The knowledge made her want to throw something. Anything. Instead she balled her hands into fists. "Whatever. If he fucks with me, I'll kill him."

"He's not going to pick a fight, Murray. We both know that. The punch you threw almost knocked his jaw out of joint."

"Good."

"He's not going to cause trouble," Wayne repeated. "If anyone starts anything, it'll be you. And it'll be because you think you have to."

Murray swallowed his words and bit back all the things she wanted to say about Joe. She didn't understand him, but It didn't make him any different than Caleb Walker.

Wayne watched her stand and walk to the door as he leaned on the bed. He went over to the ashtray and lifted his cigar. Picking it up, he sniffed the air. "Lemons, huh?" He inhaled and savored.

His long silver hair fell across the sheets, giving the strands a darker gray cast against the bright whiteness. He lifted his hand and massaged his temples, dreading the night ahead of them. Maybe they'd help some people the Federation wanted to kill.

That's if Murray didn't tangle with Joe. But keeping Murray at bay would take much more than simple words. Her need for secrecy was as great as her fear of men. Both of those two worked against Joe. He just hoped Joe knew how to handle it.

He shook his head and exited the RCI, heading for a drink. "Shit." He needed to get drunk right about now. He knew Murray too damn well. She'd pick a fight just to prove that she had a warrior's spirit.

Chapter Ten

"Guard you left side, kid," Joe snapped as he sparred with Henry in the yard. Although the sun had gone down hours ago, the lights provided enough artificial sunlight. He held the blade in the air, focusing on Henry as the kid circled him.

"I am," Henry yelled back. Sweat spilled down his forehead and into his eyes. He blinked, trying to clear his vision.

Joe lunged toward him and tapped the blade against Henry's side. "Then I shouldn't be able to get inside your space. Get the sword up."

Henry stopped moving. His eyes grew wide as he stared past Joe. "Come on, Henry. Let's get back to this."

The kid planted his feet and lowered his sword. "Maybe some other time. Right now you've got company."

Joe turned and came face to face with Murray. He wiped the sweat from his forehead with the back of his hand. "Well, well. I see you're awake. Feeling-"

"Cut the crap, Joe. I want you to leave." Murray held a

sword in her left hand.

"Friendly as usual." He refused to look away from her cold, green eyes. "But I don't want to leave. I want to find out what's going on with New Life just as badly as you do. I've got a run to go on tonight."

The agitated frown dissolved into a wilder expression. Her eyes widened and she gritted her teeth. "I said leave!"

Joe rolled his shoulders. "And I said I wasn't going anywhere."

She lifted the sword and swung it. Joe blocked it. She switched angles and thrust. It came close to Joe's side before he thrust his steel in her path. "Get out of here!" She kept swinging. Joe kept blocking. She danced around him, her green eyes always trained on him.

She swung wide and the tip of her blade skimmed Joe's arm before he jumped out of the way. Blood immediately rose to the surface. Joe felt the burning pain. Then he saw the blood.

Murray swung again. The rage in her face waned under the sweat and dirt. Her green eyes blinked. Pain surfaced in them. And fear.

Lifting her sword, she stepped toward him and swung. Her strokes kept coming. He moved his weapon, using it to break her swings, never to assault. Her circular steps darted toward him and away with each thrust, parry or swing. "Fight me, damn you!" she screamed, thrusting the blade at his chest. He broke the movement with his own steel.

"No, Murray. I'm not here to fight you." He grabbed the

131

hand holding her blade. "You want to make me your enemy, but I'm not going to play the part. I didn't mean to find things you wanted to hide. But if you keep picking fights with me, neither one of us is going to stop New Life. Is that what you want?"

She stopped swinging and stared at the darkened ring of sweat on the neck of his tee-shirt. Under his armpits, she saw similar stains. She looked at his calm face, and wished she could break that stillness. She took a step backward, still watching him. "Damn you. Damn you to hell."

She gripped her sword so tightly. Then she stalked away, almost running into Wayne as she passed, glaring at the cigar in his mouth.

"Still got all your limbs attached?" the healer asked.

Murray walked away without answering. Joe watched her go. "Barely. She's pissed."

Wayne nodded. "I came to warn you." He pulled the cigar away from his lips. "Women. You spring their butts from certain death, and they come at you with pointed objects." He put the cigar back into his mouth and shook his head. "What's the world coming to?" Wayne peered at Joe's arm. "You're bleeding."

Joe touched the gash on his arm. When he pulled his fingers back and looked, blood covered them. "Yeah, thanks for the warning, but she already gave me one. Fortunately for me, she didn't put it where she first tried or I wouldn't be breathing."

Wayne lifted the torn part of his shirt. "You have a habit of attracting sharp objects, you know that? Let's get some solution on that," the healer said.

Joe sheathed his blade and nodded. "Just lucky, I guess. Murray wants me to leave. I refused to go."

"Good. Just be sure and wear padded clothing around her."

Joe brushed the hair away from his eyes and thought right then the little souvenir from Murray's rage didn't feel good, even if standing up to her did. He just wished he had done it for another reason besides the fact that he was a man and she feared him.

***

Joe stood in the front room of the Palace with a small group of others, waiting to go on the run. Murray stood on the other side of the room, purposely ignoring Joe. She held one of the Parkinsens, checking the clip to make sure she had plenty of ammo. Henry hovered near Joe. He stared ahead, his feet taking small steps and his hands moving around in tiny motions as he mentally ran through some defense moves.

All of them wore black clothing, even Wayne. Because his silver hair would shine, even in moonlight, Wayne tucked it into his shirt and then slipped on the black hat. About half of them were armed with blades. The others carried the Parkisens.

Joe reached into his pocket and double-checked to make sure the gun hadn't fallen out and waited for Murray to get the ball rolling. As he stood in the middle of the room, he rocked from the balls of his feet to his toes and back again. A low mumbling of voices hummed around him.

"I need to see you for a minute," Murray said, appearing at his side. For once she didn't glare at him. Her face looked pale against the black shirt, and the turtleneck hid remembrances of her encounter with Malachette.

Henry started to follow, but Murray touched his shoulder. "I want you to stay put, Cammo."

"Henry," the kid said, glaring at her. "Why don't you just call me Henry? It's my name."

Murray moved her hand, her fingers brushing his neck as they lifted. "Fine. Stay here, Henry." She turned and motioned for Joe to come with her.

He followed her into a small room away from the others. "Yeah. What is it?"

She rubbed her forehead. "I want you to stick to my brother like glue. He's never been on a run before, so the two of you should be good together-"

"He's what?" Joe repeated weakly. He thrust his hands through his hair, not able to believe what he was hearing. "What about the night I found him?"

"He has this thing about looking at stars. He often slips out during Lock-down. Malachette caught him that night."

Joe closed his eyes and the kid's face appeared, then the Spanish boy's. He should have known. When would he learn not to assume things? "But he found you quick, like your group had been out on a run together."

Murray looked at her gun, checking it again. "Yeah, we were together looking for Cammo. I was worried about him because another Resister came up missing the day before that." She looked up from the gun. "You and Wayne wanted him to go.

134

You said he was old enough. So you'd better cover his ass."

"Yeah, I will." Joe turned away from Murray.

"Joe."

He stopped walking. "What?"

"I shouldn't have been so angry at you earlier." Her voice cracked slightly. He knew what the words must have cost her. "You got me out of a tight jam when you didn't have to. I shouldn't have taken things out on you like I did. I'm sorry."

Joe turned back to her and saw her flushed cheeks. Her fingers clutched the gun as though she clung to it to keep from drowning. "I don't blame you, Murray. I'll look after Henry."

He stared at her a moment longer, at her half-open mouth which looked like she wanted to say something else but didn't have words. Then he turned away and headed back to the group.

"What did she want?" Henry asked as Joe came back into the room. He chewed loudly on a piece of gum.

"For me to keep you in line," Joe responded in a serious voice. "Why didn't you tell me you hadn't been on a run before?"

Henry shrugged. "You didn't ask. And then you convinced Murray I could go. Why would I want to tell you a fool thing like that when you would have changed your mind?"

Joe rubbed the bridge of his nose and said, "Because it would have been nice for me to know, Henry."

"So now you know." He blew a large bubble, which popped a second later.

"You stay close to me. Anything happens to you, Murray will have my ass."

"Maybe that would do her some good."

Joe stepped closer to Henry until inches separated their faces. "I'm going to remember that you're still at a stupid age where thinking is optional, kid." Joe watched Henry abruptly stop chewing gum and stand perfectly still. "But so help me if I hear another comment like that come from your mouth, you'll wish to hell you never learned to speak. Do I make myself perfectly clear?"

"Yes." A bright crimson splashed each cheek, and Henry looked down at the floor.

Joe stepped away from Henry, and as he looked around the room, everybody stared at him. Everyone except Murray, and she had just re-entered the room, forcing everyone to look at the walls and start talking amongst themselves. She stopped walking and caught Wayne's attention, asking what had happened.

Wayne shrugged, as if to suggest it wasn't important. Murray, completely unconvinced, nodded slowly. She walked to the front of the room and looked around. "Is everyone armed and ready?"

An uneven chorus of 'yeses' broke the tension in the room. Murray nodded and gestured toward the door. "Let's go. We'll head north on Jackson and south on Meridian. The damn Lifers usually like that part of Dal-worth."

A soft murmuring agreement spread through the group as they headed out the door. As promised, Joe walked beside Henry. An uncomfortable tension spread through him as he thought about the Parkinsen in his pocket and the kid walking next to him.

136

It stuck to his gut, clenching his stomach nervously.

Murray walked a couple of paces ahead of them, behind two of the other Resisters. Out of the group, only three people were easily identified, considering all the black: Henry, Wayne and Murray. The longer Joe watched Murray, the more he wondered how he could have mistaken Murray as a man. *It's all in the attitude*, he guessed.

As they walked outside, Joe noticed the empty streets outside the facility, and he smiled slightly. At least the Lifers had the good sense to sleep sometimes.

The small group divided into two separated parties and loaded into two separated jets. Joe selected the vehicle without Murray. As he closed the door, he exhaled a sigh of relief. The last thing I need right now is her hovering over the kid.

"Joe," Henry said in a voice so quiet that the other Resisters didn't hear him.

"Yeah?" Joe looked at the kid, but Henry refused to meet his gaze, preferring the darkened window.

"I didn't mean to make you mad earlier. I know what I said, but I meant it differently."

Joe frowned and gripped his seat as an uncomfortable tension threaded through his muscles. "It's okay, Henry."

"I meant that maybe you and my sister could like hook up or something. She been through so much shit that she's stopped believing somebody like you exists."

"Someone like me? Are you crazy?" Joe echoed incredulously. "Kid, you don't even know me. And I didn't even know Murray was a woman until a few hours ago. This is a little more complicated than you might think. And I can't save anybody. Not your sis-"

DON'T SAY IT, JOE, Wayne's voice filled his head, interrupting him. HE NEVER BELIEVED IN ANYBODY BEFORE YOU, AND HE'S GOT ENOUGH FAITH TO GIVE YOU AND MURRAY SOME.

Joe looked around the jet and spotted the back of Wayne's head. I DON'T WANT HIM TO BELIEVE IN ME, he thought.

GREAT, Wayne continued. GOT ANY POPCORN SO I CAN WATCH YOU FALL ON YOUR FACE?

"What were you about to say?" Henry asked. He stared at Joe curiously since Joe had stopped speaking in mid-sentence.

"Nothing, Henry." Joe felt his shirt collar closing in, strangling him. He raised his hand and deftly tugged at it.

"Have you ever done this before?" the kid asked.

Joe watched the road and saw images of South America. Full moon nights in sweltering heat. Trees that scented the air exotically. A different world, a different time, a different war. Same damn killing. "Something like it."

The jet slowed and then stopped. Joe felt acid clutching his stomach with needled claws. The Resisters in front of him stood up and one by one climbed out of the jet. As Joe stood , he turned to Henry and said, "Stay where I can see you. I mean it."

Henry rolled his eyes and sighed. "You sound just like Murray."

"Don't test me," his voice dropped to a threatening whisper.

Joe climbed out of the jet and clapped his hand on Wayne's shoulder. "What are we looking for anyway?"

Wayne glanced at Joe. THANKS FOR NOT TELLING THE KID. The healer projected his words into Joe's mind. "Something you can't see." When Joe frowned at him, Wayne quickly added, "I'm looking for mental footprints they've left behind, Joe. Once I detect them, we'll know the direction they're headed."

More mumbo jumbo. "So how's the other group going to find the Lifers without your abilities?"

"Murray."

Joe felt the temperature around him drop about ten degrees. He stopped walking abruptly. "She can do the same thing you can? She can read my mind?"

"Which means you'd better not have any wild fantasies about her while she's in the room."

Joe moved his hand from Wayne's shoulder and his back muscles stiffened. "Thanks for telling me at this late stage in the game."

Wayne stopped walking and scrutinized Joe's face. "Already had a few, huh? Is that why she came after you with a sword?"

"There are times when I really don't like you," Joe muttered, shaking his head.

The healer patted his back. "If I had told you before, you would've put your guard up around Murray and confused her readings. She had enough fear of you without that, Joe. She didn't want to believe in you. Still doesn't. But you can't hide

139

your scars anymore than she can hide hers. It's the pain which draws her to you. And the pain that keeps each of you from letting anybody get close. You're two halves wanting to be whole."

Joe shrugged away Wayne's hand. "Don't get maudlin on me."

"I said the same thing," Henry interjected, smiling broadly as he threw an arm around each of them.

Joe glared at him. "Oh really. Somehow I thought it actually had something to do with sex. Or lack of it on your sister's part."

Wayne's body stiffened. He closed his eyes, focusing on something within.

"What is it?" Joe asked, removing the kid's arm.

Wayne's eyes opened and he looked down the silent street. Lifting his hand, he pointed at a row of gutted houses. "There. The Lifers are on the move."

Joe looked at the surface stillness, then back at Wayne's concerned frown. The healer raised his hands., "We've got action ahead."

The group of Resisters stilled. Henry scuffed his shoes against the concrete nervously, and the thongs on Wayne's socked feet left a shuddering coldness deep inside Joe. He felt like he'd been on some crazy ride and had dropped a few feet, leaving his stomach hollowed.

"How many?" one of the Resisters asked, stepping toward Wayne. He pulled out his gun and checked his clip. The other

Resisters with guns mimicked the action.

Taking a deep breath, Wayne closed his eyes again and squinted, trying to focus the mental image. "I sense three...no, make that four."

Wayne opened his eyes and scanned the row of houses ahead. Frowning, he finally lifted a hand and pointed to the second house. "I think they're inside that one."

"You think?" Joe asked. "Can't you be a bit more sure?"

"This isn't an exact science." Wayne nodded. "Besides, I have to get closer. The Lifers aren't secretive about their persuasive tactics." As the healer started walking toward the house, Joe noticed the other Resisters flank around him, forming a barrier around him with their bodies. Joe pulled at Henry's arm and headed toward the back of the ensemble.

"Why are we lagging behind everybody," the kid asked in an edgy voice. His fingers hovered close the hilt of his blade. "I want to be in the middle of the action. This is boring."

"Precisely," Joe said, smiling grimly. "Considering this is the first run for both of us, we're not going to be at the front."

A disgusting sigh came from the kid. "You'll let me come, but you won't let me fight."

Joe stared at the house as they moved forward, thinking, *There'll be plenty of days to fight. Too many, kid. You just don't know it yet.* "That's right," he snapped. "Now get ready."

Two Resisters walked up to the door and looked back at Wayne. In the full moonlight, Joe saw the questioning expression of raised eyebrows and shoulders, double-checking to make sure they were at the right place. Wayne nodded them on.

The others moved around the sides of the house and hid in the midnight shadows. Joe walked to the left, making sure the kid dogged his footsteps. The sound of glass shattering jarred Joe's nerves. Then he heard a female scream. "Leave him alone!"

More glass. Something heavy slammed into a wall, thudding loudly. "Are you stupid, bitch? You know why we're here. The question is, what are you going to do about it? Get the implant or stop breathing?"

A child wailed. "Shut that kid up!" another male voice growled. "Or we'll do it for you."

"We can't afford the implant-"

The Resisters threw open the door and ran inside. More glass breaking. Bullets ripped through the night. Screams. More Resisters darted inside. Joe yanked out the gun and ran toward the door. As he crossed the doorway, he saw the bodies first, then looked at the foreheads. Lifers. Four of them with huge holes in their chests where the Parkinsens had done the job.

Wayne looked around and spotted the woman, draping her body across an unconscious male. She cradled a baby in her arms. Her body convulsed with tears as she clung to him with a tightly. Blood spilled from gashes on his forehead and drenched her hair.

Wayne brushed past Joe, toward the man. As he bent over, he nodded toward two of the Resisters who pried the woman away, despite her screaming. The shrieking jarred the baby from his blank stare and his voice peeled through the forced stillness.

"Leave him alone!" she screamed. Her face looked as white as flour, except for the spots of blood and a cut lip. She writhed her body, trying to escape from the Resister's grip. Each movement jarred the baby, snapping the head back and forth. He screamed.

Joe stepped toward her, gesturing for the two men holding her to release her. His legs felt awkward, heavy. "We're here to help." He pointed at Wayne, who leaned over the man, probing the cuts on the man's head. "He's a healer."

She clutched the baby to her chest and stared at Wayne with dull hope flickering in ash-grey eyes. "Can he heal him? Can he?" She licked her lip, cleaning off some of the blood.

Joe looked at Wayne's bowed head. Thick lines creased his forehead, and he slowly shook his head in a negative motion.

Chapter Eleven

One of the Resisters came toward Joe, motioning for him to lean close. As Joe tilted his head toward the man, the Resister whispered, "We've got to get out of here. More Lifers will be here soon. The Parkinsens give us away every time."

Joe nodded and looked back at the woman. "We've got to get you out of here," he said in a gentle voice. "More of New Life's men will be here any moment."

She exhaled loudly in fear. Her eyes widened and her gaze veered sharply toward the door. "Can you heal him? My husband?" Her chest heaved up and down rapidly. Tears pooling in her eyes spilled down her face, mingling with the drying blood.

Joe's fingers started to curl into fists until he noticed the woman focus on the movement of his hands. He forced his palms open and stepped toward her. "Not here. We have much better facilities at the compound. We have doctors there-"

"No!" She took a giant, uneven step back and clutched the baby tighter to her. The infant's wail had turned to a whine. His

144

face looked ghostly white. She leaned her head on the baby's. "You're just like them. You're going to make us get the implant."

She turned to run, but two Resisters caught her. She screamed loudly and struggled as Joe pried the baby from her arms. "No! That's my son. You can't take him." She inhaled and exhaled sharply as though hyperventilating. "Please God don't put that implant in him!"

"I'm not going to put anything in him," Joe said. He bent his head to the baby's cheek, waiting for the soft caress of breath. At first he couldn't feel the scant movement of air. Then he saw the baby's lips move slightly.

"Don't you hurt him!" the woman screamed. She yanked against the Resisters, trying to jerk free. Joe looked around the room and spotted a blue blanket in the crib. Stepping around the trash on the floor, he made his way to it and picked it up.

Wayne looked at Joe and nodded toward the woman. Joe mouthed the words "Sedate her." The healer gave a quick head shake and walked toward the woman. He reached into his belt and pulled out a syringe. Then he plucked a small vial from his belt.

"No!" she screamed. "No!" Her hysterical voice made Joe cringe. Hearing his mother's voice rising, the infant wailed.

Joe cuddled the baby tighter. "Shh. She'll be fine." From the corner of his eye, Joe saw Wayne thrust the syringe needle into her arm. Her cries dwindled to sharp silence as she slumped forward into one of the Resister's arms.

Wayne capped the syringe and put it back onto his belt. In

passing, he touched the baby's forehead. "Let's get out of here."

Joe wrapped the baby in the blanket, covering the head to block the cold wind. As he started toward the door, Joe's gaze landed on the dead male--the child's father. Joe mentally traced the bloody lines on the victim's forehead and saw the shape of a pentagram which had been carved into his skin. Probably his skull, too. New Life wanted to own him one way or another.

The baby stirred and whimpered. Joe pushed the infant's head just under his chin, quieting the child. Feeling the small bundle of warmth against his chest, Joe knew that for once, he had entered the right war. If there ever was such a thing.

He stepped over a splintered chair and glanced at the Resisters. *Where's Henry?* His stomach dropped when he realized the kid had disappeared. *If anything happens to him, I'll never forgive myself.* Joe followed Wayne outside, and the Resister carrying the woman pulled up the rear. Once outside, he caught another Resister by the arm and asked, "Where's Henry?"

The man pointed around the house. "Over there." Glancing at his watch, the Resister said, "But he'd better get his butt over here. We've got to fly."

"I'll get him." Joe walked around the house and spotted the kid sitting on a lawn chair, staring at the sky. As Joe approached, Henry didn't move. "Come on. We've got to go."

The kid blinked once. Twice. "It never ends, does it, Joe? The Lifers killed that guy."

Joe nodded. He leaned his chin on the baby, drawing strength from the silent peace there. "Yeah. They killed him."

"They would have killed that woman and baby, wouldn't they? Just like they tried with Murray."

Joe gritted his teeth and looked back at the hoverjet. Only two resisters remained outside, waiting to board. "We can talk about this later, Henry. We've got to get back to the compound before the Lifers regroup."

The kid stood and walked over to Joe. Reaching up, he touched the soft folds of blanked swaddled around the infant. "What do you think the Lifers want?"

Joe shrugged and placed his free arm around the kid's shoulder. "I just wish to hell we knew, kid."

***

Joe stood in the RCU doorway, watching Wayne and two other Resisters check out the new patients. The healer leaned over the child, listening to the heartbeat. He ignored the baby's grip in his long, silver hair. Wayne's skinny fingers brushed all over the child as a female Resister held the infant against her chest.

"The blood came from the father," Wayne said, wiping a moist cloth across the baby's forehead. "He's a healthy fellow with a good grip." Wayne extracted the strand of hair the baby had been yanking. "He's just a little exhausted and dehydrated."

Joe exhaled slowly and leaned heavily against the doorway. "What about the mother?"

"She's sedated, thank God." Wayne nodded at the Resister carrying the baby and she set the child down in a large box filled with bedding. Another remembrance that life didn't grow inside walls like these. Joe shook off the thought.

Wayne stepped over to where the mother slept on a bed. The healer gingerly touched her temples, searching for wounds amid the dried blood. "She's got some gashes all right." His eyes met Joe's. "But I think she was actually lucky because the Lifers were playing games with her more than trying to hurt her.."

Joe thrust his hands into his pockets and stepped inside the room. He peered over Wayne's shoulder. "Is she-"

"Get out of the way!" Murray barked as she strode into the RCU. Two Resisters followed her, carrying bodies. Blood trailed after them, staining the floor a translucent red. Murray stopped in front of one wall and pulled down on two handles, lowering a bed. She quickly walked to another portion of the wall and repeated the motion. "Set them down," she ordered sharply.

"What have we got here?" Wayne asked, hovering near one of the Resisters as he deposited an unconscious woman on a bed.

"Two women," Murray replied in a tight voice. She crossed her arms over her chest. "The usual." She looked at the victims and then closed her eyes while gritting her teeth. "God, New Life is so damn twisted."

Joe stared at her chest, noticing how she held her breath. He kept thinking, *Breathe, Murray. Just let it out*. As if hearing his thoughts, she exhaled quickly and inhaled, holding the air once again as her fingers raked through her short, spiky hair. Blood stained her jacket and pants. Joe looked down at his own bloodied hands. Unnerved by the victim's blood, he walked to the sink and washed his hands. Even after they were cleaned Joe still felt the skin sticking together from where the blood had been.

The other Resister placed the second woman in the vacant bed. As her head touched the pillow, long, black hair haloed around her bruised face. Her ripped shirt fell open, revealing more bruises on her neck and chest.

Murray flinched and looked away. "Heal them, Wayne," she said in a thick voice. "Don't let the run be for nothing." She strode from the room in long, sharp steps, pounded out like her fist slamming a knife into Malachette's chest.

GO AFTER HER, JOE, Wayne's voice filled his head.

"I'd rather not commit suicide right now," Joe said, glaring at the healer. Still, his body had turned toward the door, as though he would walk out at any moment.

GO AFTER HER. YOU'RE THE ONLY ONE WHO STANDS A CHANCE OF PROVING TO MURRAY THAT NOT EVERYONE IS LIKE CALEB OR MALACHETTE.

Joe massaged his forehead as though that would get rid of Wayne's voice. And his conscience. "You must have proven it to her. She believes in you." He crossed his arms over his chest.

Wayne fingers lingered at the black-haired woman's forehead as he examined her, but he looked up at Joe with tired eyes. THERE'S A DIFFERENCE IN TRUSTING SOMEONE BECAUSE YOU KNOW YOU'RE STRONGER. SHE IS STRONGER THAN ME. I'M A HEALER, JOE, NOT A FIGHTER. THE ONLY REASON SHE BELIEVES IN ME IS BECAUSE SHE COULD PUT A DAGGER IN MY HEART AND I COULDN'T STOP HER.

Joe sighed in exasperation. "Thanks, buddy. Maybe she'll knock my jaw the other direction this time to even up the pain." He walked out of the room with the feeling of acid eating through his stomach again.

WHERE IS SHE? Joe thought, hoping the healer would still be reading his mind.

IN THE YARD, Wayne replied. SHE'S WATCHING THE STARS, TRYING TO FORGET....

Joe headed toward the yard. TRYING TO FORGET WHAT? THE RUN? MALACHETTE? WHAT?

The silence in his brain felt odd, empty. SHE'S TRYING TO FORGET THAT ONE OF THE WOMEN LOOKED A HELUVA LOT LIKE SHE ONCE DID.

Joe's steps quickened. HOW IS THAT ONE DOING?

SHE'S DEAD. SHE WAS DEAD BEFORE MURRAY BROUGHT HER HERE. JOEY JUST CARRIED HER BECAUSE MURRAY REFUSED TO LEAVE WITHOUT HER.

Silence. Joe opened the door and found Murray sitting on the ground, holding her sword. With her legs crossed over each other and eyes closed, Joe suspected she was meditating.

He slowed down, suddenly not sure what to say. And he wished for once he could read minds like Wayne. *Why in the Hell does he keep insisting I can heal her? I can't even heal myself.*

He leaned over and started to call her name. Murray's eyes flew open and she lifted her sword, sharply swinging it up at his neck and stopping as the point of the blade jabbed the skin under his chin. "You're just like Caleb. Maybe you haven't proven it yet, but I know better."

Joe stood perfectly still, trying to ignore the blade pricking his skin. He looked her straight in the eye. "Am I? Then I guess you'll want to slit my throat before I turn into him, won't you?" He folded his hands together and waited.

Hostile green eyes glared at him as he folded his hands together. He slowly sat down next to her, despite the blade cutting his neck. Sweat beaded on his forehead and rolled down his temples. The night smelled of sweat and blood and he didn't want to keep breathing like this. He had spent half his life killing people. He couldn't do it for the rest.

Murray's hand faltered. The blade wobbled and fell away. She dropped it and closed her eyes as she thrust her head into her hands. Despite the way her back rolled into an impenetrable fortress he couldn't touch, despite her controlled pain, despite the silence breathing between them, Joe saw the glimmer of the Murray who once had been. And he ached to restore her.

He reached out and touched her back. She flinched hard and gulped air. He almost jerked his hand away from her, but forced his fingers upward, touching her hair as the short wisps by her neck curled slightly from sweat. The winter air chilled her skin.

"I meant what I said, Murray. I didn't come here to fight you. I'm not Caleb." He spoke softly. "And I never will be."

Her shoulders softened as his hand rested there. She lifted her face and looked at him. "I don't trust people easily," she said finally, her green eyes focusing on his chin.

"You mean you don't trust men easily." He moved his hand

from her shoulder and placed it on top of hers. "You do what you have to to get through Hell. Sometimes pieces of you don't ever make it back. Sometimes they come when you stop believing they survived." He touched the scar on her inner wrist.

Murray stared at the ground in front of her. Her hand trembled where his fingers traced the pink line. With a soft sigh, she closed her hand around his, holding it. "I didn't want to believe in you. I thought if could just make you angry enough you'd act like Caleb. I was prepared for that. I'd spent hours practicing with a blade." She clenched her eyes shut and squinted so tightly that her face contorted in pain. "The fact that you wouldn't act the part was the only thing I couldn't handle."

Joe squeezed her hand and looked up at the sky. "Sometimes it's easier to deal with anger than anything else, Murray. Anger gives you rage."

"Why did you stay?"

Joe looked at her face. "Because of Henry. I've danced with my own demons." He turned her wrist over and traced the scar. "I've been there, too. But I couldn't give up. I wouldn't. And then I saw Henry. I knew I had the chance to get him away from Malachette. I couldn't change the past, but I could save the kid."

Murray's hand slipped away and rested on his knee. "Do you still fight those battles in your dreams?"

"Yes." Joe closed his eyes and saw Miguel's rough wooden cross, remembering when he had laid the child to rest. He knelt before the fresh grave and buried his hands in the dirt. From behind Joe heard quick footfalls. He stood and turned to see Aleana racing toward him.

"You bastard!" She lunged toward him and pummeled him with fists. He tried to catch her hands, but missed. Aleana drug her nails across his face. "You killed my son!"

"I didn't-"

"No!" she jerked away from him. Her waist-length chestnut hair billowed in the air. "He loved you like a father. I took you to bed like a husband." She leaned over and spat into his face. "And you killed the only part of me that matters!"

Joe took a deep breath. Murray's hand lifted from him. He stared, memorizing how she drew her knees to her chest and curled her arms around them. He said, "They'll always haunt me."

"No matter what you do, the memories don't go away. I thought I could forget what Caleb had done. Yet, I've forgotten nothing." Her shoulders sagged and she closed her eyes. "What did Wayne say about the dark-haired woman I brought back?"

"She's dead."

Murray shuddered. "I knew that was coming." She leaned her head against his shoulder, resting. "How's Cammo?"

"He's okay. Not so gung-ho for the next run, I bet."

The door of the compound opened slowly and Wayne stepped outside. He draped his arms around his chest to block the chilly air which cut through the thin shirt he wore. "Murray, there's something you should see ASAP."

Murray pulled away from Joe and stood up. "What is it?"

153

She bent over and picked up her sword. "Joe already told me about the woman so-"

"It's not about her," Wayne cut her off quietly. He nervously tapped his right foot on the ground. "It's Caleb. He's using a new strategy. There's something you need to see in the Broadcast Room."

Murray's shoulders stiffened and she stalked inside the compound. The threesome quicky made their way to the Broadcast Room. As they entered it, the wall-sized television screen flashed a recent picture of Murray holding a Parkinsen.

"So they finally have proof I have a gun. So what?"

Wayne nodded for one of the Resisters to start the video. "...this woman is believed to be the killer. According to witnesses, she met with Renault in a bar before the murder." The image on the screen flashed to a female newscaster. "Renault had been the vice-president of New Life for four years. This woman is a suspected member of a cult group referred to as The Resisters, and this murder is suspected as a retaliation against The New Life Company, or more accurately, the popular Longevity Implant."

Gasping, Murray slowly fell into a chair. Her hands patted over her body, checking for her Parkinsen. "Oh God. Malachette kept my gun." Her head rolled forward. "He used it to kill Gabe." Her arms quickly wrapped around each other and she rocked back and forth. "Caleb just set me up for a capitol crime. If the Peace Officers catch me-"

"They won't," Wayne said quietly as the image flickered

154

and died. "You're getting out of Dal-Worth tonight." He walked behind Murray and rested both hands on her shoulders. "We can handle it without you. We'll break into New Life and get the information we need."

Murray reached up and touched the healer's hands. "I can't run from the past. Besides, there isn't a state where Caleb and his henchmen can't find me. I can't go."

Joe paced around the room nervously. "Come on, Murray. Be reasonable. Caleb's probably sponsoring a hefty reward for your capture. Hell, he's probably giving away credits toward buying a Longevity Implant as rewards for clues to your hiding place. He's getting everything he wants. You and new victims for the implants. What a bargain, huh?" Joe rubbed his temples. "Get the hell out of Dal-worth right now, Murray. I'll bury the pieces of Malachette and Caleb when I'm done. Don't worry."

As a blush flamed into her cheeks, Murray shook her head and rose. "Yeah. Just walk away, right? I'm supposed to forget what he did to me? It's insignificant, right? You'll even the score for me?" She walked past him. "Thanks but no thanks."

She sauntered to the doorway and paused before going out into the hallway. "I'm going to bed, not leaving Dal-worth. I have a fight with Caleb and Malachette. I intend to finish it."

Unless he finishes you first, Joe thought as Murray disappeared. "Damn," he swore under his breath.

"Yeah, damn," Wayne echoed, watching the other Resisters leave. "She's so stubborn."

Joe sat down in the chair Murray had occupied. "So what

now?" He looked at the healer while his fingers nervously tapped his leg. "She can't stay. It's asking for trouble."

"Are you going to be the one to make her leave?" Wayne asked, his eyebrows arching incredulously. He walked over to a filing cabinet on the east wall and opened one of the drawers. After sifting through a few files, his fingers paused, resting on a particular one. He glanced at Joe and then pulled it out. Crossing the room, he tossed it into Joe's lap.

"What's this?" Joe stared at the folder.

"Murray's past. Take a good hard look and then try telling Murray she can walk away."

Joe's fingers caressed the file surface nervously. As he opened the file, Wayne disappeared out the door. Color pictures slid out and Joe quickly reached to catch them. As he picked up one, he stared into Murray's photographed face. Not that he would have recognized her had Wayne not told him. The long hair and younger face would have implied someone else. And then the purple bruises flowering all over her head hid what should have been a beautiful woman.

Joe slid the photo back into the file and slammed it shut. He closed his eyes and tried to think of something else to make him forget. He set the file on the floor and began pacing, almost wishing he could feel a small ache in his knee.

He looked at the folder once. Twice. Three times, but he couldn't make himself pick it up. "Jesus, Joe," he muttered to himself. "You've seen mountains of bodies before. Why can't you face this one?"

BECAUSE YOU'RE AFRAID YOU WON'T BE ABLE TO SAVE HER EITHER, Wayne's voice jumped into Joe's mind.

Joe clenched his fists as though that would get rid of the healer's voice. YEAH, Joe thought, hoping Wayne was still reading his mind. IT DOESN'T LOOK LIKE I CAN HELP HER. NOT WHEN SHE'S DAMN SURE HEADING FOR TROUBLE BECAUSE SHE KNOWS IT'S THERE.

STAY AND HELP HER FINISH IT, Wayne replied.

I NEVER SAID I WAS LEAVING, Joe thought, picking up the file. He crossed the room and opened the drawer. He, he slid it between two files. MURRAY'S GOT A SHADOW WHETHER SHE LIKES IT OR NOT.

WELCOME BACK TO THE LIVING, JOE, Wayne replied.

Joe rolled his shoulders and exited the Broadcast Room, heading for his chambers. He rubbed his neck, feeling the knotted muscles ache. "What a day," he muttered. "I need some sleep."

Chapter Twelve

Murray twisted her body against the sheets as she fought the dream. Caleb's hands. Malachette's laughter. She kicked, trying to untangle her legs from the sweaty covers. "No," she cried. She jerked upright and looked around her room.

Sunlight peeked around the curtains. She lifted her hand and pressed it to her chest, as though that would slow her heart. *It's just a dream,* she thought. It was the same thought she used as a mantra, day in and day out. Never again. Caleb had only the power of dreams and mist. He could never hurt her again.

She forced her legs over the side of the bed, ignoring the cramping of her left calf. Although she'd learned to expect sore muscles after a run, she hadn't gotten used to it yet. Just like the guns, the killing, and everything else New Life had forced her to in this world.

She touched her hair, pulling at the spiked ridges which had allowed her to blend in so well as a man. Her fingers stretched outward, as though feeling the longer strands she'd once worn.

Maybe after Caleb and Malachette were dead she'd grow it out. Then again, maybe she liked everyone thinking she was a male better. It kept the fear at bay.

Her hand drifted downward and rubbed away the goosebumps rising on her flesh. A chill crept down her spine. The tank top she wore didn't keep the winter draft away. *Tonight we get answers.* She pulled the curtains back from her window and looked outside, past the gates to where the protesters stood. *So many damn signs waving in the air. They've doubled or tripled in number.*

"Murray?" Joe said, rapping his knuckles on her door.

"Yeah?" she replied, squinting as she tried to read the words printed on poster board as the Lifers bobbed the signs up and down. Hinges creaked as the door swung open. Dead silence. Murray turned and looked at Joe. "What were....." Her voice trailed off as she looked at his pale face. "What's the matter? You look like you've seen a ghost."

Joe clutched the doorknob tightly, unable to let it go. *No,* he thought, *actually I've seen your back. The map of scars left by whips and who the hell knows what else.* He flinched and dropped his hand.

Murray's eyes narrowed slightly. She reached over to the chair and grabbed a denim shirt, hastily tugging it on. "I don't want your pity, Joe. I've lived without it this long. I think I'll keep on managing." Her fingers fumbled with the buttons.

Joe swallowed hard. He laughed harshly. "So you think it's all about pity, huh?" He stepped into the room. "I don't pity you.

159

Never have. I just feel the same damn thing about you as you felt for that woman you brought in last night. It's like pouring rubbing alcohol on an open wound. It bubbles and burns until the wound feels raw. And you only wanted to clean it." He pointed to the window. "What were you looking at?"

Murray's hands stopped moving. "The protesters. Looks like the number has doubled. Probably due to that great broadcast last night. Anyone who wasn't anti-Resister will have a quick change of heart after having heard it."

Joe brushed past her and looked outside. "You guys sure know how to throw a party. Unfortunately we're the kids nobody wants to play with." He looked back at her. "I guess I have a gift at setting you off, don't I?"

She picked up her sword. "You've got to be good at something, I guess. What did you come here for? To talk me out of staying?"

Joe sat down in the chair across from her bed. "I don't think I could talk you out of anything."

"You're learning." She fastened her belt and the sword sheath around her waste. Then she picked up the replacement Parkisen and put it in the holster on the other side. "So why did you come?"

"To send you to the lab. They've got information about that disc you got from Renault."

Murray nodded and stepped toward the door. As she walked through she shot one last look at Joe. "You coming or what?"

Joe stood up. "Yeah."

160

They walked down the hall together. Joe kept pace with Murray's rapid steps. "What do you think they found?" he asked.

Murray shrugged. "I don't know. Caleb is so twisted it could be anything. Anything at all."

They arrived at the lab and Murray yanked open the door and barged inside. "Swell, what have you got, Larry?" she asked the Resister sitting at the computer terminal.

Larry looked up through thick glasses. His curly hair frizzed around his face. "A copy of some of the patient records from New Life's databases."

Murray leaned over him and rested her hands on his roll-away chair. "Yeah, and what's in them? Why would Renault give them to us?" She tapped her fingers against his chair furiously and stared at the computer screen with intense scrutiny.

Larry touched some keys. The screen changed to a menu of options: patient records, DNA sequencing, projected DNA combinations, compliance ratio, patient labeling. "It gets better, trust me." He waited a moment until Murray nodded that she had read the screen before pushing another key.

The screen listed several names with dates besides them. Dates within the previous month. "What is this?" Murray asked, reading off names, feeling an emptiness growing in the pit of her stomach.

"A list of all the people who have had the implant done last month." He scrolled through what appeared to be an endless list.

Murray closed her eyes, but her mind kept seeing the white letters forming names against the black background. "There must

161

be thousands of them."

Larry nodded. "Twenty thousand, five hundred and sixty four, to be exact."

Joe walked up behind Murray and patted her shoulder. He half expected her to flinch from feeling his palm touch her, but she never moved. He smiled and gently squeezed reassuringly. Maybe he did have a snowball's chance in hell of teaching her something about people.

About him.

"But Dal-worth's New Life couldn't have done that many," Murray insisted.

"No, that facility didn't," Larry agreed, switching screens. The new data on the screen showed the various New Life facilities divided by states and numbers of surgeries.

Murray took a deep, unsettling breath. "How can we begin to stop this?" She felt Joe's fingers massaging her neck, and she rolled her head from side to side, trying to relax. Murray stared distractedly at the screen. "I just don't understand what Caleb is doing with these people."

"At least we finally understand what kind of information the disc is storing." Larry pushed his glasses higher on his nose before hitting more keys and opening a single patient file. The screen filled with numbers placed in a semi-logical order. "This is the person's DNA. The disc is encoding it."

"Why? What would Caleb want with it?"

Larry shook his head. "I don't know. The patient records is the only segment of this disc we can access. The other sections shut the system down."

Joe dropped his hand and Murray stood upright. She crossed her arms over her chest and frowned. "I don't like this. Why would the system shut down?"

Larry closed out the file and looked at Murray. "There's probably a security code in the program that aligns with a particular system. Of course ours isn't it."

"You mean if we take it with us tonight and get inside one of New Life's computers with it, we might be able to access all of the data?" Joe asked.

Larry nodded. "It's a good possibility."

Murray looked at the New Life emblem on the screen and said, "Good work, Larry. Make sure you've got whatever you might need ready for tonight."

He nodded. "Yeah. I'm ready. Been ready for years."

She glanced toward the door and found Joe edging into the hallway. "Where are you going?" Murray asked. She placed her fingers on her waist, as if she didn't know where else to put them.

"To check on the people we brought in from the run last night." Joe thought he could hear a baby crying down the hallway.

Murray nodded and fell in step beside him. "I'll go with you." Her frown deepened.

They walked to the RCU in silence. Murray kept enough distance between them so that another man could pass through. You do what you have to to get through Hell, he'd told her. *And right now she's doing it*, he thought. *She's going back to see*

163

women who remind her of the past.

The baby's cry softened as they arrived. Joe peered around the room, searching for the infant. First he spotted Wayne, standing beside the medicine cabinet. Then he found the boy nestled in his mother's arms, nursing. Feeling a thick lump forming in his throat, Joe walked over to the woman and touched her arm lightly. "How are you feeling?"

She looked at him with tear-filled eyes. "I'm okay. My baby's okay." She nestled her chin against the top of the baby's head. "My husband ...." The words choked her, and her face crumbled under the weight of grief. Sobs ripped through her.

"I'm sorry," Joe whispered, putting his arms around her. "We did everything we could." He closed his eyes and listened to the sound of grief winding through each breath. It helped somehow for him to absorb her grief, as though displacing some of the pain for Miguel.

"You have a beautiful son," Murray said, softly. She approached timidly and stared at the child. "May I hold him?"

The woman nodded slowly and held out the baby for Murray, who quickly cuddled the baby against her chest. The motion seemed so pure and natural. Again, Joe wondered how he could have mistaken Murray for a man.

"Thank you," the woman whispered, her fingers clinging to Joe. "You got us out of there. Away from those people."

Joe withdrew slowly. "You're welcome." He walked over to Wayne and stood beside him. The healer's silver eyes focused on Murray's devotion to the baby. THIS HAS GOT TO BE

DIFFICULT FOR MURRAY, Joe thought, wondering if Wayne would get the message.

YOU HAVE NO IDEA. SHE ALWAYS WANTED A LARGE FAMILY. SHE'S HAD TWO MISCARRIAGES IN THE PAST, ANOTHER REASON CALEB SENTENCED HER TO DEATH. SHE COULDN'T PRODUCE A CHILD.

Murray hand the child back to his mother. "I'm so sorry about your husband." She kept staring at the baby and once her arms had emptied of the child, she folded them around her body.

YOU'RE SOFTENING HER, JOE, Wayne's voice echoed in Joe's mind.

SOMEHOW THAT'S WORKING BOTH WAYS, AND I'M NOT REAL SURE I LIKE IT. Joe's fingers touched the bear. He gritted his teeth and pulled away from it. WHAT IF I FAIL HER?

Wayne frowned at him and shook his head negatively. YOU CAN'T FAIL. EVERYTHING THAT MATTERS IS IN YOUR CONTROL. THE ONLY THING YOU CAN'T STOP IS HER DEATH OR YOURS. BUT THAT'S NOT FAILURE.

In the mother's arms, the sleeping baby let out a small sigh and scrunched his face before slipping back into the stillness. WHAT ABOUT MIGUEL?

BAD THINGS HAPPEN. YOU LOVED THAT KID. JUST LIKE YOU'RE STARTING TO CARE FOR MURRAY.

Joe nodded and looked back at her. He found himself staring at the smooth curves of her facial profile. His path of vision moved lower, tracing the swell of her breasts. Her flat stomach. She looked up sharply at him, as though something had changed. Confusion swirled in her green eyes. Her breathing sped up slightly.

She's reading my emotions, Joe thought. *Which means I have some explaining to do.* He walked over to her and touched her shoulder while leaning close. He ignored the fact that Murray's back was rigid enough to form a wall and whispered in her ear. "I'm a man. Murray. I won't deny that. And you're a woman. What you're reading is natural, and it's good. The only thing that makes it feel so damn bad is that you want to put me into Caleb's mold." He rubbed her arm. "And I don't fit."

He touched her hair softly and kissed her earlobe before walking away. As he exited, he expected to feel something sharp dig into his back or strike him over the head. The Murray he'd known just a couple of days ago would have, he mused.

***

Caleb stood in front of the wall mirror in his office at New Life. His fingers plucked at his tie and rearranged his suit jacket and black silk shirt. His fingers brushed over the stubble covering his jaw and cheeks. Suitably blood-shot eyes peered back and he smiled at the lingering effects of too much booze and women.

He could look like a martyr, even if he wasn't one. "Mr. Walker, Kim Blount from Dal-Star Six is here to see you for the interview."

Caleb walked over to his desk and sat down in his roll-away leather chair. He pushed the speak button on the intercom. "Very well. Please send her in."

"Yes, sir."

Caleb leaned back and folded his hands in lap, waiting. As he watched the door, it opened, admitting a tall, thin female reporter. Caleb admired her hips as she walked toward him. He forced himself to rise and purposefully banged his shin on the desk as he stood up and pointed out a chair for her to sit in.

She nodded, acknowledged the chair. "I'm Kim Blount." She offered her hand to him.

"Caleb Walker." He shook it.

She sat in the chair in front of his desk which he had earlier pointed out. "I have to admit that I was completely puzzled with your phone call. I mean, why call a news station instead of a Federation Peace Officer?" She brushed a strand of hair behind her ear and then pulled a small tape player out of her purse, setting it on his desk. "Do you mind?" She pointed to it.

"No, no, that's fine." He leaned back in the chair. "It helps your accuracy, I'm sure." He stared at her face. "I was shocked to see Murray's picture on the news bulletin, too. That's why I called you so quickly."

Kim pulled out a pad and pen. As she held them ready to write, she asked. "Mr. Walker-"

"Caleb," he corrected. "Just call me Caleb."

"Caleb," she repeated slowly, offering a stiff smile. "Why were you puzzled?"

Caleb cleared his throat. "Because my wife has been missing for six years. I had believed her to be dead." He shifted his weight in the chair, pretending to be uncomfortable.

167

Kim looked up at him. "You didn't even know she was alive? Or where she had been?"

He shook his head. "No. As I told the peace officers, I believed the Resisters had taken her hostage and had planned to turn her against me and my company. But I couldn't prove it." His voice rippled, as though he would break down. "But I never thought my wife would change, and I felt that they had killed her because she wasn't any use to them."

Kim scribbled furiously. The strand of hair she had tucked behind her ear fell forward into her face. She stopped writing and looked up, asking, "So what do you think happened to her? Why would she have killed Renault? And where is she now?"

Caleb stood and stared at Kim's long legs and black skirt which crept to the middle of her thighs. "The Murray I knew and loved wouldn't have killed anybody." He walked over to his bar and poured himself a glass of whiskey. "Would you like something?"

Kim shook her head negatively. "Thanks anyway."

He lifted the glass and drank, but not quickly enough so that some of the liquid dribbled down his chin. Nice touch. Now she probably thinks grief has driven me to drink myself to death.

"Where do you think she's been all this time?"

Caleb wiped the liquor away with the back of his hand. "With the Resisters. They've probably brainwashed her. Without her medication--"

"What medication?" The reporter looked up at him, the pen in her hand hovering over the paper, waiting for his response.

Caleb refilled his glass and downed it just like before. He closed his eyes, savoring the taste.

"Caleb, I know this might be difficult to talk about, but Gabe Renault's family deserves to have the truth come out."

Clever girl. Gabriel didn't have any family, just a stupid cat. He opened his eyes. "Before she was abducted, my wife had begun suffering from paranoid delusion. At times she even suffered from depression." He returned to his desk and sat down. "I think the Resisters kidnapped her, turned her against me by focusing her delusions on New Life. It changed her forever."

Caleb reached out and touched Kim's hand. He allowed moisture to pool in his eyes. "But whatever she's done, it's not her fault. If she did kill Renault, it was because the Resisters ordered it. She was used and she's probably confused and frightened." He blinked and forced the tears from his eyes. "She needs her medicine and the security of her home. Deep down I know she still loves me. I know I can get the old Murray back."

He squeezed Kim's hand. "Please tell the world about my wife's suffering so that her judgment will be kind and she can return home. Tell the people I love her still." He forced himself to begin hyperventilating.

Kim looked at him with two tear streaks lining her face. "I will, Caleb. I promise."

***

"So what's up with you and my sister?" Henry asked. He jabbed his sword at Joe while they sparred together in the yard.

Joe quickly lifted his weapon and blocked him. "Not much."

He swung at the kid's chest and watched Henry's blade meet his, wavering slightly. "Focus, Henry."

The kid gritted his teeth, dipped his sword and jabbed toward Joe's mid-torso. "I am focusing!"

Joe deflected the strike easily and from the corner of his peripheral vision, he noticed someone walking behind the kid. The ridges of dark hair told him it was Murray. She held her finger over her mouth, gesturing for Joe to keep quiet. Then she silently drew her sword and waited for Joe and Henry's swords to intersect again. As steel met steel, she prodded Henry's buttocks with the tip of her blade, saying, "If I were a Lifer, you'd be dead right now. You didn't hear me approach or draw my weapon. Joe's right. You're not focusing, Cammo."

"It's Henry." He flushed and stopped sparring. "And you're not a damn Lifer. You're my sister--a natural pain in the butt." Gritting his teeth, he lowered his sword and turned to glare at her.

"But you didn't know that when I crept up behind you."

Henry rolled his eyes. "Yeah, yeah. You win. I'll try to watch my back tonight. What time are we breaking into the New Life building?"

Murray looked past the kid and straight onto Joe. "We're not. You'll be staying with Wayne on this one." She frowned at Joe, as though daring him to challenge her,

Henry stepped closer to his sister. "Why not? Didn't I do a good job on the run? I listened to Joe." He turned to face Joe. "Tell her I did good."

Joe came forward and touched Henry's shoulder. "You were

great, Henry. But this is completely different than a run. The only people going on this trip are the ones who have to--a handful of fighters and computer hackers."

The kid lifted his blade. "But I am a fighter. You know that. You've been teaching me."

Joe wiped his sweaty forehead. "Yeah, I do know that. And one of these days you'll be damn good at it, if that's what you still want. But right now, you're not ready for something like this."

Henry shoved his sword into his sheath. "You'll probably never think I'm ready, will you? Thanks for the faith in me, Joe." The kid stalked away.

Joe and Murray watched Henry re-enter the compound. Joe sighed and slowly shook his head. "I think I just became a responsible adult in his eyes."

"Yep," she replied, stepping up to where the kid had been standing. She raised her sword in an open challenge to Joe.

His grip tightened uncomfortably on the sword's hilt and his throat felt dried out. How many times are we going to go through this anyway? He lowered his sword and stepped back. "I'm not going to fight you. We've covered this ground before."

Murray rolled her shoulders, trying to loosen the muscles. "I didn't come here to fight. I came to spar. And you're the only one out here."

Joe moved his fingers and tried to ignore the slight numbness from the cold air. Joe stood where he was, unable to decide the lesser of two evils. He glanced at her sword tip point directly at him, waiting for his answer.

Murray flashed him a bemused grin. "Let's see. You either think you could actually hurt me. In which case you're wrong. Or you think I'm biding my time until I can cut off a few male decorations for my collection. In which case you're still wrong. I have little or no patience and I would have done that already had it been my intention."

"So what is your intention?"

Murray reached out with her sword and tapped his blade. "To spar. Nothing more. Nothing less. Unless you think you can't handle the action because I'm a woman."

Joe stepped toward her and raised his blade. "You know better than that, Murray."

Her first swing came hard and fast at his left side, followed by a low thrust. Joe moved his blade, deflecting each stroke which came in a rapid succession. Murray's steps around him came quick and light, in rhythm with her body's inner dance. Her arms show no signs of fatigue as she parried, and he waited for the slightest indication of her slowing down before advancing his own swing at her body.

Murray's sword danced in front of him. With each stroke he met her steel. From time to time, he saw her eyes, the green flashing in the afternoon sunlight like the steel. But with each swing her facial expression remained unchanged. Her body performed the ancient movement of weapons because it had been taught, it had been hurt and it had been healed.

As Joe looked at her, he realized that for once in her life, Murray had separated her rage from the weapon in hand. Their swords crossed each other, overhead. He lowered his and looked at the ground. "I think that's about enough for now." He caught her staring at the leather gauntlets around his wrists.

"Why do you wear those?"

Joe glanced at the scuffed leather. He shrugged. "Oh, I don't know." He smiled at Murray kept looking at them. "You like them?"

She raised her shoulders indifferently and looked away. "They're interesting."

Joe pulled one off and then removed the second. "Here, take them."

Murray ducked her head at his offer. "No, that's okay."

Joe proffered them more firmly. "I want you to have them. For luck."

Murray slowly reached for them while alternating her path of vision between Joe's hand and his face. Her fingers brushed his palm and he placed his free hand on top of hers.

"I don't know that they'll work," he said, "But we'll need all the luck we can get tonight."

Chapter Thirteen

A subtle movement in the doorway alerted Joe and Murray that they weren't alone. They turned in unison to find Wayne hovering near the door. He massaged his forehead as though trying to rid himself of a headache.

"Wayne, what is it?" Joe asked. His fingers tightened around the blade.

The healer dropped his hands to his side. "More bad news I'm afraid," he sighed. "Caleb's up to some new tricks."

"More tricks?" Murray asked. The smile Joe had seen on her face earlier disappeared under a cold frown. She stepped toward Wayne, clutching the gauntlets tightly in her grip. When the healer looked at the ground and failed to respond, Murray snapped. "It can't be that bad. Just spit it out!"

Wayne's shoulders sagged slightly, and the way the sun spilled across his sliver hair and pale face made him look older than he actually was. "You were featured on another Dal-Worth news report a moment ago. A special bulletin." The healer spoke slowly, drawing out each word as though he didn't want to have to say the next one.

"And?" Murray prompted anxiously.

"They have finally matched your name to that picture."

Murray paced a circle around Wayne. "Why is that bad? I expected it. I mean, I'm still Caleb's wife by law. It doesn't matter that I'd slit his throat if given half a chance. We knew this would get back to him because of who he is. And of course he revealed to the media my identity."

Wayne nodded and watched Murray's sharp steps. "Yeah, but that's not the bad news. He's claiming the Resisters abducted you six years ago, and that all this time he had believed you to be dead. The Resisters have been brainwashing you, Caleb claimed. And that they are using you to get to him."

"What?" Murray stopped pacing in mid-stride. "You can't be serious." The color drained from her face.

Joe walked up behind Murray. "So that story might actually destroy any credibility Murray would have in the future when she talks to the press about New Life." Joe reached up and touched Murray's shoulder softly, reassuringly.

"Yeah," Wayne agreed, walking toward Murray. "But that's not all of it. Wayne also said his wife had been on a prescription drug for delusions and depression. He said he feared that the absence of the drug and the brainwashing of the Resisters made her kill Renault."

Murray's mouth dropped open. She shook her head vigorously in denial. Wayne held up his hand and went, saying,

175

"But Caleb didn't think Murray was responsible for her actions. It was a moment of incoherence. He asked for the public to be lenient on her and return Murray Walker to his home where she might be treated for her illness."

The gauntlets slipped out of her hands and fell to the floor. "The Federation can't even protect me from him. Caleb owns it, just like he owns me." Her lips parted slightly and trembled. Her knees buckled and she started to fall. Joe saw her going down and slid his arms under her, lifting her body against his.

"I knew she wasn't going to take this very damn well," the healer muttered, staring at Murray's ashen face. "And I didn't even tell her the worst of it."

"The worst?" Joe prompted, walking toward Murray's private chambers. Her head laid against his chest, and, as he carried her, he realized just how little she weighted. An image of his first encounter with her came to mind and suddenly he couldn't ever imagine mistaking her for a male again. "So what didn't you tell her?"

Wayne fell in beside him. "A few minutes ago Cammo ran outside of the Palace. I tried to follow, but he lost me quickly. The protester throwing punches my way didn't help either."

Joe stopped walking as he felt like a boulder fell out of the sky and crushed his lungs. Every breath seemed more difficult than the last. "Henry? Where is he?" It was a stupid, pointless question, but the only one he could think to ask.

"Well, if I knew that, would I be panicking?" The healer opened the bedroom door.

Joe carried Murray to her bed and gently set her down. He looked at her peaceful face and knew she'd wake soon enough. Probably too soon. He slid her arm from around his neck and placed it across her body. Her hand rested between her breasts. "Anything happens to him, it'll kill her." His words came out as a hoarse whisper.

He stalked over to the window and looked out at the crowd of protesters. More of them than before. "Helluva day to run away, kid. You just surrounded yourself with more enemies than you'll know what to do with," he muttered sofly.

"What about you?" Wayne prompted softly as he lingered by the door. "He still reminds you of Miguel.."

Joe winced. He balled his fingers into fists and brushed past Wayne, heading toward the door. "I'll find him. I don't care how long it takes."

The healer grabbed his arm. "No. You were lucky to find him once. I don't think you'd be so lucky this time. You haven't studied the kid's habits, where he goes. He's done this before." Wayne glanced out the window. "I'm just worried about him outside with all those nuts. Besides," Wayne pointed at Murray, "You'll have the best shot of keeping her from flying off the deep end when she finds out the kid has vanished. You can be there for her when she wakes." He let go of Joe. "I've already dispatched a crew to search for Cammo. Not that anyone will find him until he's ready to be found."

Joe rubbed the bridge of his nose, trying to forget the last angry words Henry had shouted at him in an unforgiving voice.

Thanks for the faith in me. Joe's path of vision returned to Murray's face, tracing the afternoon sunlight across her profile. "You're right," he muttered to Wayne. "I'll stay with her. I mean what do I know about the kid anyway?" His throat constricted and he closed his eyes. How many times had Miguel asked him to be his father? And in the end he had given the child the one thing no one could take back, a bullet.

"You know that you wanted to keep him safe, just like Miguel. "The kid's gotten in your blood. Cammo always had a way of doing that."

Joe let out a humorless laugh. "Yeah. Let's just pray your boys find Henry before Malachette does." He sat down in the chair across from the bed and thrust his head into his open palms, unable to watch as the healer left the room. Yeah, he was supposed to keep Murray from going off the deep end. Who was going to restrain him?

As the healer left, he closed the door quietly, leaving Joe staring at the floor. Moments passed in a thick silence. "Mmmm," Murray moaned, turning to her side. Her arms crossed in front of her chest, as though she were trying to defend herself. "Stay away," she mumbled.

A nightmare. Joe wearily walked to the bed. His fingers barely touched her arm. "Murray, wake up. You're having—"

She grabbed his wrist and yanked him down before curling her fingers around his neck and squeezing, cutting off his air. He pushed back, hard enough to break her grip. "Stop it!" he said, grabbing her hands.

Her body stilled. Her fingers became limp in his grip. Her chest heaved up and down and she closed her eyes. "Damn him." Rage and pain twisted her voice. "He wants to put me back into a corner of his little world. And if I won't stay put, he'll kill me. Well, I'd rather be dead!" she spat.

Joe cringed from her words. He loosened his hold on her fingers and turned her wrists upward. Tracing the scars on her arm with his forefinger, he looked at them. "Yeah. I know."

Her eyes opened at the sound of his raw voice. She inhaled slowly and held each breath, letting it out in wispy gasps through slightly parted lips. The corners of her eyes filled with tears. Overflowed. Her body began trembling and she couldn't stop it.

He reached up and wiped away the tears. "But you're not going to give up, Murray Walker. Whatever happens I'll be right behind you. And if you don't kill Caleb, I will. Not because of New Life. Not because he deserves. I'll kill him so you can live." He lowered his hands back onto hers and watched the fear in her eyes swirl into confusion. Her body kept trembling, but he knew it came from another emotion besides fear.

Her green eyes stared at him and he leaned forward, caressing her lips with his. At first she didn't respond. Then her mouth parted, inviting him inside. He drew closer, softly rubbing her arms with his palms. His fingers unbuttoned her shirt.

She closed her mouth and pulled away. "Don't." Her hand slid in front of his, blocking him.

He kissed her ear. "Why?"

She shut her eyes. "Because I don't want you to see me.

Caleb left so many...scars. I don't want you to see them all." She ducked her head away from him. "I wouldn't be someone you'd...find beautiful." She licked her lips.

Joe moved his head back slightly and trickled his fingers through her hair. "The scars won't matter, Murray."

Her throat moved and she swallowed and peered at him with large eyes. "I can't."

Joe's fingers moved and touched her chin. "No, you're afraid. You think love and pity are the same, and I'm about to prove they aren't." He lifted her face to stare into her eyes. "I know I don't have any right to ask you to trust me, but I have to. For both of us."

Her fingers fluttered to her lap. Joe touched her breast and she trembled. He leaned over and kissed her throat, thinking, *You will believe, Murray. I won't give you room to doubt.*

***

Henry sat in the ancient evergreen beside the New Life Building. Despite the frigid wind, blowing through his clothing, despite the gnarled bark prodding his buttocks, despite the slow, sweeping regret at leaving the Palace, Henry forced himself to sit still and wait for nightfall. *One way or another I'll be going on this mission.*

"Let's see you try to stop me, Joe," he muttered, lifting a pair of binoculars to his eyes. He heard the grass rustling beneath him and he looked down to see four resisters searching the grounds for him. Right idea, wrong hiding place, he thought, watching them move closer to the building and then back away.

The kid continued to observe them until they disappeared. Shrugging, he picked up his binoculars again and looked through them, focusing on windows in the fourth floor.

"Man," the kid whispered, shaking his head in bewilderment at the numerous rows of computers and operators. Too many to count. "You'd better bring more than a few nerds, Murray. Or you'll never be able to figure out what's what in the systems."

He lowered his path of vision, trying to focus on the computers, wanting to read the screens, but the monitors were turned from the window. "What are you hiding?" he mused aloud.

"I had wondered what those Resister dogs were sniffing at," a loud voice called to Henry. "I suspected it would be one of their own. Your kind always seems to run in packs."

Henry cringed at the sound of that voice. Slowly, he forced himself to look down and found Malachette standing at the base of the tree holding a gun. The binoculars slipped out of his grip and thudded to the ground besides Malachette.

"Your aim is lousy, boy."

Henry's empty fingers fluttered through the air, reaching until he clutched the tree. "If I was aiming, I'd have hit you."

Malachette laughed. The expression transformed his scars from lines to pitted recesses in his face. "Remember the last time we met? I told you we'd finish this. I told you there'd come a day you didn't have someone to save your butt. Remember?"

Clutching the tree, Henry tried to think of some witty comment, but his throat felt dry and his body trembled. His heart slammed against his chest so loudly everyone must have heard it. *He's going to kill me!* "Yeah, so." He looked upward, wondering how fast he could climb. Not fast enough to dodge a bullet. He stood up and grabbed the limb above him.

"It's here and you're in deep shit."

Henry ignored him and flung his body over the branch above. "I don't think so."

Malachette laughed again. "The only reason I haven't killed you is because Caleb thinks your miserable life is worth something and that Murray might be interested in you."

Henry's leg slipped and he almost fell. The rough bark bit into his hands as he worked to pull himself back up. "You leave my sister out of this!"

Malachette circled the base of the tree, constantly eyeing the kid. He lifted his gun and fired. A bullet whizzed past Henry's head and lodged into the branch he reached for. "But your sister is the issue. Caleb wants her. He doesn't care how many pieces she comes in. And I'm going to use you to get her."

As Henry swung his body over the next limb, he looked down and saw Malachette gun aimed at him. The gun fired. Pain ripped through his leg. Henry's fingers slipped. Blackness came and clawed through daylight as he started to fall.

Malachette watched as Henry slipped from the tree and thudded to the ground at his feet. He smiled the kid softly moaned and passed out. Lifting his hand to his mouth, he whistled loudly. A few seconds later, Lugnut and Spare Change joined him.

Malachette pointed at the kid and said to Lugnut, "Pick him up. He's got an appointment to see Mr. Walker right away." He leaned over and grabbed the binoculars. As his fingers felt the dirt on the lenses, Malachette quickly dusted them off.

"Okay." Lugnut rolled his eyes. He bent and hefted Henry's body over his shoulder, ignoring the kid's screams that punctuated the stillness. "Sounds like he's in pain." Lugnut smiled.

That's nothing compared to what he's going to be feeling, Malachette thought as he walked around Lugnut and looked the kid over. "Something probably snapped when he fell." Malachette spotted the twisted arm, broken bone gouging through flesh. He reached out and touched Henry's arm.

"Get away from me!" the kid screamed, trying to move the broken bone out of Malachette's reach.

Malachette smiled and he cinched his fingers tightly around the broken place and squeezed. "Helluva deal, huh, kid?" He jerked his fingers away and started walking. Although Henry tried to kick Lugnut, the beefy man ignored him.

As they rode the elevator toward Caleb's office, the kid lapsed into silence. His body hung limply over Lugnut's shoulder and his face turned red as blood rushed to his head.

Yeah, save your energy, Malachette thought, stroking his chin. *You'll need it to scream for your sister.*

They walked into the hall before Caleb's office and spotted Caleb talking to his secretary as he handed her a disc. "I want this taken down to the fourth floor and given to Warren Rodriquez.

183

Tell him the dump section has been assigned in this group."

The slim blonde nodded and took the disc. "As you wish, Mr. Walker."

Caleb stood up and walkd around the desk toward her, slipping his hand on her buttocks. "As I wish. How quaint. There are many things I wish for."

The secretary squirmed, trying to tactfully remove his hands. "I'd better get these to Mr. Rodriquez."

Caleb nodded and kept his hand in place. "Yes, you'd better. And then you can come back to see me."

She took a step back. "But I have so much work to do. I-I can't get it done unless I spend time at my desk."

"The only work you need to do," he said, tracing his fingers down the cleavage of her low-cut sweater, "is to keep me happy. That way you can keep your job." He narrowed his eyes and sneered at her. Do I make myself clear, Ms. Taylor?"

She flushed and peered down at the floor. "Yes, sir. I'll be back." She walked out of the room, staring at his feet. Malachette whistled in her passing as his group headed into Caleb's office.

"We've brought you a gift," Malachette said, leaning on Caleb's desk.

Caleb wrinkled his nose and pointed to the blood dribbling on the floor. "Damn it. He's bleeding. He'll stain the frigging carpet."

Spare Change quickly took of his coat and wrapped it around Henry's leg where the bullet had clipped him. "There.

That's taken care of, Mr. Walker."

Caleb frowned and stepped toward Lugnut. As he stood before Henry, he reached down and thrust his hand into Henry's hair, yanking his head back. "Well, well, what do we have here?"

"Murray's brother." Malachette pulled out his pack of cigarettes and lighter. "That's what the other Resisters were doing outside. Beating the bushes looking for his sorry ass."

"You know better than to smoke in here," Caleb said in a quiet voice. From the corner of his eye, he watched Malachette slide his smokes back into his pocket. Satisfied, Caleb yanked harder until the kid's eyes opened and saw him. "It's been a long time, Henry. Since right before Murray almost died." Caleb's grin broadened as the kid's eyes widened in fear. "I can't tell you how much trouble you caused by freeing your sister. So I'll make you feel it instead. Bone by bone."

Henry tried to spit in his face, but the drops landed on Caleb's suit. "It doesn't matter," the kid said in a broken voice. "She's still alive. You didn't kill her and that's all that matters."

Caleb yanked out a handkerchief and brushed away the spittle. "Now, now. Is that anyway to greet family? I am still your brother-in-law." Caleb released Henry's hair. "But I'll be a widower soon, thanks to you."

Henry's body stiffened. His mouth froze in a petrified o before he finally managed to say, "I'll die before I lead her here.."

"No, actually after. You won't have to lead us anywhere. She'll come right to us." He looked at Spare Change. "Get me the video camera." He turned to Malachette. "You get the plastic for the floor."

Malachette nodded and opened a cabinet door. He grabbed a huge roll of plastic and spread it across the carpet while grinning menacingly at Henry. The kid started struggling.

"Put him down," Caleb ordered, pointing to the plastic.

Lugnut grinned and dropped him. The landing knocked the air out of Henry's lungs and he lay on the ground, gasping. Malachette yanked out his knife and pointed it at the kid's throat. "Let's not be stupid, Henry. The fact that we want your sister is keeping you alive right now. And you like breathing, don't you?"

Spare Change handed Caleb the camera. Caleb lifted it to his face and started filming. "Make him scream for his sister." Malachette prodded the kid's throat, drawing a thin line of blood. Henry took a deep breath and clamped his mouth shut. He closed his eyes.

"Okay, kid, have it your way." Malachette stood and slammed his foot into Henry's crotch. The kid whimpered and moved his good hand in front of his groin.

"I said make him scream!" Caleb thundered. His face turned red as he yelled.

Malachette flushed and moved toward the kid's broken arm. He lifted his foot over it and brought it down on the broken bones. Henry screamed and screamed and kept on screaming.

Caleb laughed and focused on a close-up of the kid's face. Satisfied, he clicked the camera off. "Shut him up," he ordered over Henry's agonized cries.

Lugnut leaned over and slammed the gun butt across the kid's head, knocking him out.

"Thank you," Caleb said, smiling as he handed the camera to Lugnut. He looked down at his suit and picked off some minuscule pieces of lint. He smoothed the jacket out. "Now it's time for Murray's message. I know she's dying to hear from me after all this time."

Lugnut picked up the camera, focused it on Caleb, and began recording.

***

Sunlight waned around the curtains of Murray's chambers, suggesting the approach of sunset. Joe absently ran his fingers through Murray's short hair and brushed her back softly. With each passing caress, he felt the tracks of scars lining her body, and his anger deepened toward Caleb. She'd slept for about an hour, and the whole time Joe had laid on his back, absorbing the feel of her head pressed against his chest, trying to ignore the guilt ripping out his gut. He should have told her about Henry.

"Murray," he said softly.

Her back tensed slightly and she looked up. "Yeah?" she pulled the sheet tighter around her naked body."

"There's something I have to tell you that Wayne didn't."

Murray curled closer to him. "The other shoe's about to drop, isn't it?" Her fingers brushed through the hair on his chest.

"Yeah, I guess so." He took a deep breath. "Henry has run away.

Murray tried to sit up, but he held her to him, unwilling to

187

release her yet. "Let me go," she said, squirming. Her breath quickened. "I have to find him. Malachette is out there."

"So is a search party. They're doing what can be done."

Murray yanked free and glared at him. "I have to. Why didn't you tell me sooner?"

Joe pushed his head against the pillow. "Because I knew you'd want to go, and right now you're the hottest news story since the Longevity Implant."

Gritting her teeth, she jumped from the bed and jerked on her clothes. "But Malachette. What if-"

"You can't live with 'what if,' just what is," Joe said calmly as he sat up. "I should know I've made a life out of it."

As she buttoned her shirt, her fingers fumbled. "I can't believe you didn't tell me. Is that why you wanted this little 'diversion?'" She picked up his gauntlets from the floor and threw them at him. "You sonofabitch!"

Where did that come from? Joe rose quickly and grabbed her arm. "No, this wasn't a 'diversion.' I made love to you. Not to stop you from going after Henry, but because I wanted to. And you wanted me to. You try to fit me into Caleb's mold, and I keep breaking it down a little farther. You think if you say the right words, I'll do what he did, but that's not going to happen."

"Go to hell." She yanked free and snapped her pants.

He brushed through his hair. "You're right. I should have told you. But you were falling apart, Murray. All you needed was one more thing to send you half-cocked into the sunset." He walked around the room, pacing toward the window. "Maybe then you'd get your death-wish." He turned and walked back, grabbing her. "Look at me, Murray. Tell me that's not what you're aiming for."

She stopped fighting and shook her head. "You're crazy."

"Am I? I've been walking around here for days, and I've seen the way you act. I know what you're trying to do because I've tried it, too. Why do you think I was living on the street, scrounging for my next meal in someone else's trash? I once had money, a job, a house. But I didn't think I deserved any of that. I wanted to kill myself, but I couldn't even come right out and do that." He let go of her. "And I don't think you can either. So you pick fights you can't win, thinking someone else will pull the trigger. I'll be damned if I'm going to stand by and let you destroy yourself. I killed a kid. And you think you don't deserve the right to live. Look at me!"

He closed his eyes and his shoulders rolled forward. He expected her to walk away, not to feel her head press against his chest. "It was an accident, Joe. I've seen inside you and I know what's there. I just never expected to find it, never expected somebody to say all the things you've said to me."

Joe wrapped his arms around her. He smiled and said, "Yeah, and I never thought I'd be saying them, especially not to someone I once thought was a guy. Let's go wait for Henry."

***

A silent tension threaded through Joe and Murray as they sat in the front room of the compound. They had been there for hours. Joe looked at the round clock on the wall. 11:10. He rolled his shoulders, trying to forget the fear eating away at him as he paced the room.

Murray stared ahead blankly, as though seeing nothing in front of her. "It's my fault," she said, resting her head in her hands. "I keep treating him like a kid."

Joe turned and knelt down in front of her, trying to catch her attention. "Well, he isn't exactly a man yet. And no, this isn't your fault." He clenched his fingers into fists. *It's mine.* His steps quickened.

Wayne burst into the room. "I just finished briefing everybody." He looked from Murray to Joe and back again. "The search party hasn't made it back?"

Joe stopped pacing. "Haven't seen them."

The healer walked forward and looked out the window at the stale yellow lamplight filtering through the inky blackness. "The men are getting ready now, Murray. We'll have to leave soon."

She nodded woodenly. "I know. Just a few minutes more." She sat in the front part of the chair with her back as straight as a wall. Her fingers lay still in her lap.

Joe walked toward the door. "I'm going to get a breath of fresh air." Neither of them spoke. Wayne sat down beside Murray and leaned against the chair wearily. Joe opened the door and stepped outside, quickly pulling his coat tighter around him as he felt the first snap of cold of wind. Looking up, he saw the star-sprinkled heaven and remembered the kid. A lump formed in his throat, making swallowing difficult.

The forlorn silence surrounding Joe was broken by shoes

hitting pavement. Joe looked up at the gate and spotted the search party. He ran to meet them. "Where's Henry?" he asked the first resister he spotted out of ten.

The man shook his head. "We still don't know. We looked all afternoon, but couldn't find any signs of him." The other resisters went around the two of them and headed inside. Joe gritted his teeth.

"Did you check around the New Life Building?"

The resister nodded. "That was one of the first places. He wasn't there." He brushed past Joe and headed inside.

Joe looked up at the stars again and thought of Henry. *I just hope the stars keep you warm, kid. Wherever you are.*

Chapter Fourteen

Joe stared at the shiny windows of the New Life Building as he sat inside the hover jet, waiting. Despite the cold air outside, he felt too damn warm with his coat on, and sweat trickled down his back. He visually traced the outline of the structure rising sharply into the midnight sky. Forty stories of lies.

"Doesn't look like much of a fortress, does it?" Murray asked, leaning across his lap toward the window.

"Looks are deceiving," Joe replied. "You of all people should know that." The glass fogged from their breath.

"You bought it, didn't you?"

Joe grinned ruefully. "Yeah. For a little while." The jet began to slow down and then stopped 200 yards from the building. "How long do you think it will take the first squad to deactivate the alarm system inside the basement?"

Murray leaned against the seat. "Since they've studied this system, probably ten minutes max. Barring complications."

Life is a complication, Joe thought, watching as twelve men climbed out of the two jets. The black-clad figures melted into the night. Murray pulled out a small set of headphones with a unobtrusive microphone and put it on. Then she connected the cable to a black box on her belt. "Speed Demon, come in," she said to the microphone. "Time for a sound check."

"Speed Demon reporting. Got you loud and clear."

"Ditto," Murray said. "Clear." She closed her eyes and rested against the seat. Her lips pursed together into a thin line. Her fingers brushed over each other nervously.

"You're thinking about Henry, aren't you?" Joe asked.

Murray opened her eyes. "Yeah."

"You know it's not your fault." Joe stared at the inky stillness outside the jet.

"No, I don't know that. It's my fault Cammo took off. I should have at least prepared to keep him inside the Palace."

Joe shook his head. "You can't keep anyone anywhere by force. The kid would've ditched you sooner or later." Joe smiled as he remembered Henry looking at the stars.

Murray closed her eyes again. "I just wish-"

"Don't," Joe said in a soft voice. "This isn't the time for regrets, Murray. We've got to concentrate. The kid will turn up eventually. When he's ready to be found."

They lapsed into silence. Murray's fingers silently tapped her leg. Moments dragged by. She kept looking at her watch. "They should be there by now. The other party should be gearing up for the riot. Just a few minutes more, the guards will be busy and we'll be in."

More silence. Minutes stretched. She tapped the box, checking to make sure it was on. "Why aren't they radioing in?"

Joe rolled his shoulders, trying to shake the stress knotted there, but it kept getting more and more tangled with each passing second. "Things don't always go like you expect them to. Give the guys time to breathe. They won't let us down."

"Whatever." She set her hands in her lap to keep from touching the communication device. Then she leaned over him again and tried to look out the fogged windows. Lifting a hand, she wiped away the water condensing on the glass. "I just feel like we're sitting ducks right now." She pulled out her Parkinsen and checked the clip, making sure it was loaded and ready.

"Storm Rider, come in," the radio blasted.

Murray jumped from the sudden loudness and then said, "Storm Rider here."

"This is Speed Demon. We are inside. Repeat. We are inside castle walls."

"Will do," she replied. "Clear." She pulled off the headphones and attached them to her belt before standing up. "Let's get a move on things, men. The first wave has cleared the alarms. We're ready to rock and roll."

Joe watched the others stand and waited until the rest of them unloaded before joining Murray as she stood just outside the jet and jerked a black ski mask over her head. Then she slid a pair of night vision goggles around her head. Joe pulled out his mask and goggles. He put them on. As the group headed toward the building, Joe shadowed Murray, step for step.

The jet lifted and hovered above them for a few seconds before flying away. The sleek, black metal disappeared into the dark sky. *So much for a quick getaway,* Joe thought. The Resisters broke into a run and Joe joined them, darting around the numerous trees. By the time they arrived at the east wall within sight of the basement door, Joe's breath came in labored gasps, reminding him how long it had been since he'd run that far. Always before his bum knee had kept him from running. Now he moved like the wind. And the cold air nearly choked him, burning his throat and chest each time he inhaled.

A bomb exploded in the distance. Sirens wailed through the night. Joe grinned at the sound of the other resisters doing their work. Nothing like a little fireworks to heat things up.

At the door, Joe noticed one of New Life's guards lying behind some bushes. The leg sticking out almost tripped Joe. He pushed the body deeper into the shrubbery and fell in behind the rest of the Resisters.

Two of them held their Parkinsens ready as they stood on either side of the doorway while the others darted into the room, heading through the tangle of heating and plumbing valves which wound through the basement. Joe watched the green lines of heat glowing from the others as they ran. The first one reached the door and waited for a second to arrive. He yanked it open and ducking inside.

"Go!" one of the Resisters whispered urgently to Joe, waving him toward the opposite door. "We'll cover you."

***

195

"What the hell is going on?" Caleb roared, stalking into his office from his bedroom. He yanked the silk tie of his gold robe tighter.

"Got some unwanted visitors, Mr. Walker," Spare Change said, holding out a glass half-full with amber liquid.

Caleb took it. "Inside or out?"

"Both," Lugnut replied.

Caleb sat in his chair before the desk and quickly turned it on and bypassed the security code. He moved his mouse to the camera icon.

"Which floor?" a female computer voice asked.

Caleb glared at Lugnut expectantly. "The basement." Caleb repeated his bodyguard and waited.

The view changed from the New Life logo to a black and white screen showing the basement. The stillness was only broken by periodic blurs running down the passageway between metal ducts and pipes.

"Why isn't the alarm working?"

"Some of the Resisters overrode it in the basement."

"We'll just have to resort to the backup." Caleb shook his head and clicked his tongue. "For shame, Murray. I thought you were brighter." He turned to Lugnut. "Activate the heat cells."

"As you wish." The bodyguard quickly strode over to the first wooden cabinet and pushed three buttons.

"Charge the doors, too," Caleb ordered, staring at the screen.

Lugnut pressed another button. "Done. Do you want some guards sent down to finish them?"

The founder of New life caressed his chin thoughtfully.

"No. Let's just watch them play for a few moments."

"As you wish."

"Good," Caleb purred, leaning over his desk. "What's going on outside?"

"A band is detonating some small bombs," Spare Change replied. He crossed this thick arms over his chest. "Probably just a diversion, but we dispatched a crew to handle the situation."

Caleb smiled and said, "That's what I like to hear." He lifted his glass and took a long drink.

***

Joe started running, trying to ignore the way the almost pitch-black room closed in. The hot air curled around him and sweat drenched his shirt. As his boots hit the concrete floor, Joe rolled through each step, stifling the noise. He wound through the maze of ducts, following the Resister just ahead, focusing on the shimmering green lines revealed by the goggles.

The man stopped running as the tile beneath him lit up a bright green. He screamed, and Joe stopped cold. The glow coming off his body changed from a soft green to a bright white as he started to fall. Most of his body landed in the single tile, but his left arm stretched onto the next tile, the last one before the doorway into the building. That tile remained dark. Joe backed up, and took a running start. As he reached the glowing tile, he jumped, praying he could miss it.

His feet landed just after the where the other resister's arm lay. Joe reached the door. He started to reach for it, but then recoiled as screams echoed in the room. He looked behind him and saw the glow rising from numerous tiles. The traps hadn't been in place the whole time. Someone watched them. He slid his hand into his pocket, searching for a coin. As his fingers closed in on one, he pulled it out and threw it at the door. As the coin touched the door, it lit up with the same bright green. The glow started with a small black box beside the door. Probably the heart of the alarm. Joe raised his gun and aimed at it. As the bullets struck, the green glow abruptly died.

So much for that little display. Joe opened the door and pushed through to where the other Resisters waited in a small room at the bottom of the stairs. The smell of sweat filled the air. Shouldered amid a group of much-taller men, Murray had pulled off her goggles and mask. Sweat beaded and glistened on her forehead. Her hair spiked upward from where the mask had been. Joe moved to the side of them. He pulled his goggles downward until they hung around his neck. With another jerk, the mask came off and he shoved it into his pocket. He inhaled and savored the feel of air brushing his bare skin.

"What's going on?" Murray asked, nodding toward the door.

"I think Caleb's watching us because he's setting traps. You guys ran right over the floor and didn't have any trouble. Yet sections of the floor suddenly became electrically charged. The guy in front of me stepped on one of the tiles, and it started glowing as it fried him. The door also had an alarm on it. I just blew away the charge so I could get in here. We need to watch our backs."

Four Resisters burst in after him. As the last one came across the threshold, Murray looked up at the stairs and grabbed the rail. "Let's go."

Falling into step with the others, Joe ascended the stairs. They passed the first three floors. On the fourth, Murray stopped and waved to signal they had arrived at the right level. She yanked out her Parkinsen and gestured for another Resister to cover her.

"Throw a coin at the door," Joe said. His heart pumped loudly, filling his ears with a constant throbbing.

Murray pulled a coin from her pocket and tossed it at the door. As it struck, not only did the door turn flame-colored, but branches of electricity forked through the air around the doorway. The Resisters jumped back, and Murray bumped into Joe.

"Nice touch," Murray muttered with clenched teeth. She lifted her gun and pumped bullets into the door until it returned to its normal silver color.

Murray reached for it, but the Resister closest to the door, stopped her. "I'll check it." He took a deep breath, and touched the knob tentatively before wrapping his fingers around it and opening it and barreling in with his gun drawn. Murray darted inside with the rest of the men following her.

As the point man charged down the hall, one of the floor tiles lit up a green color. The Resister stopped running and looked down at the square as two shafts of metal shot out from the walls and impaled his chest. The rods cut through his body so forcefully, his feet left the ground as he was jerked toward an opening in the other wall. He screamed as the poles shoved him inside and the wall panel slammed back into place.

"Sonofabitch," one of the other Resisters said.

"Everybody crawl," Joe said, dropping to his knees. "Now."

The Resisters fell to their knees and started crawling down the hall with them. Joe pulled up the flank. Two Resisters passed the first tile after the green one. For a second they paused and waited. Nothing. "He's toying with us," Murray said. They followed the hallway, bypassing doors on both sides of them.

A tile under a pair of Resisters in the middle turned yellow. Then it slid away. The men started to fall. Joe leaned forward and caught one arm. Looking down, Joe saw the other Resister had caught the first one's foot. "I need help," Joe growled.

Murray and another Resister grabbed the man's other hand. Joe felt hands cinch his feet, holding him in place as the three pulled the Resisters back up. As the two men crawled back onto solid ground, they looked white as ghosts.

"We're getting there, Scott," Murray said, patting one of them on the back. "It's not much farther now. The next door on the right should be it."

The regiment began crawling again. Joe lingered behind the two Resisters who had almost fallen. He looked down as his hand touched the tile right in front of him. It turned blue. Joe yanked his hand off and pulled back. Knives shot upwards and cut through the ceiling.

Joe stared at the small holes above. Sweat beaded on his temples and trickled down his face. *You're a dead man, Caleb Walker,* he thought.

"You okay?" Murray looked over her shoulder at him.

"Couldn't be better." Joe crawled around the trapped section of the floor. Each time he placed his hands on the tiles, it was tentative touch, as though expecting something to fall apart or sharp objects to assault him. Sweat poured down his face, stinging his eyes.

He blinked, trying to clear his vision and looked up to where two resisters had reached the door. "This is it," Murray whispered. "Blow the door."

"No," Joe said loudly. The hair on the base of his neck raised up, as though he knew this trap would be different. The element of surprise had to be there. "Throw a coin at it."

Murray rolled her eyes and pulled out another coin. She leaned close and tossed it at the door. As the gleam of silver struck, it zipped back, speeding like a bullet, striking Murray. She covered her face and slumped over.

"Murray?" Joe said, crawling toward her. One of the other resisters leaned her back and moved her hand. Splotches of blood covered her fingers.

"I'm all right," she said, dabbing at a small gash in her cheek. "It's just a scratch."

"So how do we get around it?" another Resister asked.

Murray reached into her pocket and withdrew a coil of wire with two small boxes on either end. With careful fingers, she stuck a box to each side of the door and stretched the wire against the doorway. She flipped a small switch on one of the boxes. A small humming filled the air.

"What is that?" Joe whispered, crawling closer to Murray.

"An energy absorption unit. Just don't touch the wire and we'll be fine." She reached up and turned the doorknob. It didn't budge. "It's locked. Murray looked over her shoulders, scanning the Resisters until her gaze settled on one of the men who had almost fallen through the floor. "Scott, pick this lock."

"Coming." He maneuvered through the others.

***

Caleb calmly stared at the computer screen, frowning as the small group crawled into the computer room. "I want the alarm specialist personnel fired tomorrow." Caleb rapped his fingers on his desk. "Then track his crew members one by one and eliminate them for building a system even my wife could slip through."

Lugnut walked toward Caleb. "I think the outer security breach has been resolved. Do you want to dispatch the men to the fourth floor to deal with the intruders?"

Caleb lifted his glass and took a drink before responding, "No, not yet. I want to see what Murray's up to. He stared at the screen, watching his wife and another Resister sit at one of the terminals. "Besides, they're not going anywhere."

"But the computer--" Spare Change started to say.

"Is fine," Caleb snapped, slamming his glass on the desk. "They don't have the access codes to look at or change anything. Be quiet and watch."

***

"I can't get in," Larry said, as he stared at the screen. "Without the password, this is useless."

Murray leaned over his shoulder. "Try immortality." She stared at the blinking cursor as the computer hacker typed her suggestion.

PASSWORD INVALID. ACCESS DENIED.

Murray's shoulders slumped. "Try Hitler."

The same message glared at them in green letters. Murray took a deep breath. "Try Auschwitz."

CLEARANCE ACCEPTED.

"We're in," Larry said, smiling.

"Any luck?" Joe asked from the hallway.

Murray didn't answer as she stared at the shifting computer screen. "Murray?" he whispered. Her fingers rested on the back of the chair where Larry sat.

Joe turned to another Resister crouched in the hallway, watching for guards. "Got it covered?" The guard nodded and Joe slipped inside the room next to Murray. "Are you getting any answers?" he asked, looking at the screen. A picture of an older woman in a red suit jumped out from the screen. That hair's got to be dyed, he thought, looking at the carrot-colored shoulder-length locks. "What is this?" he asked.

"A patient record," Larry said.

Joe turned toward Murray, and he frowned at her facial expression. "What is it? What do you see?"

Murray lifted her hand and slowly brought it to the last line on the screen. Her finger brushed the glass where bold green letters flashed, MENTAL CONTROL WEAK. CANDIDATE SUITABLE FOR TERMINATION ONLY. CANDIDATE

203

SUITABLE FOR TERMINATION ONLY!

Joe exhaled sharply as though somebody just kicked his stomach. "Jesus H. Christ."

Closing her eyes Murray let her hand drop. "What else can you find besides the actual records?" she asked Larry.

"Let's see," the Resister replied, closing out the file. The original five-option menu popped back up. Larry scrolled down to the last one: PATIENT LABELING. "I'm sure something is here." He pushed the enter key and revealed a new menu: COMPATIBLE OPTIONS AND DATE.

"Go to options."

Larry nodded and scrolled down a line. The computer prompted him with ENTER PATIENT NUMBER.

"What is it doing?" Joe asked, leaning toward the screen.

Larry shrugged and inputted the number 25.

The computer blinked it's response. PATIENT NUMBER 25 IS DECEASED. HE WAS CROSSED TYPED AND EXECUTED WITH A HEART ATTACK AS PER CALEB WALKER'S ORDERS.

Murray wrapped her arms around her body. "Pick a number in the millions."

Larry stopped and popped his knuckles before typing in a new, larger number at Murray's request. The computer screen blanked out for a moment and then a file popped open. The picture of a male in his early thirties jumped onto the screen. Joe ignored the image and looked down at the last line. It flashed the same cryptic message. MENTAL CONTROL WEAK.

PATIENT IS SUITABLE FOR TERMINATION ONLY.

PATIENT IS SUITABLE FOR TERMINATION ONLY!

"Scroll down," Murray barked.

Larry hit the arrow key and saw a new list at the bottom. The list appeared to be numbers, just like what they had seen on the computers back at the compound. Larry's fingers lifted from the keyboard. "Jesus is right."

"What is it?" Joe asked, standing upright. "What do the numbers mean?"

"Can you access patients by name? Do you see any council members on there?"

" It's going to take too much time to look here."

"How long will it take to establish the uplink?" Murray asked?

"Not long. Then I'll scramble his codes."

"Make it quick, Larry. I know he's watching us." She walked toward the door.

Joe walked behind her and grabbed her arm. "I still don't get it. What are those numbers? What is Caleb doing?"

Murray stopped and looked at him. "He's building his own master race. He's going to be bigger than Hitler. Bigger than God, Joe." She laughed angrily. "He's using the implants to mentally control people. Those who don't respond to the implants are being terminated by accelerating weaknesses in DNA. It all looks natural, but he's killing them. If somebody has a trace of cancer in his DNA, the implant helps it. Heart disease, whatever."

Joe could feel his mouth hanging open and he forced himself

to shut it. "But why the federation council members?"

"Because they make all the decisions, Joe. Control them, you own the world."

"We've got company!" the Resister yelled from the hallway.

"Have you got it?" Murray asked, running toward the computer where Larry sat.

Larry pointed at the screen. "Almost there. Hold them off."

Murray darted toward the door and yanked out her gun. Joe grabbed her arm. "Stay with Larry. Get the disc."

Murray nodded and headed back. Joe poked his head out the door. A bullet ripped into the doorframe and he ducked inside.

"Got it!" Larry shouted, yanking out the disc. He handed it to Murray. "Let's go!"

Joe looked at them. "I'll cover you. Get out of here!" He darted out into the hallway, almost tripping over the body of a fallen Resister. He started firing. A bullet clipped into a guard's forehead. He slumped against the wall and slid to the floor.

Joe kept firing. He heard their footfalls hitting the floor and then silence. He turned and ran back toward the way they had come. Bullets flew past his head. Joe ran down the stairs.

"After him!" someone shouted above him. Below him he could still hear Murray and a few other Resisters running.

"We've got to get out of here," he muttered.

As he reached the basement, a bullet ripped his shoulder and he groaned and slammed against the wall. He forced himself to open the door and go through. His arm burned and he gripped it.

I thought I was through with this shit. He stopped and hid behind a heating duct, waiting for the men following him. When three of them appeared, he fired at them, gunning two down. The third fired back and ducked behind a huge support column.

"Damn," Joe whispered, cursing his aim.

He waited, listening for movement. A slight scraping sound came to his left. Joe turned and fired. The guard's body thudded to the concrete.

Gripping his shoulder, he started running again, heading for the other door. As he opened it, he heard more guards coming after him from the stairwell door. He exited into the night and prayed he could run like the devil.

The burning in his chest rivaled his arm by the time he saw the jet. Bullets exploded around him. Murray cocked her gun and leaned out the jet. She picked off the men chasing him . When he reached the jet, she yanked him inside and slammed the door.

Bullets lacerated the metal as they took off. Joe's fingers clamped the seat and his vision started to get blurry.

"You're bleeding," she said, touching his wound.

"I guess I shouldn't have tried to catch that last bullet," he muttered, clenching his teeth as she jerked off his jacket. A huge oval blood stain drenched his shirt. She tore it open and dabbed her finger at the wound.

He flinched and said, "Have you seen enough?" He tried to tug the fabric together, but she jerked his hand away.

"I've got to stop the bleeding. At least until we can get back to the compound." She pulled out a rag from a compartment between the seats and pressed it to the wound. As she applied pressure, Joe groaned. Lightheadedness swept over him.

Murray looked up at him and sensed the disorientation. "Don't you dare pass out."

Joe blinked, trying to resist the weighted feel of his eyelids. "Yeah, what's the worse thing you could do?"

She slipped her hand under his chin and jerked it upward, forcing him to meet her gaze. "Not a smart question to ask a woman who hates men."

Joe smiled. He could feel sleep wrapping around him. "Not all men, Murray. You don't hate me." His mouth felt heavy, as though he could barely speak. The words sounded distant.

Her eyes looked like ocean water. He had always loved the ocean. Her lips softened, almost grinning. "Damned if I didn't try, Joe Ramsey. But you had to be different."

Her face separated into three equal images and spun in a small circle. "I always am," he muttered, thinking about the wonderful illusion he was seeing that made his stomach roll with nauseau. He closed his eyes, ignoring Murray's voice calling his name. He felt so tired. And then he slipped into a river of blackness.

***

Caleb paced the room, stopping only when he heard his office door click open. He looked at the head security guard crunched between Lugnut and Spare Change. "Do tell what happened, Mr. Rinehart. How did you let a woman slip away."

"She killed two guards. We did everything we could."

"Not quite everything," Caleb said pleasantly. "You know the story, boys. Finish it."

"But Mr. Walker," the guard yelled, as the two bodyguards dragged him from the room. "I did my best." The door closed behind them, muffling the guard's loud screams.

"And it wasn't good enough." Caleb stalked over to the window, focusing on this blackened screen, prompting a password he didn't know. *You'll pay for that one, Murray. In blood.*

Chapter Fifteen

Inside the Resisters' computer lab, Murray leaned over Larry's shoulder as he sat at a terminal. "Your hovering isn't going to make this go any quicker," he said softly.

Although normally large enough for at least fifteen men to move around comfortably, the lab currently overflowed with Resisters. Some of the men crossed their arms over their chests. Some thrust their fists to their hips. Some of them slid their hands inside pockets. All of them waited.

"Give me some space, Murray. I can't breathe," Larry complained. His fingers stopped tapping keys and he reached up to push her away from the screen. "I know you're anxious. We all are." He stretched his arms out in front of him, trying to ease the cramping in them.

Murray flushed and stepped back. One of the men behind her cleared his throat. She raked her fingers through her hair. "What did you find out about the council members? There's only ten of them and they control all of the Federated States."

Larry took of his glasses and rubbed his forehead. "Yeah. Seven of them already have the implants. Caleb has a majority in his corner."

Murray clenched her eyes shut and shook her head. "What about the uplink? Did you get all the information we wanted? Is it enough to nail Caleb and stop New Life?"

Larry rolled his eyes. "I can only answer one question at a time." He stared at the screen as the New Life Incorporated pentagram popped up along with the usual menu. "We're in the system and I've copied some of the files. Now I'm getting ready to download the information to other compounds." He scrolled down to the bottom and selected the last option. The blinking cursor asked him to select a patient.

Murray exhaled the breath she'd been holding. She wrapped her arms around her body tightly, as though holding it together with them.

Wayne walked over to her and embraced her. "You did it, Murray. You got the goods."

She closed her eyes and embraced him tightly. "Joe and I did it. Together." She pulled back and asked, "How is he?"

Wayne watched Larry begin to download patient information to other Resister compounds through the modem. "He's fine for somebody who makes a hobby out of bodily injury. Probably still sleeping. Having a wet dream or something." He pulled out a cigar and shoved it in his mouth.

Murray's arms fell limply to her side. Her lips tugged into a frown and she chewed on the lower one. Her eyebrows furrowed together to complete a worried expression.

"Why aren't you hitting me? I mean what's the point of annoying you if it doesn't work? What's up with the stone face?" He gestured toward the computer. "You did what you set out to do." He dropped his hand. "What's bothering you?"

"Cammo."

Wayne reached out and touched her shoulder. "You know how he is. You can't keep him locked inside any more than yanking a star from the sky. He's got to grow up and he's got to do it in his own way. Besides," he continued squeezing her shoulder softly. "He's been gone longer than this before. Remember when he disappeared for three days last month? The kid's a natural-born free spirit."

"Hello New York!" One of the Resisters yelled loudly. Murray looked at the screen just in time to see the download had finished to that state. "Soon everybody's gonna know the truth!"

A loud chorus agreed with him. One of the men came up behind Larry and patted his back. "Way to go, man."

Larry gestured to Murray. "It's all in the team." He clicked off directions and downloaded the information to a second site. There were at least fifty compounds, one for each of the Federation states. All of them would get the same information, and when the last download completed, a simultaneous pirate broadcast would show the stolen information and tell the world about New Life and its lies. Soon the Longevity Implant would simply become a memory.

Murray looked down at her watch, not to read the time, but

simply to break the cycle of staring at the screen. "It's going to be hell out there once people find out what they've been given. I just wish Cammo would come home."

"He will. In his own time." Wayne lowered his hand from her shoulder.

"But what if this time things are different?" Her fingers balled into tight fists and she shoved them into her pocket to keep them still. "What if Malachette-"

"Don't," Wayne interrupted. "Worrying yourself isn't going to change anything or bring Cammo back." He turned her shoulders so that she faced the screen and couldn't look away. "Just keep thinking about that, Murray. You beat that sonofabitch at his own game. His corporation is about to fall into a million pieces." Murray watched the small clock on the screen signaling that the current download was half-completed. She sighed and turned away, leaving a room full of Resisters planning a celebration.

She just wished she could believe enough to celebrate.

It can't be that easy, she thought. Her boots scraped the floor as she walked toward the RCU, echoing over the hammer of her heart, a frantic sound hinting at the storm blowing within. The war was far from over. Caleb wouldn't give in that easily. She rubbed at her temples, feeling the faint beginnings of a headache forming there. She needed aspirin. And a helluva lot more faith than she'd ever had.

***

Laughter rippled in Joe's dream. It grew louder. Damn it

was hot. That South American sun felt like it was baking him alive. Joe looked up toward the sound rippling in the air. He saw the alleyways. In front of him he sensed Miguel's tiny body. The air tasted metallic, like blood. He scanned the empty windows, searching the off-white curtains billowing in the hot breeze. He finally spotted the man, four stories above him.

"Good shot, senior! Do you always murder kids?" He pointed at Miguel. Sunlight glistened off his pale skin and light blonde hair. The hair raised into the air sported a flashy gold watch. Probably expensive.

Joe raised the gun an aimed at him. You sonofabitch.

Joe turned over, struggling to break from the dream's undertow. *He felt the gun in his grip. His finger pressed the trigger.*

His leg exploded in pain. Joe's gun dropped a few inches and discharged. The bullet splintered into the wall. More laughter. He groaned.

"Adios, Asshole," that voice said. Joe turned his body and saw the man who had shot him. The same one he'd been chasing. Joe fired. The bullet struck the man in his chest. He fell swiftly.

Joe looked up at the empty window where the cream curtains billowed like ribbons. "Hablar that, you sonofabtich."

He moved his leg and bit his tongue to keep from screaming. Blood poured from his shredded knee. I may never walk again, he thought. His fingers trembled and he tried to set his hands on the ground away from the seeping blood, but it covered his skin.

Miguel.... He looked at the little boy's gaping chocolate

eyes. His vision strayed to the teddy lying in his slackened grip. Joe's throat constricted. "No," he whispered, shaking his head. "God, no! What have I done?"

The dream dissolved, leaving him sitting upright in a bed. Murray stood in the doorway of the RCU. Her hand rested on the doorframe. Her midnight hair laid down slightly, and Joe thought it must be growing out.

"Still dancing with those demons, huh?" She watched him lean against the pillow.

"Yeah," he finally said, trying to slow his breath. "They kept treading on my toes." The sweat on his body made the covers cling to him. His hand crept toward the place where the bullet had clipped his shoulder. Instead of a wound he found a scar. "Lucky me," he muttered.

"Yeah, you are lucky." She leaned against the wall and crossed her arms over each other.

Joe threw his legs over the side of the bed. He tried to block the image of Miguel's face, but it wouldn't disappear. "Any news on Henry?" He stood up, wearing only underwear. The lights illuminated numerous scars across his muscular body.

"No news yet." She walked up behind him and traced a long, thick scar across his back. "Guess I shouldn't have been so worried about the marks on my body. Seems like I'm not the only one with a few." She withdrew her fingers. "I guess I'm just vain."

Joe turned and caught her wrist. "You're anything but that. Besides, they don't say much, Murray. Just that you've been alive and that you finally understand what living means."

Joe slowly released her hand and grabbed his clothes, tugging on his pants first, then his shirt. "Where is Wayne?"

"With everybody else in the computer center."

He picked up his socks and boots. While he put them on, he asked, "What's going on there?"

Murray sat down on the bed next to him. "Larry is transmitting the data we recovered from New Life to other facilities where we have friends who can help call attention to the lies. Once we have sent the information to all of our links, we'll jam the local signals and broadcast the information via the media."

Joe nodded approvingly. "So that will be the end of Caleb Walker and New Life."

She stood up and walked to the cabinet. She opened the door and pulled out the bottle of aspirin. Dropping two tablets in her hand. She replaced the bottle and closed the door. The glass showed her reflection and her fingers toyed with her bangs, trying to spike them up, but they seemed longer. More feminine. She frowned and tried harder to brush them into place.

"I like the way your hair looks."

She ignored him and headed to the sink to get a paper cup filled with water. "You'll be on your way soon."

Joe got to his feet and came behind her. He wrapped his arms around her and rested his chin on her shoulder. "I was on my way when I met you. Maybe I'm still on my way. But I'm taking you with me. Henry, too, when I find him."

Murray grabbed a paper cup, filled it with water and took the pills. After drinking the water, she crumpled up the cup and threw it into the trash. "Talk's easy, Joe."

He kissed her neck before pulling away. "So maybe I'll try walking on the water next time. It might get your attention."

Murray walked to the doorway and paused there. "You coming?"

"Where?"

"To the computer lab. I want to check Larry's progress."

Joe took her hand. She tried to pull away from him but he refused to let go. "Why not?" he asked, looking down at their intertwined fingers. "Everybody else knew you were a woman long before me. It's not like you're going to surprise anybody."

She stopped resisting. Her stomach felt like needles pricked it, but she recognized the way a nervous stomach felt. *Joe's right,* she thought. *I won't surprise anybody. Except me.*

Together they walked hand in hand and entered the computer lab. Although many voices were raised in an uproar, when they crossed the doorway everyone abruptly stopped speaking and stared at them. Murray hastily dropped Joe's hand. "What is it? What is everyone looking at?"

Wayne stepped toward her. He looked pale and old in the unnaturally bright lights. "There's something I have to show you." He barely spoke above a whisper but in the dead silence of the room it sounded like a shout. He reached for Murray's hand, but she wouldn't let him take it.

"What? What is it?" she demanded, thrusting her hands to

her hips. "Did the download fall apart or something? Did New Life jam us?"

Wayne didn't respond. He reached for her hand again and latched onto it. "No. None of those. We just received a transmission, Murray. I think you'd better have a look."

She stalked over to another computer beside the one busy downloading the data. The words "message saved" flashed in scarlet letters. She punched a key and called up the message.

Henry's screams shattered the silence and his writhing body filled the computer screen. "For the love of God," Murray whispered, clenching her fingers tightly to back of the computer chair. Her knees buckled and Joe caught her arm, offering support. "Where is he?"

The image changed abruptly, switching to Caleb's smiling face. Joe looked up at the screen and blinked three times, as though that might clear the haze of familiarity washing over him. The dream. He remembered the face in the dream. "Good shot, Senor. Do you always murder kids?"

"Who the hell is that?" Joe asked, drowning out Caleb's first words.

"Caleb Walker," Wayne whispered in his hear. Murray's body shuddered and she breathed in spasmodic gulps.

"...Now that I have something you want," Caleb said, gesturing to where Henry lay on the floor, collapsed in deathly stillness, "Perhaps you'll accord my wishes. If you and your little friends had just hung around my building a little longer, we could have thrown quite a little party. Too bad. Still, I believe in second chances. I expect you to meet me at 1600 Meridian at four a.m. If you're not there, I'll know the kid means nothing to you, and I'll give him to Malachette. Just like I gave you away." He smiled at her coldly. "Come on time and come alone. And bring the damn codes with you. You fuck with me and I fuck him up." The focus moved from Caleb's face back to Henry's prone body lying on the carpet. Then it flickered to darkness.

Murray looked at her watch and found that she had less than two hours. Her throat felt dry and her stomach cramped violently. She darted through the people and headed out into the hallway before throwing up.

"You okay?" Joe asked. He stood a few feet away from her. His fingers balled into fists and he thrust them into his pocket.

"I'll be fine. Once I cut out his balls." She wiped the residue of vomit from her lips, but the hot taste of it still burned her mouth.

"Don't you mean once we cut out his balls?"

Murray stood upright and stalked back to her room. "You heard the message. I'm going alone."

Joe grabbed her shoulder. "The hell you are."

Murray yanked away from him and whirled about to glare at him. "So you're a hot shot, Joe. But you're not risking his life. It's my fault he's in there. I'll get him out."

Joe laughed angrily. "Yeah that's a good one, lady." He slammed his fist into the wall and flinched from the pain. "You go in there, you'll come out a corpse. Henry, too." He closed the distance between the two of them and grabbed her shoulders, ignoring the way she tried to shirk him off. "I've met your damn husband before. In South America, sweetheart. Hundreds of men much bigger than you died in his war. He doesn't just own New Life, he owns parts of the world. He made a fortune from his 'little' drug cartel. That's how he fronted New Life." He removed his hands. "It took me a while to make the connection, but I never forgot his face. And I always planned to get that sonofabitch."

Murray folded her arms across her chest. "Why didn't you tell me any of this before now? Didn't you think it was important?"

Joe pointed back into the computer lab. "Because the man I knew went by the name of Kristof. It wasn't until I heard Caleb's voice and saw his face that I recognized him."

She leaned her head against the all and closed her eyes. Purple shadows colored the skin beneath them. "I have to do this alone. I can't risk Cammo's life."

He stepped next to her and leaned close so that she couldn't look away from his eyes. "Do you really think he'll let your brother go? Honestly? I don't. You'll watch him die and then you'll be next." Joe laughed bitterly. "He's counting on your trust in his word. But I'm not willing to give up that easily. If Henry might die, he'd rather do it fighting than just giving in."

Murray pulled away from the wall and glared at him. "How do you know what he'd want?"

"Because he'd at least want some chance to keep breathing. If you walk in there by yourself, he's got none at all."

220

Joe watched Murray close her eyes. Her fingers curled into fists. "I suppose you have a better plan?" Glacier green eyes opened and peered at him.

"You'll walk in by yourself. I'll follow with a group of Resisters. Once you're inside, we'll raid the place, and I'll put Caleb Walker in the ground permanently."

"Murray," a Resister said, running down the hall. The short, portly woman ignored Joe and stared at Murray expectantly.

"Slow down and talk," Murray ordered, grabbing her shoulders. "Tell me what's going on."

"Federation forces are on the move and headed this way." She pointed toward the Broadcast room. "The media has been showing raw footage of our trip to the New Life Building." She turned and headed back to the room with the two of them following fast on her heels.

Once back at the Broadcast Room, the woman waited until Murray and Joe sat down before flipping on the screen. "I recorded this because I knew you'd want to see it for yourself."

The black screen flickered and a newscaster's face appeared, saying, "This woman, Murray Walker, has joined the group called The Resisters and has voluntarily assisted them in both breaking and entering and murder, as you'll see by this next footage."

The image switched to the midnight blackness outside the New Life Building, illuminated only by the light of the camera as it filmed. A handful of black-clad figures came into view. One stopped. Murray. She turned and held up her gun. Two flashes of white discharged into the night. Both guards crumpled to the ground. The camera zoomed in on Murray's face, her angry frown and clenched jaw.

"The Federation Peace Officers-"

"Turn it off," Murray snapped, standing up. "And start the alarm. We're about to have company, I'm sure." She darted out of the room, running toward the computer lab. Joe followed her. He stood outside the door, waiting as she asked loudly. "How are the transmissions going?"

Larry turned toward her and pushed his glasses higher on his nose. "We're finishing the last one now."

Red lights flickered around the room and a loud wailing siren split the silence. "The alarm!" one of the Resisters yelled.

"Yeah," Murray replied. "The Federation officers will be here any minute if they aren't already. We need to get to the tunnels and get out of here. ASAP."

Joe poked his head in the room and gestured to Wayne to come to him. The healer, who had been standing in the back of the room, talking with two Resisters came forward. "What is it?"

"What all is in that file on Murray?" he asked in a low voice. He watched Murray's back, hoping she hadn't heard him.

"Well, I don't have her shot records, but I don't think she's got rabies." Wayne stubbed out his cigar in an ashtray. "What are you looking for?"

"Evidence against Caleb. The news crew just released footage of our assault on the building. Murray was showed killing two of the guards."

"Yeah. I've got evidence." Wayne folded his arms across

222

his chest. "Caleb likes to record everything, and I've got a copy of the footage when he almost killed Mur."

Murray walked back to them. She touched both of their shoulders. "Get your stuff together. Now."

Joe nodded. "That's exactly where we were going."

Murray walked past them and headed to her chambers at a dead run. The rest of the Resisters flooded from the room, making their way around the two of them. Joe looked at the healer. "Can it be added to that download which Larry will be broadcasting?"

The healer nodded. "Yeah. We just need to tell him."

"Get it. I'll explain to him." Joe walked up behind Larry as Wayne darted from the room. He asked, "How's it going?"

"Almost through. Just got to get the local download ready."

"Yeah. I've got something to add to that." Joe said and cleared his throat.

Larry stopped typing and slowly turned. "Something to add?"

"Yeah. Wayne's bringing it. It's evidence about Murray, about what Caleb did to her. Right now she's as good as dead unless the public sees what kind of a monster Caleb is. The Federation Peace Officers will execute her publicly without a trial. They don't need one since someone filmed her killing two of the guards at the raid."

Wayne stepped back inside and handed Larry the disk." The computer expert took it and looked down at the label which read, "Caleb 1." Then he slowly looked back at Joe. "Does Murray

223

know about this?"

"No," Joe said, staring at the ground. "She'd rather die, I suppose, but I'm not so loose with her life." He folded his arms over his chest. The alarm wailed again. Joe waited until it died down before asking, "Will you do it?"

Larry turned back to the screen. "Yeah. Get out of here." He pushed the disc into the drive.

Wayne grabbed Joe's arm. "We've got to get to the tunnels. It's the only way to get out of here."

Chapter Sixteen

"Where do these lead?" Joe peered into the overwhelming blackness stretching to infinity before them. Although Joe's head didn't touch the ceiling, he found himself stooping slightly because it seemed uncomfortably close to him. The side walls also caused him to feel claustrophobic. Wayne reaching up and shoving a huge metal bar under a latch to lock the entrance didn't help to lessen the sensation.

"This will take us to a private storage facility my nephew owns," Wayne responded. He pointed his flashlight toward the tunnel ahead. "It's a three-mile stretch to that point."

Joe's breath funneled outward into the cold air as they began running. He pulled his jacket closer around him to keep warm. "So what's there?"

"Jets to get us to the rendevous point with Caleb." The healer flashed his light at his watch and frowned. "It'll be close."

The image of the kid lying so damn still on the floor jumped into Joe's mind. The screams. He shuddered and forced it away.

"We'll get there. Murray will go first and then I'll go in after with a team. When I get done, Caleb Walker will be a corpse."

The two of them lapsed into silence and focused on running. Joe's heartbeat quickened. *Nothing like feeling like I'm going to have a heart attack*, Joe thought. *When this is all over I'm going to get into shape.*

"You've changed her," Wayne said finally as he pointed the flashlight ahead, searching for Resisters. The small beam barely penetrated the thick darkness.

Joe unzipped his coat, beginning to feel hot from running. "What do you mean?"

The healer chuckled. "You have eyes, Joe. You have a heart. Tell me you haven't noticed her softening from time to time. Before you came she'd been sleeping through life, only waking long enough to curse Caleb's name. Now she's waking up. And remembering things besides her husband and Malachette. You know, the maudlin shit."

"Good," Joe replied. He wanted to say that once he'd gotten Henry free and finished off New Life, he'd give her more things to remember and less to forget, but Joe's voice failed him. He cleared his throat and blamed it on the fact that because he was huffing and puffing while running, even breathing was hard, let alone speaking. He would let the future speak for itself. "Did you bring any Trianna?"

Wayne touched his backpack. "Yeah." As Joe glanced at the healer, he spotted those damn thongs on his feet.

"Aren't your toes cold?"

Wayne grinned and shrugged. "Keeps me awake."

Joe stopped running and began walking. "I'm out of shape," he muttered.

The healer slowed his pace and waited for Joe. "Helps to have a knee that lets you run, doesn't it?"

Joe nodded. "Yeah. Thanks to you."

Wayne patted Joe's shoulder. "No, I should be thanking you. You didn't have to stay and help. This wasn't your fight, but you never left. You don't have to get the kid, but you are. We should thank you, Joe."

Joe wiped the sweat from his forehead before it rolled into his eyes. "Tell that to Murray after that footage rolls. Somehow I think if it does get her off the hook, she's going to kill me."

***

Murray stood in the storage shelter, waiting for Joe. She alternated her weight from one foot to the other and kept glancing down at her watch. 3:15. With every passing minute, her stomach tightened and she felt like she could barely breath. *You have to do this for Cammo.*

She looked up at the trap door, narrowing her eyes as though by simply focusing she could make Joe and Wayne appear. "Where are you, Joe?"

"Murray?"

"Yeah. What is it?" She turned from the trap door toward the speaker. Randy Dartman stood before her, handing her keys.

"These are for your jet. I've briefed the others on the way the two-party rendezvous will go down. We're waiting for Joe."

She looked back at the trapdoor. "Yeah. Just waiting for Joe," she echoed. Her back muscles ached from the tension, and every nerve in her body sang from the stress. *Hang in there, Cammo*, she thought, *I'm coming.*

She looked down at her watch again. Damn. What was taking those two so long anyway?

As if answering her question, the trapdoor flipped open and Wayne's head popped into sight as he climbed up the ladder from below. Murray quickly walked toward them. "Taking your sweet time these days, aren't you?" she growled, watching as the healer cleared the door and Joe followed him.

As Joe looked at her, the hard line of her shoulders curved when she spotted him. *You're right, old man*, he thought. *She is softening.* "Glad to see you, too. No, we didn't have any problems. Thanks so much for asking," Joe replied in a caustic tone. Looking away from Murray, he glanced around the huge open steel building. Four large jets sat waiting, and approximately twenty Resisters sat around them on the cement floor.

Murray glared at him. Her arms folded across her chest and she tapped her fingers on her arm impatiently. "You're cutting things awful damn close, aren't you?"

"Close is what I do best." He frowned and looked for the rest of the Resisters. There had been many more of them. "Where is everyone else?"

Murray pointed at the closed exit doors. "I sent them on to other facilities. They couldn't have accomplished anything else from here." She looked at her watch. 3:30. Time to go. Her stomach lurched and she shuddered from an unexpected chill. "I guess I'd better head toward the meeting place. The others have been briefed on this mission. They're ready to follow you." Her steps came down faltering and uneven, tapping loudly on the floor. As she headed toward one of the jets, her arms fell to her sides and she clenched her fingers into fists.

"Murray?" Joe called out. He pulled out the gauntlets he had tried to give her earlier.

The echo of her footfalls ceased as she stopped walking. Her chest and back tensed as though she held her breath. Finally she replied, "Yeah?" and slowly turned to face them.

Joe threw the gauntlets at her. "For luck," he said, watching her fingers stretch through the air and catch them. "We won't be far behind you."

As his words echoed in the large, almost empty building, Murray's shoulders slowly loosened even more. Her lips tugged upward into the first traces of a smile Joe had ever seen her wear. "I know."

The other Resisters began rising from sitting positions, and once upright, they checked and double-checked their Parkinsens. Eyes averted, the men refused to her gaze until Murray had passed. Randy stood closest to Murray's jet. As she opened the door and climbed inside, he walked up to her.

"What is it?"

His fingers rubbed the door of the jet. "I just wanted to tell you that you've been the best. And we won't fail you."

Murray gestured to the other Resisters to open the doors. "Thanks, Dartman. I know you'll do your best."

Randy moved his hand and stepped away as the huge metal doors swung wide and parted in an ancient grinding sound. Murray started the jet and headed out the door, disappearing into blackness.

Once the lights of her jet vanished, another Resister walked up to Joe and handed him a communication device. He slipped on the earphones and mike and clamped the box to his belt. Joe looked at Wayne. "Tell everyone to board and get ready. We're about to fly away."

The healer nodded and walked toward the Resisters. Joe turned on the box and said, "Storm Rider come in."

"Storm Rider here," Murray said.

Joe closed his eyes and listened to her voice. It reminded him of silk fraying at the edges. "How are you holding?"

"I'm holding just fine," she snapped. "And how bout you?"

Joe cringed at the sarcastic wall she'd just slammed him with. "Cut the crap, Murray." He shoved his fingers into his pocket and touched the bear. His fingers wanted to pull away from the softness, but he wouldn't let them. "I didn't ask you in front of the men because I know you want everyone to think you're made of steel. I asked how you were doing and I meant it."

Silence. "Murray?" His back muscles started to ache from the tension building there.

"I'm nervous," she replied. Her voice sounded diminished.

230

Static broke through, humming.

Joe shook his head, thinking that anyone else would have used the word terrified but Murray wouldn't even allow herself to tell the truth. "The men are boarding right now." He watched the black-clad figures slipping inside the jets. "We'll be following you in a matter of minutes."

"Joe? Promise me something."

"What?" His breath caught as he sensed she wanted to ask him something he wouldn't like.

"If you can't free us, you'll kill us."

The air rushed out of Joe's lungs and his solar plexus stiffened. He blinked. "Murray-"

"Promise me," she demanded. "You said this would work. Maybe it will. But I'd rather die than live through his version of hell. And I'd rather Cammo died than survive Malachette's torture. Now promise me!"

Joe gritted his teeth. "It won't come to that, Murray. But if it does, I'll call the order."

Wayne gestured for him to board. "I'm getting on the jet."

"Just can't seem to stay away from me, can you?" Her voice had thickened. She sounded like she was crying.

"No, I had to be different, remember?"

"Yeah. I remember. I'll see you soon, Joe."

Joe listened to the silence for a moment before turning and walking to the jet. He slipped inside and sat down next to Wayne.

The healer braided his long silver hair and dropped the long tail inside his shirt. "How is she?"

Joe leaned against the seat and tried not to remember her voice breaking. "Fine." But he knew she wasn't. Still, Joe would make sure she turned out fine, one way or another.

The jet moved toward the door and slid into the midnight blackness, rising after the building had been left far behind. Joe's stomach rolled from the combination of the sudden motion and nerves eating away at him. The windows fogged over from the cold air outside. Joe forced himself to lean back against the seat, but his stomach muscles clenched, refusing to relax.

"I'm almost there." Murray's voice filled his ears. "The location is Mikel's Tavern."

"How many jets are parked outside?" As Joe spoke, he felt Wayne's gaze resting on him. He tried to measure his words so that they came out calm, steady.

"Ten."

Joe frowned. *At four in the morning?* The hair raised on the back of his neck in warning. *Something is seriously wrong with this picture. It's a trap,* he thought. "Murray, don't--"

"I've landed," she said, interrupting him. "I know what you want to say Joe. It's what I want to hear. But I can't do it. I can't turn around. I'm getting out now."

"Murray," he said. "Don't go in there."

"Too late, Joe," she said in a tired voice. "I'm opening-"

The air turned to static buzzing loudly in his ears, and then silence. "Murray?" he repeated, louder. His stomach hollowed and dropped. He closed his eyes and the air caught in his chest, expanding until it hurt.

"What is it?" Wayne asked.

"I don't know. The air just went dead. Static and then nothing at all." Joe moved his hand to the arm rest and clamped his fingers onto the plastic surface, rubbing at the cold smoothness. He pushed his back against the seat harder, trying to ignore the way the sudden silence cut through him. He rubbed his eyes and the fog of days since he'd first met Murray washed over him in waves of exhaustion, baptizing him in pain. He remembered his fingers brushing her skin, tracing the length of her neck down to the point between her naked breasts rising and falling in rhythm with his own heart. "Murray," he called again.

No answer.

He opened his eyes. His heart hammered loudly, thundering in his ears until it was all he could hear. He felt red heat washing over his face. He gripped the arm rest so tightly his fingers hurt. *If anything happens to her or the kid , I'll never forgive myself.*

"What did she say?" Wayne demanded impatiently. "Christ, Joe. You look like you've seen a damn ghost. What's going on?"

"She said the meeting spot is Mikel's Tavern and that there were lots of jets parked outside."

Wayne scanned the backs of the men sitting inside the jet in front of them. "Sounds like trouble."

"Yeah. She was cut off in the middle of saying something. It was too damn sudden." Joe's throat constricted and he wondered what he should have said to her.

They both stared out the window and waited. Joe's fingers traced the shape of his Parkinsen. As the vehicle slowed, Joe

233

looked for the tavern. "It looks like trouble, too."

He looked at the parking lot, squinting his eyes to count the vehicles. When he came up with six, instead of ten, the lead in his stomach dropped farther. He'd counted Murray's jet in the group.

Although they could see the tavern, its windows illuminated with faint light, the driver had parked the jet far away enough to escape detection. Joe stood up with the other Resisters. "Some thing isn't right here. Murray just told me there were ten jets in the lot. Now there's only six, including hers." He passed from one fact to the next. "Everybody knows the drill, right? We figure out where Murray and Henry are, we take Caleb and his men by surprise and we get the two out, right?"

The men nodded in agreement. He had known they would, but Joe needed to vocalize the plan, as if that would make it go down without problems. "Let's go and do this right. For Murray." He led them out of the jet and waited for the last one to exit before they headed toward the tavern in a ragged line.

Joe's body began tingling. He could feel one of New Life's mental broadcasts washing over him. He gritted his teeth and tried to fight it, but the resistance simply made him feel light-headed. It came anyway. NEW LIFE IS THE ANSWER TO DEATH. OVER SEVENTY-FIVE PERCENT OF THE POPULATION HAS ADDED YEARS OF LIFE. COME JOIN OUR TEAM TODAY AND GET FIFTY NEW REASONS TO SMILE.

As the voice drifted away, Joe rolled his shoulders, trying to loosen them. He shook his head, shirking the faint trickles in his mind. "Damn Caleb Walker and New Life," he muttered savagely. He spotted Murray's jet, the driver door cocked open and the interior light illuminating a small dome into the blackness.

Joe looked for guards, but the lot appeared empty as he ran toward it. Plumes of steam puffed from his mouth. Dull footfalls hit on the pavement behind him, telling Joe the others followed closely behind him. He plastered his body against the jet and slid toward the open door. His fingers skimmed the cold metal. As he made it to the driver's door, he peered inside.

The communication box lay on the seat and the wire to the earphones half-wrapped around the steering wheel before dangling in the cold night breeze.

She's inside. With Caleb. Joe gritted his teeth and stared at the tavern. *If anything happens to her or the kid, I'll never forgive myself.* He looked at the other Resisters and pointed toward the tavern. He headed for the bushes beneath a barely-lit window.

"I'm coming, Murray."

Chapter Seventeen

Gun in hand, Joe darted to the east wall of the tavern and plastered his body beneath the dimly-lit window beside a bare-branched bush. Each passing second dug into him like nails piercing his skin. The cold air burned his chest as he inhaled. Then, as he exhaled, it slipped away in a grey stream of mist, melting into the night. *Murray is in there. She has to be.* But why was someone waiting for her in the parking lot? They knew she'd come inside for the kid.

Taking a deep breath, Joe slowly moved from his scrunched position to standing upright where he could peer into the window. Scanning the room, he noticed five men besides Caleb and Malachette. The group sat still, watching the television mounted to a wall. Henry's still body lay crumpled on the floor face down. The windows pulsated with a gyrating beat pumping from the juke box, rattling the glass panes.

Where is she? Joe wondered. *Where is Murray?* Joe ducked back against the wall and gestured for Wayne to move from behind the jet where he was currently hiding to the spot beneath the window beside Joe.

After looking both ways for guards, Wayne bolting forward, holding his Parkinsen with both hands. He stopped right next to Joe. "Did I mention that I was a healer not a fighter? Do you see them?"

"He's still got Henry, but I'm beginning to wonder if he's had Murray taken some place. I don't see a single trace of her. He could have her in back, but I don't think so. Caleb and Malachette would be entertaining themselves with her if she were here, and all I see them doing is watching the frigging television."

The healer's silver eyes focused on Joe. "So what now? Where is she? We can't just open fire and get rid of Caleb until we find out what he's done with her. Besides that would be too easy to get rid of him. I think Mur should get a chance to finish him off."

Joe chewed on his lip. "I wish to hell I knew what he did with her." The cold wind blew through him and he thought of Murray's short, spiky hair and the lattice of scars crisscrossing her back. "We've got to go in there and make him talk after we get the kid back."

"How is Cammo?"

Joe tried not to remember the kid lying on the cement floor. "Unconscious, I think."

"Not for long with the noise we're about to make." The healer waved to the other Resisters, telling them the time had come. Joe pointed at Wayne's Parkinsen and said, "Take

Malachette out of the game. I'll give Caleb something to think about."

He and the healer slid up the window and took careful aim. Joe focused on Caleb's left leg. Wayne moved beside him, leveling the gun at Malachette's head. As Joe began to squeeze the trigger, pain blasted in his back and chest, but he didn't let go of the gun. He groaned and yanked the trigger, spraying glass everywhere.

The night erupted in more bullets and chaos. Joe slumped toward the ground as another bullet clipped the tavern wall next to him. Fire surged through the back of his shoulder, taking his breath away. He reached for it and felt blood. Joe's body began tingling with a mental message coming. THIS IS THE FEDERATION TASK FORCE. THROW DOWN YOUR WEAP-

Something stopped the message. More bullets. The air was thick with them, like bugs flying in all directions. Strangled screams punctuated the night, and the scent of gunpowder filled the air, burning Joe's nostrils.

"How bad is it?" Wayne asked, slumping next to Joe. He fired into the blackness toward the Federation officers. Three of them fell from his wave of bullets.

"Not good," Joe muttered, gritting his teeth as the burning spread through him. He was seeing spots dancing in front of him and the world felt lopsided. He saw the healer thrust his Parkinsen into the air and kill three more of them. It was an ambush. *So what had happened to Murray?*

The bullets stopped raining down on them. Silence spread through the air, clinging to the gunpowdered stench. Joe peered out into the blackness, waiting for them. From the darkness he saw more men coming. They mixed in with the growing spots filming over his vision. He lifted his gun, ready to fire.

"Joe? Wayne?"

Just more Resisters, he thought. Joe closed his eyes and forced himself to rise. The pain almost doubled him over and he heard moans coming from his mouth that didn't sound like his voice. He coughed and blood came out, spewing dark and thick on the ground.

Wayne leaned over and helped him up. Moving drove the pain into sharp, stabbing sensations and shallowed his breathing to short, wheezing gasps. "Did you get Malachette?"

"Right on the star. I knew those damn pentagrams would be good for something. What about Caleb?"

Joe coughed again. "His leg." He tried to walk, but he started slipping toward the ground. As he began gasping air, the cold temperature bit into his lungs, and he felt like he couldn't inhale fast enough.

The healer caught him and braced Joe against a wall. "I'm the one who's supposed to get hit. I'm the amateur, weekend-warrior type, remember? You tough guy types aren't suppose to pass out. Jeez, when I tell Murray, you'll never live this down." Wayne spoke fast, too fast. "You're losing too much blood. I'm gonna have to use some of the Trianna on you or you won't make it." Wayne yanked off his backpack and reached inside it, grabbing the bottle of medicine and a rag. He pulled out his knife and slit the front of Joe's shirt. Joe looked dully at the buttons, but Wayne said, "Just think of it as air-conditioned. You can wear it in the summer and stay cool."

"You tell Murray I'm a wimp and I'll rearrange your anatomy." The world began spinning harder around Joe, whipping him around like a carousel spinning out of control. "Everything is spinning." His head lolled forward, and he didn't have the strength to lift it. Something cold touched his chest and shoulder. Joe flinched and tried to move away. Blackness started to come for him. His vision had become one big circle of darkness. And he felt smothered. Each breath hurt.

"Joe, stop fighting me." Wayne's voice. Fingers tapped his face, driving away the darkness. "Hold on. It only takes a minute. Then you'll be good as new. I promise."

Joe didn't feel like he had another minute. Not without sleep. He forced his eyes open and thought about breathing. In and out. In, out. Stay awake. The blackness wavered, forming grey lines. Then the light peeled the skin of darkness. The grey became the yellow drifting from inside the windows. The feeling of fatigue rescinded, too, but it left the biting cold wind, dragging ice claws across his exposed chest. Joe blinked, trying to drive away the residue of weakness which had washed over him.

"The wimp lives," Wayne said, patting his back. "Come on. Let's go."

Joe yanked his shirt together and tucked it inside his pants, trying to keep it pulled shut. "We've got to get the kid." Joe looked at his empty hand and then at the ground where his Parkinsen had fallen in the dead grass. He bent over, picked it up and then glanced inside the window.

Three men standing. Caleb, Lugnut and Spare Change. Malachette lay on the floor behind the bar. His head rested in a puddle of blood flowing outward in small trickles.

Joe focused on Caleb. The breath slammed out of his chest as he saw Henry pinned in the crook of Caleb's arm. And the glittering, bloody steel that Caleb held poised at the kid's throat, waiting to cut.

He moved back down. "There's only three of them left. Caleb holding the kid with a knife pointed at Henry's throat. Looks like Malachette's dead behind the bar."

A small cluster of Resisters swarmed around Joe, silently awaiting their orders. "We'll hit the door." Joe pointed at Wayne and said, "You stay here. Cover us. They'll be expecting us since that's the only way inside. You pick off the lugs holding the guns."

Wayne nodded. "I always love hunting season."

"Just remember who you're suppose to hit." Joe moved with his men as they lined up on either side of the door. Two of them stepped forward and kicked in the door wooden door. It swung wide and slammed against the walls. Bullets snapped around them, exploding in one of the Resisters head. He slipped to the ground. More bullets.

Joe and the others ducked back as bullets peppered the air. He counted to three, jumped from his temporary sanctuary and started shooting.

"Do you really want to kill him?" A voice asked.

Joe sucked in a sharp breath as he stared at the only man standing, Caleb. Wayne had done his job, clearing the way for them. Now, Joe's gut clenched. Caleb held a death-grip on the kid and smiled as he saw Joe stare at the blade. Joe and three Resisters stepped across the splintered threshold, toward Caleb.

"That's far enough," Caleb ordered, prompting the blade higher on the kid's neck. "Keep moving and he stops breathing. Got it?"

Joe stopped and motioned for the others to obey. "Yeah. We got it."

Caleb's grip loosened slightly on the blade. "I don't know what you think you can prove. In a week every last Resister will be publicly executed for the good of society. You can't make a difference here. And you can't even save Murray."

Joe forced the fingers holding the gun to loosen, even though he really wanted to raise it and pull the trigger. "I'm not here to prove anything. I'm here to kill you. Take a good look at me, Caleb. Or Kristof. Which do you go by these days?"

Caleb squinted his eyes and the smile vanished. Joe had no doubt his mental gears were turning furiously. Joe laughed raucously. "You don't even remember me, do you? Do you remember the Mexican kid? The one I killed because I was chasing your delivery boy?"

Caleb's grin snapped back and he slowly bobbed his head obligingly. "Yeah. The alley thing, right? Pity that you killed one of my most loyal men. Still, it looked good for the Federation. He was a drug runner, after all." Caleb leaned over the kid and said, "And we can't have drugs corrupting the minds of the future, can we?"

Joe slipped his foot forward slightly, trying to move without being noticed. "He was just following your orders. And it was okay so long as it helped fund New Life, wasn't it?"

Caleb rolled his eyes and prodded the knife into the kid's neck. "You're boring me." His lips turned upward into a vicious sneer. "And I don't like being bored. You may be a difficult man to kill, but not impossible. No one is impossible to get rid of. Not even Murray." He pushed the steel against the kid's neck, drawing blood. "Now throw down you damn gun or I'll kill him. You wouldn't want to be responsible for killing another kid, would you?"

Joe felt the flush creep across his skin. He stared into Henry's eyes, watching them widen as trickles of pain cut through him. "Where is Murray?"

"Being taken care of. Once and for all. Now throw down that goddamn weapon or I will kill him."

Clenching his jaw, Joe uncurled his fingers from around the grip of the gun and let it clatter to the floor. Caleb shuffled the kid's body so that he could see where the weapon went and Joe spotted the growing red circle on his adversary's leg. At least he hadn't missed his mark. "Now tell your men to do the same."

Joe looked at them and nodded. They threw their guns on the floor. "Step back," Caleb growled.

Joe and the others moved back and watched as Caleb came toward the guns and kicked them further into the room, away from them. "I've played your game, Caleb. Now tell me what you've done with Murray."

Caleb cocked his head to one side and scrutinized Joe's face. "Something tells me you've taken a fancy to my wife. Too bad she won't be breathing long enough for you to worry about anymore." His laughter echoed loudly, and one of the few unbroken whiskey bottles slipped to the floor and crashed, adding its voice.

"Where is she?" he demanded.

Caleb nodded to the television screen and said, "Take a look for yourself. I'm sure you'll be interested in this."

Joe scanned the room before he stepped further into it. He half-expected someone to jump out, grabbing him. His stomach rolled unpredictably. He had a bad feeling about this, he realized as sweat beaded on his forehead, despite the cold winter wind blowing through the open door. But he had to know. He forced himself to turn toward the screen for the answers.

The picture showed a huge crowd standing in the darkness. Joe's first instinct about the image was to tell Caleb he was full of shit and ask him what he'd done with Murray again. Then he saw her. He recognized the short, spiky wisps of black hair blowing slightly in the wind. He recognized the angry set of her jaw. And mostly, he recognized the fact that on either side of her stood a Federation peace officer, holding her in place, leading her toward a public execution for her crimes against the government.

He felt his mouth gape slightly and he forced it shut. His knees buckled. He whirled around and took two hasty steps toward Caleb before seeing the blade sink further into the kid's neck and watching Henry's mouth open wide in shock and pain. A small, whimpering sound came out. It staved Joe off. "You sonofabitch!" Joe's fingers curled into fists.

"Caleb laughed loudly and shook his head condescendingly. "She's my property, you stupid fuck! I'll do with her as I please, and her death will please me greatly." He pushed the knife into Henry's throat, like a huge tack into a pincushion.

Joe saw the blade sinking into flesh and the blood that surged outward. He ran forward. The sound of bullets ripped through the air. A huge hole tore into Caleb's left temple. His bloody hands fluttered and then released Henry. The kid sank to the floor and Caleb's body fell on top of him.

Behind the bar, Joe saw Malachette rising, aiming the gun. More bullets came from Wayne standing at the window. They sank into Malachette's chest, staining his blue shirt with a purple oval, growing by the minute. Malachette groaned and turned toward the window. He pulled the trigger and sprayed bullets toward Wayne. He kept firing as he fell, shredding the wall with bullets.

Joe felt to his knees and touched Henry's throat, tracing the path of the gouged flesh. His fingers trembled as he fingered the wound, feeling the warm stickiness of blood. "Wayne, get in here. NOW!"

Silence.

Joe turned to the closest Resister. "Go get him!" he growled. *That's all we need. For the medic to be hurt.* But Joe's chest tightened, as though the air had been sucked right out of it. For the first time all evening, he noticed how cold his body felt with the wind blowing in the open doors at the rear of the bar.

The man turned and ran out of the building. Joe looked back at the kid who kept moving his mouth, trying to speak. All that came out were tiny, surging air bubbles. "Don't try to talk, Henry. Just hang in there. You can tell me anything you want later. Wayne'll fix you right up." Trickles of bloody saliva ran down the kid's chin and cheeks.

He cradled the kid's head in his lap and held him so close to ward away the trembling which started inside Joe and worked it's way out. "Just hang in there," he pleaded. Damn, what's taking so long!

The Resister returned, his boots tapping on the floor. "Wayne's dead. I brought this." He held out the half-empty bottle of Trianna to Joe.

"Dead?" Joe echoed, feeling the color drain from his face. With a shaking hand, he took it, yanked open the lid with his teeth and quickly shoved his fingers into the jar and scooped out some. He coated the kid's throat.

The rest of the Resisters wandered into the room and watched Joe and the kid. Henry's face had grown pale like cooled ash. The wash of red on his throat made him look dead. The Trianna bubbled over the wound, and Joe felt drops of the warm liquid spill from the wound and soak into his clothes. Joe saw the kid's shocked brown eyes glaze over. His eye lids drooped.

Stillness. "Come on, kid. Don't do this to me. I can't handle it." Joe thought of the bear in his pocket. He thought of Miguel. And he thought he would break. "I'm sorry kid. So damn sorry."

He moved Henry's arm back into a normal position and dabbed some of the Trianna over the broken bone. Joe couldn't look. He forced his eyes to the ceiling. Not another kid. Not right now. And Murray. He looked up at the television screen and saw her sitting in the electric chair as they strapped her inside. Even with the sound of the crowds drowning out her voice, he read her lips and heard his name come out in her breath. He felt the way the letters curved to her mouth as she spoke.

Against the hard, wooden chair, she looked rather small. Her back braced defiantly against the chair, and as her fingers clutched the arm rests, her coat sleeves pulled upward, revealing the gauntlets he'd given her. Her chest rose and fell quickly. The wideness of her eyes, staring ahead diminished her other features more. She closed them and took a deep breath as the executioner fitted the cap on her head.

She looked right at the camera and mouthed, "I love you, Joe." He heard her voice in his mind. "I always did," she said.

"Oh, Murray." He clenched his teeth and shook his head, trying to erase what he saw. "I should have known. ."

The other resisters gathered around him and watched the screen. "This can't be happening," one of them said as he numbly stared. "Not to Murray."

247

Joe shoulders rolled forward and he cradled the kid tighter to him. *It can't end like this. Not like this.* He leaned his head against the kid's and prayed. *I'd give my life for his...and hers.*

The screen drifted to static, and grey nothingness replaced Murray's face. And in that unexpected sea of noise, he heard the sound of his heart. He just wanted to know if it was beating or breaking.

Chapter Eighteen

"Hang on, Henry," Joe whispered, cradling the kid's body against him. The stillness of it weighed him down. Static from the television set filled the otherwise silent room. Joe kept staring at the screen, waiting for the image to come back.

The gray haze disappeared from the screen as Murray's face bruised face appeared. Larry did it. He's showing the evidence. Naked, Murray knelt on the floor with Caleb leaning over her. In his right hand, he held a razor. "So you think you're gonna tell the whole world about me. About New Life? That I'm gonna own the Federation? Well I can't let you do that. I've got too much riding on this one. And besides, the only people getting hurt are the ones who don't deserve to live in the first place."

"I won't tell," she whimpered. Her long, dark hair fell into her face and matted against her skin, sticking to the sweat and blood. "I won't tell anybody anything. I swear! Please let me go."

Caleb laughed, pushing the blade closer to her face. The

249

harsh lights illuminated his flashy white teeth. "I know you better than that, my dear. You are my wife, after all, if only in name. I mean, we both know I don't need you for anything else. Just to look like a family man for the camera. I'll play the part of a grieving husband for a year or so, and then I'll tell everyone I've met the newest love of my life. And I'll marry the woman you knew as my mistress. The same one who gave birth to my daughter. You know, the child your pathetic body could never give me."

Murray shuddered and closed her eyes, trying to forget about the razor in her face. "I'll run away, Caleb. Just disappear."

"No. You won't. You know the implants are a lie. You know I'm not giving people fifty extra years. That's why you have to die." Caleb brushed the blade across her shoulder, cutting her. "The press will report your death as an unsolved murder. If your body is ever found at all." He watched the thin line of blood ebb to the surface of her skin. "But I don't think it will be."

Caleb lowered the blade and tracked it across her back, gouging her skin. Murray screamed and clawed at the furniture, trying to get away. As she moved her arms, the chains and manacles holding her prisoner rattled against each other. Her body stretched out long and taut. Caleb pushed the blade harder, thickening the cut. Red lines appeared.

"I'm not giving anybody fifty years," he snapped, staring at the blood on his hands, staining the cuffs of his white shirt. "But I'm certainly not giving you a chance to save the world."

She screamed loudly. The sound of it broke as the image

changed into the New Life option menu. The cursor scrolled through the list, selecting the patient records. A background voice chanted, "New Life is Killing. New Life is Killing. Caleb Walker is a murderer. Caleb Walker is a murderer."

People's faces flashed on the screen, as well as the DNA information about them and the future plans Caleb Walker had made for them.

"Joe?" Henry said, struggling to sit up. His fingers touched his throat, feeling the way the skin had pulled together into a loose pucker which would eventually form the final scar. He moved the once broken arm with ease.

"Don't touch that," Joe said, pushing the kid's hand away. Then he reached up and wiped away the dampness under his eyes.

"You're healed, but the scar is still new. It needs time to finish forming." He looked from the kid back to the television screen to the endless faces peering at him. He reached up and touched the triangular scar on Henry's forehead, thinking, *You were smarter than I ever knew, kid. This is what gave you the extra years of life. It gave you a chance to grow up.*

"Where's Wayne?" The kid moved out of Joe's reach and stood up while looking around the room.

Joe pushed his hands to the floor and rose. "He's dead, kid."

Henry's head shot up and he kept shaking it back and forth, trying to deny what he'd just heard. "No-"

"Yeah. I'm afraid he is." Joe took a deep breath and tried to forget the fatigue of grief. He pointed at Caleb's body and then Malachette as he looked at the kid's white face. "But he died

251

fighting for what he believed in." Joe rubbed the bridge of his nose. An uncomfortable thickness settled in his throat, making it difficult to speak. "He knew he might die, but he also knew it was the only way to stop New Life. He was a healer, Henry. Right up to the end. He healed the world of New Life's power."

"Where's my sister?" Henry's voice rippled. He stood on unsteady feet. The red stain on his shirt made him seem more vulnerable than the lost look in his eyes. "I want to see Murray."

That makes two of us, kid. The lump thickened and he felt the pain of it spreading through him. *Except I don't just want to see her. I want to hold her again.* He closed his eyes and kept reminding himself to breathe.

"Well, where is she?" Henry stepped toward him and shoved his shoulder. "Answer me!"

Joe shoved his Parkinsen into its holster. "She's not here. The Federation officers have taken her into custody. Last time I saw her, they were about to execute her for crimes against New Life." His shoulders sagged from the weight of the words.

"Where did you see her?" Henry demanded, stepping close enough so that inches separated their faces. "When?"

"A few minutes ago." Joe pointed to the screen. "It was going to be a public execution. Before they could start, one of our men tapped into the system and broadcasted the evidence against Caleb and New Life."

Henry staggered backward and cringed as though someone had hit him. His empty hands trembled before balling into tight fists. "We have to stop this. We have to get to her. Before-"

Joe shook his head. "There's no time." His voice sounded painfully quiet against the hum of chanting coming from the television. "It's over by now." His gut clenched and he thought the tiny grip of control he had been maintaining would snap in half. "She's with the healer."

Henry jerked away from him and grabbed Joe's gun. Surprised, Joe let it slip. His fingers curled around the air, trying to hold onto it. The kid headed toward the door. "No! I don't believe you." He started across the threshold.

"Stop him," Joe shouted, running after Henry.

Two Resisters reached out and latched onto each of Henry's arms, stopping him. One of them plucked the gun from his grip. Joe walked up at looked at the kid's red face and hateful expression. "It's over. There's nothing you can do. Going out there now will only get you killed. Especially now that the public knows the truth about New Life. And Caleb Walker."

Henry gritted his teeth. Every muscle in the kid's body tensed as he struggled against the hands holding him still. "You could have saved her. She trusted you. You should have been there!" He pursed his lips and spit at Joe.

Joe opened his mouth to say something, but the chanting from the television abruptly ceased. They all looked up at the screen and saw the image change from faces to a woman with a raging fire behind her. "...struggled to free herself, but the execution was carried out, even though it should not have been. The crowds have been out of control and the Federation officers have fled the area, probably to regroup. This execution-"

Joe grabbed his gun from the Resister and shot the screen. Glass flew and the snapping sound of the bullet echoed. In the sudden silence, he felt his knees buckling, giving way underneath him as he slipped to the ground.

It's my fault she died. I promised I'd be there. And I failed. I failed.

I failed.

He leaned over and vomited. Even with his eyes clenched shut, all he kept seeing was her face on that damn screen. Her mouth formed the same words over and over. She had said she loved him. And he couldn't respond.

Joe wiped his mouth with the back of his hand and forced himself to his feet. "You're right, Henry. It's my fault she died." He couldn't look the kid in the eye, even when he spoke to him. Maybe it was the guilt, but Joe rather believed it was the rivers of tears running in lines down Henry's dirty face. "Let's go back to the compound. I don't think we have to worry about the Peace officers anymore."

The Resisters slowly released the kid, but hovered nearby, just in case he tried to run again. Joe walked behind them partially for that same reason. Partially because he didn't know if he'd ever be able to face the kid again. He watched Henry climb onto the jet before walking around the tavern and stopping in front of Wayne's body lying face up on the ground. Branches hid the lower half of him. The silver eyes peered at the stars. Joe looked up and stared at the twinkling heavens.

For a moment he lost himself to the endless blanket of blue

overhead, but then he forced himself to look back down at the body, at the dark stain and bullet holes ripped in the black jacket. Joe reached down and upzipped the coat. As he pulled it open, he saw a canary-yellow shirt, the same one the healer had worn the day Joe first met him. The blood stain looked just like another flower. Malachette had stolen the only thing he couldn't get, a heart.

Falling to his knees, Joe picked up one of the healer's hands and tried not to feel the cold skin. "Take care of her, old man. Keep her warm and tell her that I loved her, too. I just wish I had gotten a chance to say it." As the cold air blew through him, he felt hollow, as though he would simply collapse from the nothingness inside.

He picked up the healer's body and hoisted it over his shoulder, carrying it back to the jet. Once he stepped inside, he made his way to the back of the vehicle and laid the body down. As Joe sat next to it, he could feel Henry staring at him. Taking a deep breath, Joe forced himself to look at the kid. The faint moonlight fell across the kid's sandy hair. And it reflected the film over Henry's eyes where fresh tears pooled. "He was my teacher Joe. Ever since I can remember he was my teacher."

Joe blinked and nodded. He reached across the seat and touched the kid's shoulder. "Yeah, I know. And he still is. He always will be because he lives inside of you in a place that no one can ever touch or erase. Not even you."

Henry shrugged away Joe's hand and stared out the window vacantly. He crossed his arms over his chest and leaned against the seat defiantly. Joe lifted his hand away from the kid. "I'm sorry, Henry. I never meant for any of this to happen."

Henry closed his eyes, as if to shut Joe out. "But that doesn't change any of this, does it. It still happened. Murray and Wayne are dead. And you can't undo that."

"You're right." Joe turned away as the jet rumbled forward and accelerated into the night. As they flew, Joe looked along what once had been a dark world. Now flames flickered in the night, darting upward toward Heaven's rage. And the brightest of the pyres was the New Life Building. Forty stories of flame which had once been the modern-day tower of Babel.

Chapter Nineteen

Darkness hung around the Palace as the jets pulled up. As Joe and the other Resisters climbed off, he looked around, searching for Peace officers. Nothing moved. Nothing breathed. He gestured to two of the Resisters. "Check inside."

Joe glanced at the sky around them, black with smoke furling toward the heavens. As he watched it consume the velvet sky, he felt it stirring in his lungs like ashes blowing inside him. He had failed. Leaning against the jet, he held his Parkinsen in one hand and waited, half-expecting a barrage of bullets to come out instead of the Resisters. But the men appeared at the gates with Larry accompanying them.

"What happened while we were gone?" Joe asked Larry.

"I finished the broadcast from the tunnels." Larry pushed his glasses higher on his nose. "The cops came and ransacked things while I hid in the tunnels. All hell broke loose in the square and they had to leave. The Palace is empty and demolished."

Joe nodded and ducked back inside the jet to get Wayne's body. He thrust the healer over his shoulder and carried him through the building to the yard. A slight echo of footfalls told Joe someone was following him. Half-turning, Joe spotted the kid a few steps behind him.

Henry's scarlet cheeks emphasized the angry set of his jaw. He hung his head low and he had shoved his hands into his pockets. "I can't believe the two people I loved most are gone."

Joe's chest tightened. He couldn't believe it either. He stood still, waiting as the kid finally walked up beside him. "Yeah. I know." Joe clenched his eyes shut. His shoulders ached from the weight he carried, and the air trembled inside his lungs, threatening to explode. *I failed her.* He started walking again.

"You want to help me tend to Wayne? He would have liked that." He walked outside and looked at the stars. "I thought we'd bury him here."

The kid nodded. "Yeah. I'll go get a shovel."

Joe walked to a far corner of the lot to a place where the winter grass grew thick and soft like a blanket. He leaned over and laid the body down. As the head touched the ground, the silver eyes still stared at the stars. Joe laughed softly. "You were the one who taught the kid about stars, weren't you? You taught him about windows and open air." He rolled his shoulders, trying to loosen the knotted muscles. "You taught him what it meant to be free, didn't you?" He reached down and closed the healer's eyes as Henry returned, carrying a shovel.

"Where should I dig?" the kid asked. He clutched the shovel

with both hands.

Joe looked at the ground. "Pick a spot, Henry. Any place you want."

Henry moved a few steps to the right and thrust the spade into the earth. He put both feet on the shovel and forced it deeper into the dirt before scooping outward. The kid dug fast, piling each small mound beside the grave. More than once Joe wanted to offer help, but the kid's sharp movements warded away the words. Joe recognized the language a body used to express grief. It came out in sharp breaking of earth and tireless scooping.

As the kid finished the hole, Henry stabbed the shovel deep in the ground a short distance away from the grave. His gaze met Joe's. Joe rose from where he'd been squatting and together they picked up Wayne's body and laid him inside the grave. They stepped back and stared at the healer, waiting one last second for the stillness to break. For him to breathe again.

Inertia.

Joe found himself looking at the thongs on the healer's feet, thinking the toes must have been cold. But never as cold as the chill eating away at Joe. He wrapped his coat tighter around him and folded his arms over each other.

The kid picked up the shovel and began covering him with dirt. In the background Joe saw numerous other Resisters standing in the doorway, watching the dirt sink into the hole. The pile of earth beside the grave dwindled to a small mound as the burial was completed.

"What about the marker?" Henry asked, leaning on the

259

shovel. He wiped away the sweat collecting on his forehead.

Joe studied the kid's face. Moonlight painted his bruised skin darker. But that wasn't what kept Joe staring. It was the way the line of his face seemed different. As though he couldn't rightly think of Henry as a boy anymore. The tall, thin body had begun to change into a man. But Henry already had the mind of one. And the heart.

"Joe, what about a marker?" Henry asked again. He brushed the back of his hand across his forehead, wiping away sweat.

"Whatever you want," Joe replied. "Whatever you think he would like best." Exhaustion tore through him, and he knew he wouldn't be standing much longer. He just didn't know how the hell he would ever sleep again. Not considering he would see her face in every dream until the day he died.

***

A full moon hung over the Palace. Wisps of smoke clouded it for a moment before passing. Murray stopped at the gate and stared for a moment. Her fingers touched her clothing, assessing the rips around her sleeves. The night still smouldered with rage. She slipped in the door and met the Resister standing guard.

"Murray?" Tennyson said, walking up to her. He shook his head in amazement. "It can't be." He touched her shoulder, as if checking to make sure she was real.

"Well, it is. I am." Her shoes clicked on the floor.

He reached out and embraced her. "How? The execution-"

"Luck, I guess. They weren't quite ready to fry me before Larry got the broadcast going. And afterward, the crowd rioted."

She raked through her hair with trembling fingers. "Put it this way. A small group from the crowd got me out of the chair and put a female officer in my place. That was the execution." She took off her coat. "And she was lucky compared to some of the other officers. She died quick. What about Caleb and Malachette?"

"They stopped breathing. Bullets usually do that." Tennyson looked at the floor. He licked his lips nervously.

"What is it? What are you hiding? Did Joe get my brother?" She bent over and matched his gaze.

"Yeah. Both Henry and Joe are sleeping. But some of the others didn't make it back."

Murray stood upright and held her breath. "Who?"

"Wayne."

Murray stood and set her coat on the chair in the hall. Each breath was painfully labored. She looked at the ceiling and forced herself to blink so fast the tears couldn't come. "You're sure?"

"Yeah. Joe and the kid buried him in the yard."

"Anyone else?" She chewed on her lip, biting hard enough to break the skin.

"Daniel and Kyle."

She nodded slowly and thought of the men who had been her friends. "Good night, Tennyson."

"'Night."

She walked through the compound and out into the yard. In the moonlight, she immediately spotted the swelling of freshly-turned ground. Her head rolled forward and she forced herself to

261

keep walking on unsteady legs until she reached the site. Her knees gave out and folded under her.

She touched the earth, savoring its coldnesst. Digging into it, she brought a handful to her chest and let it fall on her jacket. "Some people don't believe in angels, Wayne." She put her hands in the dirt, leaving indentions. "I do. I knew you. I mean you had your moments of humanness. God forbid I ever forget that you did appreciate your damn cigars and those shirts. But you had the power to heal and you believed I could throw Caleb off his throne. Hell, a little love and faith, what more could an angel have?"

She covered her face and the tears came streaming down her face. "I'd give you a gift, Wayne. But you packed before I got here. So I'm giving you place in my heart rent-free."

She wiped her face and stood up. Her eyes strayed to the sky, at the moon playing hide and seek behind the smoke. "Light a star for me, old man."

She walked back inside with unsteady feet, and quietly passed through the Palace. The midnight stillness felt oddly soothing as she headed toward her brother's room. For a second she paused at the closed door, raising her hand to knock. Instead, she wrapped her fingers around the knob and let herself in.

She crept to the bed and knelt beside her brother. The moonlight illuminated his face, reminding her of the father she'd lost long ago. She frowned as she realized the person she'd known as a child had disappeared. She leaned over and touched Henry's face, whispering, "Cammo."

He scrunched his eyes, as though trying to fall deeper into sleep. "It's Henry, not Cammo," he muttered, still half-asleep.

Murray smiled and brushed her fingers across his cheek more firmly. "Wake up, Henry," she said.

He turned his head toward her and opened his eyes. "Murray?" he called, abruptly sitting up. "I thought-"

"I know," she cut him off and sat down on the bed next to him. "Tennyson told me when I arrived just a few moments ago." She lowered her hand to her lap. "That's why I woke you."

Henry wrapped his arms around her waist. "I'm so glad you're back. I didn't know what to do. Wayne's gone."

Murray clutched him and stared out the window. Her eyes sparkled with unshed tears that she tried to blink away. "You would have done just fine. Wayne taught you well. And he loved you." She closed her eyes and leaned against him.

"I'm so glad you're home," he repeated.

Murray felt the tears fall, leaving a warm path. "Me, too." She tightened her arms around him, trying to keep her body from trembling with the pain stifled inside.

"Murray?" Henry pulled back and met his sister's eyes. "I said some things to Joe to hurt him. I wanted to blame him when I thought you were dead." He averted his eyes to the floor. "I shouldn't have. I know he blames himself for you and Wayne."

She brushed her hand across her face. "There's been too much guilt in these walls," she said, her voice cracking. "And I gave him so much anger when he first came." She stood. "And now I'm going to take it away. Along with your guilt. And his."

She walked back inside and down the hall to Joe's room. As she entered, she stared at his body outlined in bright moonlight. He tossed and turned, the sound of his sheets crinkling blocked out the soft clicks of his door opening and closing.

Murray stood in the doorway and stared at his bare back, visually tracing the lines of scars on his back. She smiled softly and thought he was right. Scars made you believe you could live again he had once told her. She touched her wrists, remembering the way the leather straps had felt. Then the deeper feeling came. She had once wanted to kill herself. And she wasn't the only one. Many people had wanted to take her life. But she had never once had someone who believed in her enough to fight to give it back to her. She walked toward Joe, stepping in the glow of soft moonlight. As she made it to the bed, she reached to touch him, something she hadn't thought would happen again.

She smiled and thought that the end of New Life was only the beginning of her life.

This is Maria Rachel Hooley's first novel. She is a high school English teacher who lives in Oklahoma with her husband and three children. She is currently at work on a young adult novel and a script for *New Life Incorporated*. Numerous journals and companies have published her work.

LaVergne, TN USA
19 February 2010
173701LV00006B/89/P